EATERS AND OVERLORDS

EATERS

AND

OVERLORDS

Blaine C. Readler

EATERS AND OVERLORDS

This is a work of fiction. Names, characters, places and incidents are either the product of the author's wild imagination or are used fictitiously. Any resemblance to actual events, locales, organizations, or persons, living, dead, or one foot in the grave, although inevitable and in a weird way complimentary to the author, since it shows he is not so insulated from reality that the products of his imagination are totally alien to the average mind, is nevertheless entirely coincidental and beyond the intent of either the author or the publisher.

Visit us at: http://www.readler.com

E-mail: blaine@readler.com

ISBN: 978-0-9992296-2-0

Printed in the United States of America

There are people of worth all over the Earth
who are far smarter than I.
Of those, there's a few, who, when you're blue,
wipe the tears away when you cry.

There are people with insight who let in the sunlight
and show you how to have fun.
There's an occasional star who raises the bar,
I'm so lucky I married one.

ACKNOWLEDGEMENTS

A hearty thanks to James Ward for putting to vision the words of the tale.

http://www.jameswardillustrations.com

As all regions below are replenished with living creatures ... so may the heavens above be replenished with beings whose nature we do not understand.

—Isaac Newton

But who shall dwell in these worlds if they be inhabited? ... Are we or they Lords of the World?

—Johannes Kepler,

Chapter 1

Terri stood next to the car, peering into the midday twilight that infused the old-growth forest before them. "Hey," she said, turning to Professor Siderai, "isn't this where that old man was murdered?"

Siderai wasn't actually a professor—not at a community college—but the story was that he had been on track to become one at a university back east. In any case, against his objections all the students called him "Professor."

"No," he said. "That happened near the south lot, a mile from here."

Terri tore her gaze from the organic gloom to look at him. "A mile? That's a ten-minute walk."

"You'd have to run to make a mile in ten minutes, and the forest trails wind around. You'd be lucky to get there in twenty minutes."

"Well, that's a big relief. An insane killer surely wouldn't invest twenty minutes for a next victim."

Siderai grinned. The other instructors ignored students' jokes. The Professor, though, seemed to enjoy their borderline adolescent humor. "That was a week ago. I doubt the perpetrator hung around."

The murder had made quite a splash in the small town. The killer had apparently used something like a kitchen knife. A big one. The State police had even showed up. "Maybe he, like, lives here in Mirkwood," she said. "There's a lot of places to hide in there."

The actual name was Mark Ward State Park—named after an early twentieth-century Congressman who's only apparent achievement was getting his name hung on twenty-thousand acres of dense northwest forest. In the imaginations of the town's youth, the vast expanse of trees surely harbored magic and secrets like the ancient wood of Tolkien's tales.

"It rained all last week," Siderai said, "and dipped into the forties overnight. If he's been in here all this time, he'll be begging for us to take him in. Besides, it was your idea to come here."

Terri stood, staring into the soft silence under the unbroken canopy. She hadn't been here in years. She had thought she was ready, but now she wasn't sure. The memories were so happy, and she didn't want the terrible end of them to become part of the fabric of the place in her mind.

"We can go back, if you like," Siderai said quietly.

She glanced at him and shook her head. "I need that A."

He grinned. "You need another A? You have nothing *but* A-grades in all your other courses."

"Exactly. I'm not going to blow a class in my major. I need a four-oh average if I'm going to transfer into a good university. Community college is basically preparation for—"

She caught her breath. She was about to say "a real education." She looked at him. "I mean . . . not that it's not a good education . . ."

He waved it off. "Shall we proceed? Your marmot is waiting."

"You mean my marmot excrement."

"Otherwise known as . . . ?"

"Always the Professor. Otherwise known as scat."

Terri had blown the zoology final. She'd had a terrible time with her mother the night before, and had hardly slept a wink. She knew she'd screwed the pooch when she handed in the test, but still she'd cried when the devastating, humiliating B grade was posted. She had begged and pleaded with Siderai to make it up somehow, and he had agreed to this extra-credit project—analyze marmot scat and determine as many types of plants as possible. She thought he was joking at first, but he'd said, "Animals don't live in classrooms. If you want to truly know them, you have to go where they do."

"I asked for it," she said, walking to the trail head. "Let's get it over with."

"As I recall," he said quietly, "you didn't ask, you threatened."

She stopped and spun around. He stood looking at her with one raised eyebrow. A tall, thin man, she would have found him attractive if he shaved off the ridiculous mustache. Of course, the attraction would have been a purely abstract notion, since he was gay. "I did not!" she exclaimed. "What are you talking about?"

Grinning, he walked past her and headed down the trail and into the dappled half-light of the forest. "I remember distinctly that you said that if I didn't let you make up the grade, you'd never make it into a prestigious university," he said over his shoulder, "and then you'd have to settle for a half-ass—your words—medical school, which would likely cause you to misdiagnose and kill somebody someday."

She ran to catch up. "I may have said something along those lines, but how is that a threat?"

"You hinted that I'd share the blame."

"I did not. Did I?"

He didn't answer, which was an answer.

"Hey," she said, remembering, "did I tell you I have to be back by five o'clock?"

He stopped, looked at his watch and turned to her. "No, you didn't. It's three-thirty. We'd better hustle."

"Let's hope those little rodents haven't been constipated."

"If you really plan to be a doctor someday, you may want to work on your presentation style."

They walked on in silence. Other than the occasional snapping of twigs, the only sound was the near constant angry chatter of squirrels cursing their passage through their domain. "Becoming a doctor is a long, hard road, you know," he said. "Are you sure I can't interest you in a career in zoology?"

"Just because you love animals, doesn't mean everybody does."

"A zoologist doesn't have to love animals, just the study of them."

"I won't have to do dissections or dig through scat?"

"Of course you will. You know that."

"Well, there's your answer."

"The competition is stiff in medical school. You need to

prepare yourself for some setbacks."

"Oh, I'm not worried. I've already weathered one of those."

He looked at her.

"I flunked out of UW—actually, I dropped out, but I would have flunked."

Siderai walked along with his hands in his pockets. "I find that surprising, considering your current performance."

"I'm actually trying, now."

"You didn't before?"

"I was kind of wild in high school. The group I hung out with were nerds, also super-cool—the avant-garde crowd, spiked hair, nose rings, drugs, that sort of thing."

"I would have tagged you for the academic crowd."

She gave him a sidelong glance. "My dad got me into a charter school—just before he died. What you're calling the academic crowd were the attractive kids from wealthy families."

"Attractive," he repeated, a challenge.

"Yeah. You know, pleasing to look at."

"So, why wouldn't you fit in?"

She threw him another look, but he kept his eyes on the path. "Prof, have you looked at my face?"

"Terri, come on. You have a perfectly normal face."

"That's exactly the problem. To this crowd, anything 'normal' is basically untouchable."

"Well, it seems statistically improbable that all the kids from the wealthy families would happen to be attractive."

"Sure. Some didn't start out that way."

"You mean cosmetics?"

"Clothes, orthodontics—one even had a nose job, at the age of fifteen."

They walked in silence. "Makeup goes a long way," he finally said.

"You're talking about me?"

"I'm talking about any girl, or woman."

She bristled. The idea of trying to make herself pretty with makeup nudged a small, knotted ball lying deep in her gut. "What would you know about it, anyway?" she said.

She frowned at what she'd just said, and the knotted ball jostled.

"I'm sorry—" she started.

"Because I'm gay?" he said at the same time.

"No—yeah. Look, I'm sorry. That was uncalled for."

He grinned. "You're not apologizing for acknowledging that I'm gay, are you?"

"No! Okay, yeah. Look, I can be a real bitch sometimes. But I'm trying."

"There's nothing to apologize for. Really."

More silence.

She couldn't let it go at that. It did need an apology. Or at least an explanation. "You know, before my dad died, he warned me about avoiding things—things that are difficult. He said that every time we decide to forgo some challenge, we should ask ourselves whether it's just circumventing risk—you know, the fear of losing."

"I presume he was specifically talking about you."

"Yeah. He got irritated with what he saw as my cowardice."

"Um, that doesn't sound very supportive."

She shrugged, and then chuckled.

He looked at her, waiting for her to explain.

"That's the ultimate irony—admonishing *me* about not playing the game."

Terri sensed the black curtain rising from her brainstem, and closed her eyes a moment, pushing it back down.

"I don't understand," Siderai said.

He was watching her with concern.

"I think you do, Prof." She wanted to finish the sentence, but the words wouldn't form.

"Terri," he said gently, "did your father . . . did he . . . ?"

"Yeah, Prof. He offed himself."

"Suicide?"

"The old pistol-in-the-mouth trick."

She felt weak. She almost reached out to him to steady her balance. She fought back the black curtain.

"I'm . . . I'm very sorry, Terri."

"Boohoo me," she said. Pity implies weakness. Be strong, be smart, don't make mistakes. Her dad's voice inside her head lived on. "Prof, since we're baring our souls, how did you end up teaching at a community college?"

5

He nodded, a fair question. "We think we live in progressive times, but a lot of it is facade. Blacks were given equal rights under the law in the sixties, but it's taking generations for society to catch up."

"You think it's the same with gays?"

"Oh, I don't think. I know. The evidence is all around."

Silence.

"Prof, I don't get it. I heard that you were a professor at a university—"

"An associate professor."

"Whatever. You're saying they fired you because you're gay?"

He smiled. "That would be illegal. No, I broke a serious rule. I had an affair with one of my students."

"You had an affair with . . . a boy?"

He laughed. "That is the definition of being gay."

"Ah, geez, I still don't get it. If there was a rule against fraternizing—in the biblical sense—with students, how is it discriminating against gays?"

He gave her a knowing look. "I knew of three other straight instructors that were having affairs with female students. And that's just what was obvious to me."

"Ah, I see. Uh, maybe the admin types weren't aware of them?"

"One of them was an 'admin' type. College students are not minors. There is nothing illegal about professors having affairs. It all comes down to the university culture."

Terri sighed. "I get it. I'm . . . sorry, Prof."

"Nothing to be sorry about. Animals find their natural niche in their environment. Mine happens to be teaching community college. I enjoy it. There's less politics, a lot less pressure."

"To progress?"

He laughed. "To become head of my department? No thanks. I am where my destiny calls me."

"Destiny? From a science professor?"

"Destiny, as my heredity and environment have molded my motivation values."

"That's more like it."

"And I am not a professor."

"Okay," she said, stopping. It was all so familiar, the advantage of old-growth forests—they change so slowly. "The trail dips down through a small ravine just ahead, and there's a grassy knoll on the other side, a good spot for marmots, wouldn't you say?"

"This is your project."

"In other words, you agree, but you won't tell me."

He ignored the dig. "I suggest you proceed very quietly. As soon as they see you, they'll sound a warning, and dive into their burrows, but you'll know where to look."

"For marmot poop."

"Go," he urged, waving his hands at her like she was a shooed fly.

She started forward again, stepping as softly as possible, wincing at every twig she broke. She glanced behind her, and saw Siderai following fifty feet away. It was a shame he was gay—he was rather handsome. She shook her head at the thought. She had mentally tsk-tsk'd him when he'd told her that he'd had an affair with a male student. It had seemed . . . perverse. Yet, here she was considering a fantasy of her own. It was the ghost of her father's homophobia, she knew. After his stroke, he'd done a one-eighty on the subject, and became quite vocal about his views. You either believed that homosexuality in its essence was immoral, or you didn't. If you rejected that homosexuality was a sin, then a gay professor having an affair with a male student was—should be—no worse, and no better, than an affair between a straight instructor and student—

She yelped and jumped back.

Something had fallen right in front of her. It lay there in the path, something the size and shape of a cucumber, made of metal or plastic—she couldn't tell which—definitely artificial. It tapered to a point, and reminded her of a vibrator. Not that she was intimately familiar with one. She nudged it with her toe, and jumped again when it beeped.

Siderai's pounding footsteps came from behind. "Are you okay?" he asked, staring at the interloper nestled among the leaves.

"It missed me," she said, reaching out with her foot to nudge it again, but changing her mind.

"Maybe it fell from an airplane," he said, looking up. "What the—?"

She followed his gaze, and saw only the dense green canopy, pierced by scattered points of bright light where the sky shone through. Amid the random pattern of limbs and leaves, she finally made out a regular geometric form. "A tree house. Boy, it's high up there."

"Not just a tree house. Look to the left."

"Uh, I don't see anything—wow!" She squinted against the bright patch of sky nearby. "What are they?" she asked.

There were two of them, perched on a platform made of limbs. The size of orangutans, they sat at the edge, staring down at them. Short, gray fur covered their bodies, except around their mouth and eyes—big, featureless black eyes. Furry little ears stuck straight out. The whole effect was like a cross between an ant and a koala bear.

The larger of the two pointed down at Terri and Siderai, and then back-handed the other one across the chest with a hand full of long thin fingers at the end of an equally long arm, causing him to cower. The large one cupped his hands to his mouth and called out in a warbling, complex string of tones, like a duet of violins, each playing a different jazz tune. The action was hauntingly human, and gave Terri shivers.

She and Siderai spun around at the sound of something crashing through a patch of undergrowth next to them. A third beast broke through, and skidded to a stop twenty feet away. This one looked to be the tallest yet, although Terri guessed it might simply be the broad shoulders and long, thick arms. It still barely came up to her shoulders.

But it was brandishing a sword.

Or at least a substantial butcher's knife, which for the diminutive creature served the purpose nicely.

Conan the Barbarian—for that's how Terri thought of him— pulled a knife from a braided belt around his waist, bared his teeth, and growled at them as he lifted the wicked weapons, one in each hand. From above came the intricate, competing sound of flutes and detuned violins. Conan glanced up and returned the discordant strain before turning his attention back to them, growling even louder as he shook the weapons.

"What the fuck?" Terri rasped.

"We should leave," Siderai said.

"No argument here. But, how?" He was blocking their escape.

"We'll ask it," he said.

"You don't really think it understands—" she started, but saw that he was using gestures. Siderai placed his hand on his chest, and then swung his arm out, pointing past Conan. The beast exchanged bursts of tweedling vocal notes with Moe—the one who had smacked Larry, the smaller one. They seemed to be having an argument. Conan finally cowed them with one last bellowing growl, and then stood aside. He wasn't admitting defeat, though. He raised his long arms high so that the tips of the weapons hovered above eye level as they eased past. As she slunk by, Terri found herself staring into those huge black eyes, and she realized that they were just tinted shields. Inside were steely gray eyes that studied her with clear intelligence.

Once past Conan, Siderai, who had gone first, moved Terri to the front and told her to run. She did, as fast as her feet could carry her. After a minute, however, she turned and stopped. Far behind, Siderai was following slowly, backwards, facing Conan, who paced him, weapons still raised high. Siderai raised both hands, palms out, and they both came to a stop. The zoologist and armed beast stared at each other, and then Siderai suddenly spun and sprinted off, waving for Terri to stay ahead of him.

They didn't stop until they burst into the parking area, where they turned and waited, but the only sound was the pleading whistle of a chickadee, seeming so mundane—and normal—after the otherworldly discourse of the fantastic beasts.

"Prof," Terri said, bent over with her hands planted on her knees as she wheezed deep, recovering breaths, "I don't think they were marmots."

Chapter 2

Terri watched as Siderai paced back and forth in front of the trailhead, staring at the ground, hands clasped behind him. She'd given up making comments. He'd just mumble "Hmm," nod his head, and resume pacing. She looked in her car at the time. "Prof, I'm sorry, but I have to go."

"Hmm?" he said without breaking stride.

"I have to leave, skedaddle."

"Hmm?" he said.

"Prof, I have to get home to relieve the home health care person."

He finally stopped and looked at her, blinking. "I thought your father was, um—"

"Not for my father—my mother. Alzheimer's. She'll forget it's her own house, and wonder down the street looking for my father, or her father."

"I see. I'm sorry."

"No need. She has good days, and bad days. The good thing about Alzheimer's is that she forgets about the bad days on the good days. Prof, you going to be okay here?"

"Hmm? Oh, sure. They were just defending their territory."

She was about to get into her car, and she stopped and turned to him. "Who are 'they'?"

"Hmm," he said. "Good question."

He was staring down the path, tapping his finger against the side of his nose. She sighed, and got into the car. "Prof!" she called through the open window. "Maybe they're just really big marmots!"

"Hmm," he murmured.

She chuckled and was about to drive off when a police car turned into the parking lot, hesitated a moment, and pulled up next to Siderai. She recognized Barney immediately. He was the only city cop who wore his police cap when behind the wheel. Terri threw open her door, got out, and sprinted over. Barney was four years older than Terri, and used to hang out with her brother, or rather, was sometimes tolerated by her brother and his friends. His real name was Bartholomew, and was known as Bart until he became a policeman, when his abrasive personality was given insufferable authority behind a badge. The comparison to the other Barney, the fictional one from Mayberry, was an opportunity far too enticing to resist.

He was talking to Siderai through his open window on the other side of the cruiser, and Terri heard him ask if he'd seen anything unusual.

"Hey, Bart!" Terri called, running around the front of the car. They didn't call him Barney to his face, or badge.

"Well," he said, "if it isn't Scotty. Welcome back."

Nicknames work both ways. "Terri" begat "Terrier," which morphed into "Scottish Terrier," parking finally at just Scotty. He welcomed her back every time he saw her now, a reminder that she'd failed at the university.

"Out for a, um, cruise, I see," she said brightly, throwing Siderai a warning glance.

"That is my job," he said, as though she'd completely forgotten his role. "This gentleman was just going to tell me—"

"Siderai," she blurted. "His name is Mr. Siderai."

Bart looked at her, the silent pause indicating that she was out of line. "Is that true, sir?" he asked, as if the question was on par with corroborating a murder alibi.

"It is indeed. We went for a hike together."

"And, did you see anything unusual?"

"No—" Terri blurted.

"Yes," Siderai said at the same time.

She looked at him, eyes wide.

"Most unusual," he said. "The seasonal epiphytes are proliferating and colonizing alien arboreal zones."

Bart stared at him.

"He's a professor," Terri said. "At the college."

The city cop rolled his eyes and nodded. He'd seen the type. "Nothing else? Nobody else on the trails?"

"Not a single other person to be seen," Siderai affirmed.

Bart tipped his hat to Terri, "Scotty," he said, "Professor Sadeye, have a good day."

As he drove away, Siderai said, "You didn't think I was going to give away our little secret, did you?"

"I wasn't taking any chances with ol' Barney. One look at Conan, and he'd have emptied his pistol. What was all that about seasonal epithets?"

"Not epithets—epiphytes. Mostly gibberish."

"You were gambling that he wouldn't know?"

"It seemed low-risk."

∞

"This is gonna cost a half-hour of overtime," Bertha, the health care worker, said. Terri had thought she was joking when they first met, but the beefy woman set her straight that the name was an integral part of her long Germanic family history.

"I'm, like, ten minutes late!" Terri said.

"Sorry, honey," Bertha replied, picking up her suitcase-size purse and heading for the door. "We bill in thirty-minute increments. I don't make the rules."

And you don't follow them, either, Terri thought. She was pretty sure it was fifteen-minute units in the contract. She wasn't about to argue, though. This was a person whose demeanor could keep her mother calm, or set her off on a tantrum. Instead of challenging Bertha, Terri turned the conflict inward. Her uncle Greg—her father's younger brother—was covering the cost of home health care so that she could go to college, and she felt like a worthless failure whenever she caused extra charges—or received a lousy B grade.

"How was she today?" Terri asked as she held the door for Bertha.

"Let's just say it wasn't one of her best." She walked out, but stopped and turned around. "She threw pudding in my face," she said, and left.

Her mother's sporadic nastiness was such a contrast to the patient, loving woman who had weathered so much of her own abuse at the hands of a mentally damaged husband. The HMO doctor had told Terri that he'd never seen such a predominance of Alzheimer's-induced irritability before. Terri had a theory that this was her mother's way of giving it all back to the world.

Terri found her mother sitting on the sofa watching TV in the small living room. Wisps of unkempt graying hair fell across a face intent on deciphering vague recognitions within the nineties reruns that Bertha tuned for her.

"Hey, Mom. How are you?" Terri asked. She saw that Bertha had failed to clean off some pudding smeared on her neck and shirt. How her mother had managed to get pudding globed onto her neck was one of many mysteries the disease offered up.

"The pastor called for you today," her mother said.

"He wanted me to come and work for him, didn't he, Mom?" Terri said as she tried to wipe off the pudding.

"I don't need a bath," her mother said, swatting at Terri's efforts. "What work are you doing for the pastor? Are you painting with that nice Walston boy?"

"Maybe, Mom, we'll see."

Early on, Terri had tried to straighten out her mother's twisted memories, but it had gotten to the point that now it just caused confusion and anger. The man who had called was probably Mr. Hoffman—checking if she was free to work over the weekend at the grocery store. The pastor—dead now for over a year—was Mr. Harmon. Thus, her mother's confusion. Jonny Walston was a boy she had dated over the summer after tenth grade—at least as much dating as kids with no driver's licenses can do. Joining the church's Habitat for Humanity projects, where they painted walls and fences, was a way to be together on pseudo dates. Today, Terri's mother had evidently set out on a time-travel excursion four years removed.

Terri sometimes wondered whether she would accept a time-travel ticket if offered. Turn back the dial five years, before her mother began showing symptoms they could no longer ignore, and she could be with the mom who was the calm center of the family, trying her best to protect Terri and her older brother from their father's knife-sharp disapproval and criticism. Spin the dial another five years, before her father's stroke, and she would be back in the forest glade, lying in the grass staring at the clouds, next to a gentle, supportive father describing the exotic lands where he performed archeological assessments for UNESCO. He would even let her play with an artifact he'd brought back, an odd little ornament that he wore as a pendant. He never took it off, other than during their quiet times in the glade.

Of course, it was the contrast between these two men—the encouraging, supportive dad, and the damaged berating stranger—that had sowed the seeds of her sometimes debilitating anxiety.

"How was your day, Butter?" her mother asked.

Terri smiled. "Butter" had been her nickname when she was younger, derived from "Buttercup," which her father had called her as long as she could remember.

"Fine, Mom," Terri said. "I went to Mirkwood on a school project—the same spot where Dad used to take me—"

Shit! Terri thought. She was such a dunce sometimes. Her mother frowned at the mention of the state park, and her brow gathered together over eyes swirling with fear, anger, and confusion. "Mom, it's okay. Listen, can I get you a cup of tea?" she asked, hoping against odds to distract her.

"Your father . . ." her mother started, looking at Terri as though about to make a despicable accusation.

"Mom, listen to me," Terri said, kneeling next to her and taking her mother's hand in hers. "Take it easy. Let me explain—"

She fell back when her mother swung her hand up, barely missing Terri's face. "Your father!" her mother shouted, her eyes wide with raw emotion.

"Mom, please—"

"He . . . he had a stroke!"

"Mom, come on, now—"

"He needs help!" she exclaimed, as though this was a revelation for them both. "We can't handle him anymore!"

Terri sighed. Her mother's timeline was parked where her dad had suffered the stroke, but hadn't yet relieved everyone, particularly himself, of his irascible twist of mind. Terri was sorely tempted to pull her mother forward in time, past her father's final act, but reality could produce wild and unpredictable results.

"Mom!" Terri said, pointing at the TV, "isn't that Tim Allen on *Home Improvement?*"

Her mother's head snapped to the television, and the furrow of her brow melted from consternation to concentration. "Yes," she said. "I like that show."

And that was it. Distraught confusion could evaporate in seconds.

∞

Terri was finishing her left-over spaghetti when a text came in from Siderai—he wanted to meet her at the local Starbucks. "He thinks I'm an unfettered woman of leisure?" she muttered as she in turn sent a text to their neighbor, Mrs. Freeman, who was often happy to have an excuse to get away from her recently retired husband. He was slowly driving her crazy. It said something about their situation that she would rather spend an hour with someone demented and often cantankerous, than her own husband.

Five minutes later, the doorbell rang, and Terri said goodbye to her mother, who had switched the channel to an old episode of *Breaking Bad*, and was watching with something like amazed incredulity. "I'll be back soon," she said, switching the channel to something she could understand.

At the Starbucks, Siderai waved to her from a back table. "I've been doing some digging," he said when she sat down "mostly to satisfy my sense of responsibility. I knew I wasn't going to find anything. What we saw was no known species."

"How can you be so sure?" she asked.

He shrugged. "I *am* a zoologist. My doctoral thesis weighed the comparative evolutionary advantages of arboreal versus ground habitats of primates."

"Huh, no kidding?" She'd never thought of him as lab-coat research type scientist. He was their community college instructor. "Where'd they come from, do you think?"

He shook his head. "No idea."

"Maybe they're space aliens."

"Terri, they're living in trees."

"It had a sword."

"It was hardly a sword. Besides, aggressive demonstrations are natural when protecting territory against other obvious primates.

The weapon could be a plastic toy it picked up. It probably doesn't even understand what it is, or how to use it."

"I don't know. It looked like it had a lot of practice. Hey, it wore a belt, and had a knife as well."

He shrugged.

". . . and sunglasses."

"You mean, they *looked* like sunglasses."

"I saw its eyes beneath the tinted lenses. Those weren't just any animal's eyes. That wasn't a monkey looking at me."

"Our split with monkeys are far back on the primate tree. Our closest relatives are the great apes—chimpanzees, specifically."

"Fine. That was no chimpanzee."

"When have you looked into the eyes of a chimp?"

"Touché. Still, Prof, I swear, those were the eyes of something intelligent—you know what it was like? It was like the actors looking out from their masks in the *Planet of the Apes* movies."

Again, Siderai simply lifted his shoulders.

"And how about Moe and Larry up in the tree?"

"Moe and Larry? As in the Three Stooges?"

"The larger one—Moe—smacked the smaller one—Larry—for dropping . . . whatever that thing was."

"Did you see the smaller one drop it?"

"No. But it was obvious."

"Because Moe smacked him," Siderai said in a tone verging on patronizing.

"Yes. Of course. Prof, what are we going to do?"

He nodded and clasped his hands together on the table. "I'd like to get some videos."

"You want to go *back*?"

"I don't think a drone would be very effective," he said with a half grin.

"Good luck. Watch out for the coconuts."

He raised an eyebrow.

"You know," she said. "In the movies, the monkeys throw coconuts down on the explorers."

"They aren't monkeys, and there isn't a coconut palm within a thousand miles. Besides, I doubt a wild monkey ever threw a coconut at anybody."

"Think of it as a metaphor, Prof."

He grinned. "I don't think you understand. I'd like us both to go back."

She stared at him, remembering two blades held menacingly above her head by long, strong arms.

"I need you to man the camera," he explained. "I'll make the contact. You won't be near enough to be in danger."

"We don't know how fast they can run."

"Their legs were rather short. Besides, why would they come after you? I'll be the one confronting them."

"Maybe they don't like video cameras . . . or girls."

He sighed, then looked at her. "You haven't collected your scat yet."

"Which is on the other side of the space aliens. Besides, that's not the only place marmots live."

He nodded in resignation. "It's your choice, of course. I shouldn't be pressuring you."

He made to get up.

"Hold it, Prof," Terri said, motioning for him to sit down. "I didn't say I wouldn't do it. I was just pointing out the obvious risks involved."

He watched her. "What are you getting at?"

"Oh," she said, staring at the ceiling, "what if we were to substitute this for digging through marmot shit—which, as we know, is properly called scat?"

He studied her. She was ready for him to decline, in which case she'd go along to help anyway—hell, she wouldn't miss the chance—but he nodded. "Okay, but you'll have to write up a report afterwards."

She groaned.

"You thought you wouldn't have to submit a report on the scat analysis?" he asked.

"I was hoping for, like, a hazardous duty waiver maybe."

"Sorry," he said.

"Fine, fine. Shall we meet at the trailhead at, say, noon?"

"I was hoping for an earlier start. On a Saturday there might be hikers on the trail. How about seven?"

"Seven o'*clock*? Is it even light then?"

"Okay, seven-thirty?"

"How about nine?"

"Eight o'clock, and that's my final offer."

"Or what?"

"Or you're left with, and I quote, 'an essentially failing grade'—your humbling B."

Terri sighed dramatically. "Your blackmail is probably breaking some state law, but I won't press the subject."

"Smart girl," he said standing up. "Let's hope we can entice your 'space aliens' down out of the tree."

∞

Terri turned off the car and sat staring at the wall of forest before her. Uncle Greg had no problem coming earlier than his usual Saturday morning visit. These old people—fifty, in her uncle's case—seemed to almost enjoy rising at ungodly hours. She rubbed her eyes, and then rubbed some more, wiping away the sleep.

She had parked next to Siderai's car, the only other one in the lot, but there was no Siderai. It was ten minutes past eight, and she cursed herself. What a screw-up. She couldn't even arrive on time. How much brains does it take just to make an appointment? Her father's unending disappointment in her was obviously justified.

She closed her eyes and took a deep breath, willing away the dark curtain, diverting the deeply worn trough of self loathing.

When she opened them again, Siderai was emerging from the forest. He waved, and Terri got out of her car. "Hey, Prof!" she called. "Sorry I'm late—"

He waved it off. "I got here early. I wanted to check things out."

She eyed him. "Do you enjoy getting up early?"

He shrugged. "Sure. I guess."

"Are you over fifty?"

He laughed. "No. Why on Earth do you ask?"

"No reason. How's it look down in the heart of the dark continent?"

"Quiet. I didn't go all the way in. I didn't see anything. They're either sleeping, or adept at circumspection." He reached into his car and handed her the video camera. "The power button is here," he said pointing, "that's the lever for the lens cover, and if you want to zoom—"

"Prof, I know how to use one."

He nodded and reached back into the car for a khaki vest festooned with pockets, like fishermen or Amazon explorers wear.

Terri studied the camera. "Uh, how does the zoom work?"

Five minutes later, she followed him out of the lot, and into the silent gloom of vast, endless forest, life that grew and adapted so slowly, she could easily imagine that the canopy of green above, the scattering of new growth hugging the leaf-carpeted floor, and even the soft, moss-covered angular forms of fallen trees would be exactly the same if she came back years later.

"Prof," she said quietly, hesitant to disturb the timeless calm "maybe they're mutations—you know, like gorillas that were accidentally exposed to radiation."

"Terri, think about that. I know you have more sense than Hollywood producers."

"It's not as if some gorillas mutated into giant monsters stomping around crushing cars. Just, you know, grew some funny ears, and developed a liking for cool sunglasses."

"Think about how a gorilla looks—a flat nose, large, protruding jaw, high crown at the back of its head. These creatures were almost the exact opposite in all those details—protruding nose, small jaws, and a low crown. Heck, they look more like us than a gorilla."

"Aha! Okay, maybe mutated humans."

"Come on, Terri."

"I know. Mutations operate on individual genes, and any one mutation would change just the associated aspect, like maybe just longer fingers."

"What if there were, by some chance, a whole flurry of mutations?" he asked, throwing her a glance.

"Are you testing me?"

"You're not being graded, so no risk."

"Fine." She cleared her throat dramatically. "The chances that any one random mutation would produce a viable effect are very small. The greatest likelihood, in fact, is that it would be bad. Throw a whole flurry of mutations at the victim—I assume that's a formal zoological scenario—and the poor creature probably wouldn't live long enough to be born alive."

"Too bad you didn't opt for the grade."

"I had the option?"

"We should stop talking."

She whispered, "So, we've concluded that they have to be space aliens, then?"

Siderai held his finger against his lips and moved ahead softly. Terri followed, placing each step as though walking on thin ice. When they came to a large boulder with a doomed little cypress tree growing out of a crack, they stopped. They had run past this in retreat before Conan. The spot where Larry had dropped the whatever-it-was lay a hundred yards ahead, beyond where the trail ambled to the right. Siderai pointed to a small boulder with a bush next to it, and squatted down behind the cover.

"Stay here," he whispered into her ear when she knelt down next to him.

He planned to draw the new species animals within view, and she would use the zoom to catch the activity. He set up a mini-tripod on the boulder, and checked to make sure the video camera was powered. She flinched when it beeped that it was ready.

"Okay," he whispered, "start it as soon as I reach the turn in the path—"

He yelped and tried to spin around, but fell back against the boulder. One of the animals—Moe, Terri guessed—stood there with one of his hands outstretched, three long fingers opposing an equally long thumb. He had snuck up and grasped Siderai's shoulder. Another animal stood next to him—presumably Larry, who had no fingers, just one-inch stubs where the appendages should be. No wonder he'd dropped the thingamabob from the tree house

Siderai laid his arm protectively across Terri's chest. "Don't be afraid," he said quietly, staring into Moe's probing gaze.

Larry tooted some mangled notes, and Moe replied, swiveling his little ears forward and back again, never taking his eyes from the humans before him.

Terri nudged Siderai and pointed. Conan stood nearby, both weapons drawn and ready. The brawny warrior let loose a barrage of musical dissonance, threatening in tone and volume, and Moe responded with equal emphasis. Terri had the sense they were arguing.

Conan stepped forward, and, after more musical argument, Moe stepped back. It was now Larry's turn to verbally wrangle with Conan until the warrior turned and bellowed, at which Larry stood up straight—as straight as their short, bent legs could manage—and took two steps back.

Conan turned back to them, and fear clenched the muscles of Terri's back. This looked bad. "Prof," she said, "is it time to be afraid?"

He didn't answer. He lay against the boulder staring at Conan with furrowed brow. He slowly raised both hands, as though giving himself up to the sheriff, but Conan bellowed again, and raised the sword. Siderai dropped his hands, and snorted. Terri sensed he was scared, and this frightened the bejesus out of her.

Conan lowered the points of both weapons, and then lifted them high. The meaning was obvious, and she and Siderai pushed themselves to their feet. They were now looking down at their aggressor, and he didn't seem to like that. He motioned them back down.

All three of them—Conan, Moe, and Larry—began hooting and tooting, sometimes in turn, and sometimes all at once.

"Conan wants to kill us," Terri said.

"No," Siderai said, but conviction was lacking.

"Maybe we should make a run for it."

He took a moment to think about that as Conan became particularly animated with the heated discussion, swinging his knife in circles. "I'm going to stand up and step in front of you—then you run to the left. Don't stop until you reach the parking area."

"Right, Prof. I'm just going to run off while you play martyr."

"Don't argue. Just do it."

"I have a better idea. Why don't we just both take off at once in opposite directions. At least one of us can get away."

"How is that different than my plan?"

"You have a fifty-fifty chance of not being skewered."

"And you do. No."

Their own argument was cut short when Conan walked away. He slid the knife into his belt, lay the sword over his shoulder like he was carrying a baseball bat, turned, and ambled off without looking back.

Moe said something in trumpets and flute, and they turned to him. He seemed to be talking to them, but Terri didn't have a clue what he might be saying. The beast reached behind him, into a pouch attached to his belt, and Siderai again placed his arm across Terri, both of them expecting another weapon. Instead, Moe extracted an apple, which he held out for Siderai, who looked at it in wonder, and then at Moe. The beast raised its brow, an expression that was impossible to misinterpret. Siderai took it and gave a slow little bow. Moe watched him, swiveled his little ears forward and back, and then mimicked the motion. Their host reached into the pouch, and handed another apple to Terri. She took it, but instead of bowing, she lifted her hand in salute. Moe glanced at Larry, and then repeated the action, albeit sloppily, more a tap on his forehead.

Moe then stood back and lifted his hand, one finger extended, pointing back along the trail. "That's our exit cue," Siderai said, and motioned for her to lead the way.

After a ways along the trail, they stopped and looked back. The forest was empty, no indication that they'd just had an incredible encounter. "Well," Siderai said, "I guess there's no question that they are quite intelligent."

"Prof," Terri said, "did you see their hands?"

"He glanced at her. You mean their fingers."

"Three fingers, Prof. *Three!*"

He nodded, but didn't say anything.

"Aliens, Prof. *Space* aliens."

Siderai didn't answer.

Chapter 3

"What other mammal has just three fingers and a thumb?" Terri asked as they emerged into the hazy sunlight of the parking lot. The thin white overcast seemed even brighter than raw sunshine.

"Squirrels have just four toes on their front paws," Siderai replied, staring at the horizon, hands in pockets.

"Toes, not fingers," she said. "A finger implies an opposable thumb, right?"

Terri was just guessing, but Siderai sighed and nodded.

"Besides," Terri said, "if these guys aren't space aliens, then they have to be primates, right? And I'll bet every primate has four fingers."

He nodded again. He seemed to be only half listening, lost in his thoughts like the first time.

"On the other hand," Terri said, "what're the chances that an intelligent animal would evolve on another planet and look so much like us?"

Siderai finally looked at her, and frowned. "Convergent evolution," he said, seeming to realize that she was standing there next to him.

"You're saying that on a completely different planet—another whole star system—after a billion years of evolving, intelligent life would just happen to end up looking like us?"

"Life on Earth has been evolving for over four billion years."

"Okay! Four times as unlikely! Why not intelligent reptiles, or worms, even?"

He shook his head. "That's stuff from Hollywood and uninformed science fiction. First of all, we have to define what we're talking about when we say intelligence. I think you mean an intelligence that has developed a sophisticated use of tools. By some measures, dolphins may be way more intelligent than us, but we don't think of them as on par with us because they live in a foreign environment and have a completely different social structure. We have no connection."

"Fine. We're talking about animals that use tools. That doesn't answer the question."

"I was getting to it. In the billion and a half years since life has been more than single cells, intelligent tool-using animals have evolved just once—"

"That we know of."

"More uninformed science fiction? Intelligence isn't an inevitable evolved feature, like gills, or eyes. It's a very specialized device to meet a specialized situation."

"Like, uh, let's see—the entire *Earth*?"

"Not at all. Humans have more or less taken over the planet, but that was only an after-effect to the original specialized situation."

"The irresistible urge to kill each other?" Terri said.

"Tribal warfare may indeed have been part of the picture. Chimpanzees wage tribal war of sorts sometimes. The primary component, though, was intense socialization."

"Intense socialization. I like that. Sounds like high school."

"In this case, it means that social position and interactions in the group comprise a majority component of survival advantage."

"Your place in the pecking order means life and death?"

"Indeed. Oh, indeed. Not under normal circumstances, but in times of group stress—famine, or predation, or—"

"Attacks from the Huns tribe."

"Precisely. Because we're wired for it, we take for granted the complexities of negotiation and bargaining, the subtle nuances of abstract communication, the almost magical capacity to gauge truth, lies, and trust. Early evolutionists placed a high weight on hunting—the raw advantage that intelligence provided in outsmarting the prey. That is true, but it wasn't the hunting tactics alone. It was also the social mechanizations involved—who takes the credit for the kill, and thus wields the power of distributing the meat?"

"Prof, I think we were talking about how space aliens would end up looking like us."

"It's the trees."

"The trees are intelligent?" she said. "Like Ents?"

He looked at her quizzically.

"You're not a Tolkien fan, I take it."

"I mean they obviously evolved in trees, like we did."

"The long fingers," she offered.

"With an opposable thumb. The long arms and binocular vision. And look where they choose to set up shop."

"In a tree house."

"Everything points to an evolutionary history of life in trees."

"And that helps make them intelligent."

"Absolutely. Taking up life in threes is moving from two dimensions to three. Your brain has to be able to predict ballistic trajectories, and when threatened, the number of choices for retreat are squared. And, of course, you have to watch for an individual higher up in the social pyramid dropping something on you."

She looked at him. "You're joking about the last point. You just wanted to see if I was listening."

He grinned. "So, Terri, why do they look like us?"

"Test time? Because living in trees gave their brains a head start and developed fingers and thumbs for grasping branches and collecting fruit—fingers and thumbs that they'd need to manipulate tools. Living in trees creates an animal that looks . . . well, like us."

"And, of course, mammals care for their young, which is a prerequisite if you want to live in a complex social structure—"

"Which is why reptiles aren't intelligent."

He nodded slowly, staring at nothing, sinking back into deep thought. Terri had to ask one last question. "Why do they look so different from each other?"

He looked at her in surprise. "That's exactly what I've been wondering. Why, indeed? Why would one be robust and muscular—"

"Conan."

"Okay, Conan. And another one diminutive—with no fingers!"

"That's Larry. He dropped the object at the beginning and has no fingers."

He raised an eyebrow. "The poor beasts are permanently associated with screwball comedy?"

"Fate has no conscience."

Siderai shook his head slowly in consternation. "All so different . . ."

"Hey!" Terri exclaimed, causing Siderai to jump. "So you *do* think they're space aliens!"

He chuckled. "I didn't say that . . . yet."

She leaned over and looked at his watch. "Oh, crap. I have to run." She shoved the video camera into his hands and ran to her car. She owed her Uncle Greg so much already. She didn't want to steal hours as well.

∞

Terri's mother was reading a book when she arrived. This was usually a good sign. "How's it going, Mom?" she said, sitting on the sofa across from her after saying goodbye to Uncle Greg.

Her mother laid the book on her lap. "I'm well, dear. Your uncle was here."

"I saw him, Mom."

"Are you just getting home from school?"

"Mom, it's Saturday."

Her brow furrowed. "Are you sure?"

"Yes, Mom."

She shrugged. "Do you have band practice?"

"Um, no, Mom. Not today."

Maybe she wasn't quite a hundred percent. For one summer, Terri had played bass in a band. They practiced in the drummer's garage, and Terri had to get rides from her mom. That was five years ago.

Her mother frowned again, looked off into the distance, and back at Terri. "I think I was confused." She chuckled. "For a moment, I thought you were still in high school." She frowned again, and stared at the carpet. "Your father's gone," she said softly, looking at Terri.

Terri wasn't sure she meant "gone for a drive," or really "gone." She watched her mother for a clue. "That's right, Mom," she said.

"Sometimes I think it was for the best," she said. "He was so tortured." Her mother's eyes welled with tears. "But I do miss him," she said. "Mostly I miss the father you had before his accident."

That was her euphemism for his stroke. For some reason, she had a hard time calling it what it was.

"We all miss him, Mom. And yes, he was a lot easier to live with before the . . . accident."

"He was much more than just easy to live with," she said, her voice growing louder, which made Terri nervous that it was going to evolve into a wailing session. "So much more," she added softly. "He was the perfect husband and father."

Terri was still cautious, and watched her for a clue.

Her mother took her silence for disagreement, however. "Terri, your father expected a lot from you and your brother, I know that, but it was out of love. Right or wrong, he believed that he was communicating confidence by showing high expectations."

"I know, Mom. Dad's favorite line was that your arrow lands only as high as you aim."

"The man was an angel."

"I know, Mom."

She frowned. "Before the accident."

"I know, Mom."

Her mother blinked and shook her head, as though waking up. She looked at Terri. "Where have you been, dear?"

Ho, boy. If she only knew. "I was at Mirkwood, Mom. In fact, near that glade that Dad used to take me to. Remember?"

A slow smile spread across her mother's face. "Oh yes. How could I forget? You were on cloud nine every time." She sat quietly for a moment. "He often went by himself, you know."

"Oh, yeah? I don't remember that."

"You were in school. He knew you'd pester him about going, so he sort of snuck away when you weren't here." She squinted at something beyond her vision, remembering. "He started going by himself after he returned with that damn bauble—excuse my language."

"You mean the pendant that he always wore?"

"More like an albatross hanging from his neck."

"Why do you say that, Mom?"

"He became obsessed with the thing. He would pace the floor, fingering it, with a faraway look in his eyes. He once told me that he thought it had some sort of energy."

"Like electricity?"

She shook her head. "He said it was difficult to define, like an attraction pulling at something deep in his chest." She smiled. "I called it his Precious."

"I remember that," Terri said. "Ha! I was too young to make the Tolkien connection. Is that where you got it?"

"Of course. It was all so unlike him. In retrospect, I believe that it might have some kind of minor incident—maybe on the trip where he brought back the bauble—"

"Mom, are you talking about a minor stroke?"

She shook her head in disapproval, as though Terri had talked about a fart. "The changes in his behavior were subtle," she went on. "You would have been too young to notice. It was at that time that he started going off by himself. He always claimed it was just to the glade, to be alone with his thoughts, and I never doubted him."

"You know, Mom, it's kind of ironic. Dad's life was science. He was always the stickler for accuracy. And, here he finds something mystical in an archeological artifact—"

Her mother's eyes were filling with tears again. "If only I'd recognized it at the time."

"What Mom?"

"The minor incident! Maybe they could have prevented the big one—"

"Mom, you don't even know that he *had* a mini-stroke."

"But what if he did? We could have acted on it, and he might be here right now!"

She was almost shouting, and Terri knew she was one notch away from a meltdown. "Where did he get the pendant, Mom?" she asked hoping to distract her.

It worked. Her mother blinked, thinking about it. "Goodness, I don't remember, now. He took so many trips, all around the world. I used to go with him, you know—"

"Before Ted and I were born—I know, Mom."

Her mother looked at her with concern. "Oh, honey," she said, reaching out to take Terri's hand, "there was nothing more important than you and your brother."

"I know Mom. You were ready to give up anything for us."

They'd been through this before, but her mother obviously didn't remember.

The familiar cloud settled over her mother's face. Terri didn't know what angry memory was surfacing, but she tried to intercept it. "Hey, do you remember that song you used to sing when you put us to bed? You would mimic the barnyard animals with your hands—"

"After the accident—the big one—your father basically abandoned you two, you know," her mother said darkly.

Except when he was yelling at us for some trivial infraction, Terri thought. "It took a long time for him to recover," she said.

Her mother stared at the carpet as though Satan himself was rising through the fibers. "It nearly drove him mad—it nearly drove *me* mad." Her eyes burst wide. "Maybe it *did* drive him mad! Maybe that's what drove him to leave."

Like having an accident instead of a stroke, he always "left." He never committed suicide. "Mom, what are you talking about? What drove him mad?"

"That damn bauble! He lost it during the accident, and as soon as he recovered enough to drive, he was off looking for it."

"Mom . . ." Terri said, her own brow now furrowed, "Dad had his stroke at the glade."

"Yes. Of course. That's why it turned out so bad. Who knows how long he lay there before the hikers found him?"

"Who knows, indeed," Terri said, tapping her chin, her thoughts drifting off. In Tolkien's story, Gollum's Precious, the ring of power, manages to be lost, only to be picked up by Bilbo, who carries it up, out of the dark depths of the Misty Mountains.

∞

Terri sent the text "*on my way*" to Siderai as soon as Bertha arrived. He wanted another try at capturing video before their special find was discovered, or decided to decamp for a different location.

"We had a little dramatic stroll through the memory maze," Terri told Bertha. "She's okay now. I think she forgot about it."

"No problem. *Cop Rock* comes on in twenty minutes. That should take her mind off everything."

Terri's phone tweedled, and she answered it. It was Siderai. "Stay in the car when you arrive," he said.

"Why?" Terri asked, stepping outside. "Is Conan there with his assassin knife?"

"I don't see him," Siderai said, "but I'm not taking any chances. The leader—Moe—is waiting."

"He's not getting much use of that tree house. Did he came out of the woods?"

"Not quite. I think he wants me to follow him, but I'll wait 'till you get here."

"Okay, I'm leaving now. I should be at the Mirkwood lot in fifteen minutes."

She turned back and pushed open the door to get her keys off the small side table. Bertha was stepping back, looking alarmed. "Sorry!" Terri said, grabbing the keys. "I almost broke your nose! I should be back in an hour or so."

When she pulled into the lot, Siderai leaned over into her open window. "Moe is down the trail a little ways. I'm going to check it out. Wait here until I wave for you."

"Okay. What should I do if Conan jumps out and kills you?"

"Improvise. Here goes."

Siderai walked to the trail head, and waited. After a minute, Terri thought she saw something moving farther down the trail, but the form was indistinct, as though a shadow had changed hue. A coat of gray fur provided effective camouflage in a dense forest. Siderai stepped forward and disappeared into the twilight.

One minute passed into three, and Terri was wondering what her improvising options were, when Siderai stepped back out and waved to her. "No Conan?" she asked when she came to him.

"Just Moe," he said. He smiled ruefully and held up another apple. "He gave me this."

"Maybe it's symbolic," Terri said. "Like an eatable peace-pipe."

Siderai nodded slowly. "Yes. You could be right. Very insightful."

"Uh, what if I told you I was joking?"

"I'd say you have insightful jokes. Shall we?" he said, holding out his hand to proceed.

Terri realized that she had been stalling. It was silly to think that Conan had been biding his time, waiting to lure both of them into a trap. Silly, but disconcerting all the same.

They entered Mirkwood, Siderai leading the way. Terri had thought that Moe would be waiting right there for them. She guessed that he meant to meet them at their tree house, and so she gave a little gasp when she recognized that he was indeed standing just off the path. When motionless, the gray coat was indeed nearly invisible.

Without ceremony or even a gesture, Moe took off down the trail. Although short, his legs moved more like a human's than the yawing swing of chimpanzees. Even with that, the short gait left Terri and Siderai throttling their pace. "Where's he taking us?" Terri asked quietly.

"My studies didn't include zoological telepathy," he said.

"Prof! Was that sarcasm?"

"You're surprised?" he said looking at her with a raised eyebrow.

"Yeah. You're always so . . . professorial."

"I am also gay. Aren't we known for our sharp sarcasm?"

"Wait—that's more sarcasm. Sarcasm about sarcasm. My head is spinning."

Moe glanced back at them now and then, and at one point, let loose with a musical refrain. The hairs on the back of Terri's neck rose at a suspicious thought, and she looked back. "Oh, shit," she said. Conan was bringing up their rear, little sword cocked over his shoulder. "It *is* a trap!"

Siderai turned. "He's just doing his job."

"Which is?"

He shrugged. "He's the protector, the soldier termite."

31

"You think that they're, like, huge termites?"

"That doesn't warrant a response."

They shuffled on. "We've been assuming that they're all males," Terri said.

"Maybe you have," Siderai replied.

"You've been calling Moe 'he.'"

"Only because you named it Moe."

"So, you don't think they're all males?"

"I have no idea one way or the other."

"Maybe they have no sexes—no sex at all. Maybe that's why they seem so dour."

"I'm confident that they have sexes. We just don't know how to delineate."

"What makes you so confident?"

"Convergent evolution again. Earth life developed sex over a billion years ago, before we evolved into multi-celled entities. It's a fundamental aspect of DNA-based life."

"So, you think they have DNA?"

"No. Of course not. But they surely have some means to carry species information from one generation to the next. Come to think of it, their method might just be very similar to DNA, but if so, they surely wouldn't use the same set of amino acids."

"So, eating us wouldn't do them any good. I hope they know that."

"Unless their digestive system can build up a complete set of their amino acids from scratch."

"Shh. Don't give them any ideas. Hey, so you're admitting that they're space aliens."

"I'm here to find out."

Terri saw that they were almost to the ravine, beyond which was the glade she and her father had frequented. "Uh, we're passing their tree house," she said, gazing up.

"Hmm," Siderai replied.

"Where is he taking us?"

"Terri, how can I know that?"

At this moment, Moe stopped and pointed into the brush that filled the little ravine and spilled up over the lip. When they reached him, he slipped off the path and into the thick cover. It was as though he'd disappeared. Only the slight sound of damp leaves compressed under foot, and the occasional little shake of brush revealed that he was heading away along the edge of the ravine.

Conan gave a whistle, and motioned with his sword for them to follow. Siderai turned his fanny pack around behind him and plowed in. Terri followed and was immediately slapped in the face by one of Siderai's branch recoils. It stung, and she twisted it aside angrily. She hardly took three steps before Conan signaled with a sharp hoot. She and Siderai turned to find the muscular beast pointing with his sword at a broken branch of a bush, the one Terri had yanked aside. Conan let loose with a harsh bray.

"He's chastising us for damaging the bush," Siderai said.

"That's commendable."

"I don't think they're protecting the Earth's environment—they want to conceal their presence."

"A broken twig?"

"It could be obvious and meaningful to someone who's naturally tuned in to such things."

"Like them."

"Exactly. To them the broken twig might be essentially a big sign pointing this way."

Another toot from Conan told them to keep going. Moe had stuck his head above the bushes some distance along the edge of the little ravine, and they made for that spot. As they got closer, Terri saw that the forest gorge here was choked with natural debris, as though a flash flood had suddenly dumped its torrential load. "What do you think happened?" Terri said, staring at the little mountain of leafy branches."

"I don't know," Siderai replied, "but whatever it was, it must have been fairly recent. The leaves haven't even begun to wilt."

Moe had descended half way into the ravine along the side of the debris pile, and motioned for Siderai to come down. As Terri stepped forward to follow, Conan's sword suddenly blocked her way. "Uh, problem, here," she said.

Siderai looked back. "They don't want you to come down. Maybe it's for the best until we see what they're up to."

"Sure. Leave me alone with a bad tempered space alien wielding a sword. That's for the best."

"Terri, I won't go far. Just hold tight there for the moment."

Terri watched as Moe descended farther, and then pulled away one branch after another off the pile. What this revealed caused her to rub her eyes. The mountain of branches was just a shell, hiding what was beneath—smooth, unblemished metal. Whatever it was, it was big—judging by the size of the debris pile, maybe as big as a short bus.

Moe laid his hand on the surface where it curved down vertically, and a square section flowed away. "It's the hatch from *Lost*!" Terri called.

Siderai waved her off as he peered into the cavity.

"What do you see?" she called.

"Nothing. It's dark."

Moe motioned for Siderai to move aside, and, with one smooth movement, dropped inside, demonstrating the practical advantages of a body tailored for life in trees.

"A light came on," Siderai reported. "It looks . . . like nothing."

"How can it be nothing?"

One of Moe's hands reached out and waved Siderai to come down. "How can it be nothing!" Terri called again, but Siderai lowered himself carefully inside without answering. She turned to Conan. "How can it be nothing?" she said, but the beast just stared at her through dark lenses, his eyes alert and intelligent.

The sound of a woman's voice trickled up through the open hatch. "Hey!" she called. "Who else is down there?"

Curiosity overpowered her and she took a step forward, only to be looking at Conan's sword. He moved the flat surface against her chest, and nudged her back.

From inside the hidden metal cave came faint wisps of a conversation—Siderai and a woman. Terri couldn't make out the words, and it was driving her nuts. Although solid muscle, Conan was nearly a head shorter than her. She wondered if he'd really use the sword. What if she casually reached down and broke off that dead limb from the log beside her? No, she'd sit down on the log, pretending to be tired. She could then break it off and hold it at each end to parry the sword swings until she got inside. She'd watched this a thousand times in the movies.

Ah, but what if he stabbed instead of swung?

She paused her planning when the subterranean conversation rose in volume and pitch. Siderai seemed angry, but the woman remained unruffled, as though confident that reason alone would calm him. Terri caught isolated words—"insurance," "safe," "guarantee"—but she couldn't cobble enough together to get a meaning.

If there was a fight brewing down there, Terri decided that she'd better just stay put.

She could have done it, though.

Siderai's head appeared in the hatch opening. In his face, Terri saw an impossible combination of awe, frustration, and relief. He seemed to have trouble pulling himself out until he suddenly popped up through the opening, apparently aided by a push from Moe. Siderai extracted himself from the tangle of limbs, and climbed the bank.

"What's down there?" Terri asked.

Siderai tried to wave Conan aside, but the beast held the sword higher.

Moe scrambled up the bank, and a tuneless cacophony burst out between the two beasts. The racket ceased as quickly as it had started, and Conan lowered the sword and stepped aside. He eyed the two humans levelly, his ears doing the forward/back jazz-hands flick as Siderai moved Terri along by her elbow, back towards the trail. "I'm going to scream, you know, if you don't tell me what happened down there."

"Wait until we're back on the trail," he said.

Conan followed, hooting admonishment each time they got a little too rough with the foliage. When they finally broke out onto the path, they looked back to find that their escort had disappeared.

"Prof, tell me what you found or I'm going to stomp on your toes."

He took a deep breath and let it out slowly. He looked her in the eye, seemed about to say something, then just shook his head.

She lifted one foot, poised to stomp.

"Terri," he said, "it's a spaceship."

Blaine C. Readler

Chapter 4

"I *told* you they were space aliens," Terri said as they headed back along the trail. "Wait, you're not joking, are you?"

"No, Terri."

"A spaceship!" she said. "No. It can't be. That's crazy!"

"Terri, you were right. They are not from Earth."

"It's not possible! That thing is, like, way too small."

"Nevertheless."

"Hold it. Maybe that's just, like, the conning tower. Maybe there's, like, this huge part buried under the ground."

"Terri, there's hundred-year old trees growing around it."

"Right. Maybe it's, like, been there a really long time."

"I don't think so. You know, Terri, when you say 'like' so much, you sound like you're back in high school."

She looked at him. "Are you serious? We've made first contact with aliens, and you're worried about my elocution?"

"That's better. They need our help."

"You're not my English instructor, you know—uh, you said they need our help?"

"That's right. The ship is powered with antimatter, and they're almost out—"

"Wait. Back up. Who's the woman? Where'd she come from?"

"Woman? Oh, you mean the ship."

"What? No. I mean the woman you were talking with down there."

"There is no woman. It's the ship—a computer, I guess, or their equivalent. Artificial intelligence, presumably. Although, I guess one would have to define 'artificial' in this case—"

"Prof!"

"What?"

"She spoke English. With no accent. *Perfect* English. She could be a news anchor."

"That would make sense, since she learned English watching news programs. And *Sesame Street*."

"She 'watches' programs? A computer?"

"Okay, she learned English through comparative content analysis."

"That's better."

"Do you feel vindicated?"

"I feel better, yes. How do they think we can help?"

"Moe—through the ship—started by explaining that they expected to find a base here—apparently it could somehow refuel her, I mean, the ship. They followed a beacon signal here, which is supposed to be part of the base. They found the beacon—Moe held it up for me to see. It seems awfully small to be signaling interstellar spaceships—"

"The thing that Larry dropped from the tree?"

"No, smaller—about the size and shape of a walnut. In fact, when she first mentioned a base, I thought she meant something it would rest on for display."

"So, they want us to bring some shovels and dig around for the cosmic gas station?"

"No. They seem resigned that the base isn't here—confused and disappointed, really. But evidently the low fuel is the immediate problem. There's some kind of great disaster if they run out completely, and even while sitting there buried under branches, they're slowly eating away at what's left."

"What can we do?" Terri said. "It's not like we have our own private stash of antimatter. In fact, don't scientists make it, like, one atom at a time in those city-sized colliders? And, even then, it lasts only a second before bumping into the normal kind and obliterating itself?"

"I think it's more like nanoseconds of life, but, yes, I doubt anybody keeps a stock of antimatter. How could you?"

"The container becomes the means of destruction. Sounds sort of like storing sulfuric acid in a milk carton."

"Perhaps, if the milk carton was a nuclear bomb. Anyway, I didn't go into any of this after they asked me to bring back scientists with expertise."

"They hurt your feelings, since you're a scientist?"

He didn't answer, staring at the path ahead with furrowed brow.

"Prof," she said, "I was kidding."

He looked at her. "Oh, I know that. No, I was just thinking. The reason we didn't go into the whole subject in detail was what she said next."

His brow furrowed deeper.

"Yo," Terri said. "You forgot to tell me what she said next."

"Yes, right." He sighed. "Moe didn't just want me to bring back scientists with expertise in the field, but ones that would be properly deferential."

"Deferential? Like kneeling and bowing?"

"We didn't go into details."

"Prof, that couldn't have been all."

"No. That comment made me suspicious, and I asked why they had come to Earth in the first place."

He walked along, eyes on the path, but seeing something far away.

"Prof, I'm still here."

He glanced at her. "She said they came to tame the Earth."

Terri blinked. "Tame the Earth? That's what she said?"

"Yes, those very words."

"That doesn't sound good."

"It's possible that there was something lost in the translation." He took a breath. "That's not quite all, though." He glanced at her again, frowning. "They wanted to keep you there until I came back."

Terri stopped. Siderai stopped and turned around. "They wanted to hold me hostage?" she said.

"They didn't say that, but the meaning was obvious."

"You said no?"

"Of course, Terri."

"That was the argument between Moe and Conan, wasn't it? Conan thought I should stay?"

"I can only presume, but that is what I presume."

"Prof, is it time to call, like, the FBI?"

They walked on, Siderai chewing his lip. "They did let you go without a real fight. How about I contact some acquaintances from the university before calling in the authorities?"

"You want to keep the aliens for yourself, don't you?"

He grinned sheepishly. "Perhaps. Do you think we should contact the FBI?"

"No. I want to keep them for ourselves too. On the other hand, there is that whole 'taming the Earth' thing."

"Terri, they're living in trees."

"That's true. Yet, they're cruising around the galaxy in a spaceship."

"Well, they claim it's a spaceship."

"You're right. A species completely alien to Earth might have built a language translation kiosk in the middle of nowhere, and then hidden it so nobody would use it."

"You know, Terri, sarcasm can be an effective communication tool, or it can be a blunt club."

"Sorry. Maybe they were talking about taming global warming or something—hold on."

Her phone was tinkling. It was Bertha. "Hello?" she said, answering it.

"Hello," Bertha said, "is this Terri?"

"No, I'm a homeless woman who stole Terri's phone—sorry, that was a blunt club. What's up?"

"Oh. Okay." Terri had apparently flustered her. "It's, uh, your mother. You need to come right away."

"What happened?" Terri said, her heart suddenly thumping.

"She's going berserk."

Terri breathed relief. The usual. "Throwing pudding again?"

"No, worse."

"What's she doing?"

"She's screaming . . . and kicking."

"I don't hear her."

"Yes . . . I got her quiet, but I don't think for long. You have to come home."

Terri sighed. "I'll be right there," she said, and put the phone back in her pocket. "Sorry, Prof. Sounds like my mom has dropped off the deep end. I need to go before Social Services comes to haul her away."

"Of course, Terri. Give me a call when you can."

"Okay." She sprinted off down the trail and called over her shoulder, "Maybe I can get Moe to tame her!"

∞

Terri parked in front of her mom's house and sat looking at the front door. Each time was like jumping into a lake—the water might be warm and placid, or freezing and filled with Piranhas, although that was a contradiction, since they were tropical fish.

Something tugged at the edges of her mind. The last encounter with the tree aliens had been a swirl of information, but there was something in there that had nudged her, like a children's picture game, where they have to find an object hidden in plain sight inside an everyday scene. She replayed Siderai's dive into the unknown, and stopped when she came to the beacon, the surprisingly small object no bigger than, and *shaped like* a walnut! Could it be?

The tantalizing question would have to wait. A berserk mother and frazzled health care worker were waiting.

When Terri came through the front door, Bertha was standing there, purse in hand, ready to leave. "That bad, huh?" Terri asked.

The look that she gave Terri was hard to read—it could have been fatigue, anger, or even anxious fear. "She's calmer now," she said, and pushed past Terri, closing the door behind her. This was not the Bertha Terri was used to. That Bertha would have delivered a full rundown of injustices inflicted by her patient. It was odd enough that Terri peeked through the cut glass along the side of the door. Bertha was holding her phone to her ear. She gave a quick glance back, and when she saw Terri, she hurried away down the walk.

That glance had been neither fatigue nor anger. That woman was afraid.

She found her mother watching *Ren and Stimpy* cartoons, and she sat down next to her. "Hey, Mom," she said, turning down the volume.

Her mother looked at her, puzzled.

"Mom, it's me, Terri."

She frowned. "Of course it is."

She continued staring at Terri, not completely convinced.

"Mom, Bertha seemed kind of upset. Did you give her a hard time?"

Her mother thought about it. "I don't think so. Wait, she did seem agitated once when I asked when Fred would come home. She was on the phone, and she shushed me. I don't take to being shushed."

Fred was Terri's father, which meant that the Wayback Machine was dialed at least five years. That was just about right. "Mom, remember the pendant that Dad used to wear all the time?"

"His Precious. Oh, yes. I can't decide if I want him to find it, or not."

In her mother's mind, Terri's father was still alive, post-stroke. "You said he lost it when he had his . . . accident. That was in the glade, in Mirkwood, right?"

"That's probably where he is right now, searching for it."

"Mom, how would you describe it? What does it look like?"

"You know as well as I do."

"It's been awhile, Mom. I forget."

"Well, it's about as big as a plum, but not smooth like a plum. More like giant raspberry."

"How about a walnut?"

"Yes! I thought you forgot?"

"It's coming back. Do you remember where he found it? I mean, originally."

"Oh, let's see. Where would it have been? Burma? Syria? The Yucatan? That man gallivants all over the world. Preston was with him. I remember that because they talked about it at the kitchen table. They claimed it was going to put their names in the history books."

"That little pendant?"

"No, of course not. The temple where they found it—at least, they assumed it was a temple."

Preston was her father's partner for most of the expeditions, so the fact that he had been there didn't narrow it down much.

"A temple, Mom? I don't remember that."

"Your father didn't talk about that part much. I think that was what caused the rift between him and Preston. Your father wanted to keep it secret until they could return for a detailed study, but Preston thought they should hand it over to the university and let them pick up the cost of the next expedition. Your father won out, and he spent the whole last year before the accident trying to find funding."

"Mom, I didn't know Dad and Preston had a falling out. He came by now and then after Dad's . . . accident."

"Yes, Preston is a good man. He stops by whenever he can to see how your father is faring. It's a real shame your father didn't listen to him."

Terri almost mentioned that the last time she saw him was at the memorial service, but in her mother's present state of mind, her father's suicide was still in the future.

"Dear," her mother said, "did you see your father?"

Terri looked at her. "Mom, what do you mean?"

"You were at the glade, weren't you? You would have seen him."

"Well, I was nearby. But, how did you know that?"

"You told me."

"Mom, I didn't."

Her brow furrowed in confusion. "No, dear, you are correct. It wasn't you who told me, it was Bertha."

"She told you I was there?"

Her mother's confused brow rose higher into what Terri knew was about to blow up into anger. "No. That's not right either," she said, her voice rising in volume. "How could I have gotten that wrong? I'm just not myself today. I can't seem to get anything straight, and I'm telling you, it's trying my patience—"

"Mom—Mom!" Terri said, risking a complete blowout. "Did Bertha tell you where I was or not?"

Her mother focused. "No. Damn it! I'm so flustered. She said that you were going to the park, and she asked me if I knew which part. I told her that you were probably going to see your father, at the glade. That's when she called the police—"

"She what?"

"She called the police. She told them that she had information about a murderer. I was concerned, of course, and wanted to know if you were in danger, and that's when she shushed me. Terri, I can't bear being shushed—"

"Mom! Are you sure? That was today?"

"Yes. I think so."

Pieces of the picture were falling into place—Bertha's insistence that she come home, and then her quick exit, making a furtive call as she left—probably again to the police, telling them they could come now. As Terri was leaving earlier, she'd asked Siderai on the phone whether Conan was there . . . with his assassin knife. She'd come back for her keys and caught Bertha by surprise at the door.

Ho, boy.

Bertha must have heard her say that. Terri had also told Siderai that she'd be at Mirkwood in fifteen minutes.

"Mom," she said, jumping up, "I have to leave. I'll call Uncle Greg to come over. You'll be okay until then. Just stay there and watch TV. Okay?"

"You shouldn't bother your uncle. I don't need a chaperone. Besides, your father will probably be home soon."

Terri looked at her. Everything her mother had just said was exactly wrong. "Uncle Greg won't mind. I've got to run. Just sit there and watch TV, Mom. Please."

"Terri!" her mom called as she was opening the door.

"Mom, I'm sorry, but I have to go now—"

"I remember. Your father brought the bauble back from a hiking vacation with Preston."

Terri looked at her. *No time!* She ran out, pulling the door closed behind her.

As Terri drove away, she steered with one elbow while she called her uncle. Just before making the turn at the end of the street, she glanced in the rearview mirror. A police car was rounding the turn at the far block. She held her breath as she waited for her uncle to answer, but no sirens chased her.

∞

Siderai's car was sitting in the same place when she arrived at the parking area. He hadn't left yet when she'd called him, probably having spent the whole time pacing back and forth, hands clasped behind him.

"Terri," he said, coming over to her car, "what's up? You sounded frantic."

She threw her door open, forcing him to jump back. "The police are going to be here any minute," she said, getting out.

"What are you talking about?"

"Our health care worker overheard my phone call earlier, and she thinks that we're somehow in contact with the guy who murdered that old man. She called the police, and they know that we're here."

He held out his hands, palms up. "So? We'll answer some questions and . . ."

"Exactly. How do we explain that I was talking about a guy named Conan who had an assassin knife?"

"I see. We tell them it was a silly mistake. You were talking about . . . a video game maybe."

"You don't know some of the clowns on our local yokel police force. They're just itching to make a name for themselves, and catching a murderer, well, they'd sell their mother for the chance."

"That seems like a contradiction—a policeman selling—"

"Exactly. They'll scour the whole area, and find the tree house. We have to warn Moe, so they can be ready to hide."

"Sounds reasonable. I'll go back since they've already allowed me in their ship. I guess you'll have to deal with the police."

"It won't be the first time."

He gave her a questioning look, and headed off down the trail. "Run!" Terri called, and he waved and broke into a trot.

She watched him until he disappeared around a bend, and then she turned back to the parking area—just in time to see a police cruiser pull in . . . with Barney at the wheel!

He pulled up next to her. "Well, well, Scotty, what have you gotten yourself into now?" he said through his open window.

"I don't know what you're talking about," she said, crossing her arms.

"You always were a troublemaker. You and your loser friends thought you were so cool, but you were just . . ."

"Just what, Bart?"

"Losers. Misfits. We'll see how cool you are in prison."

"What in God's name are you talking about, Bart?" she said trying her best to sound unperturbed, and all the while fighting an urge to glance down the trail.

"We're onto you, Terri," he said. "Somebody in your gang is going to the electric chair, and the rest of you are going to rot in jail as accomplices."

"Bart, what are you babbling about?"

"That poor old man, hacked to death."

"You don't seriously think any of my friends did that."

"You're right, I don't think that—I know it!"

"Based on what?"

"A confession."

"By whom?"

"You! What was it, Terri? A morbid game? Some sort of sick gang initiation?"

"Bart, have you completely lost your mind?"

He didn't like that. He had always been sensitive about his intelligence. His eyes narrowed, and he put the car in park and reached to open the door. "We'll see who's crazy once we find that tree house."

She gasped. What had she said to Siderai on the phone when Bertha was listening? *Oh my God*, she thought. She *had* mentioned something about Moe not getting much use out of his tree house.

Terri panicked. Barney had opened the car door, and was stepping out. She lifted her foot and kicked hard against the outside of the door, slamming it shut on his calf. He shrieked as she sprinted away down the path. From behind her, his howls of pain morphed into curses. "You're dead!" he shouted. A moment later a gunshot exploded the peace of the forest, and something snapped through the leaves above her head. *Son of a bitch! The bastard's shooting at me!* she thought.

She glanced back. He was standing next to his car, aiming his pistol with both hands. She dove to the ground as another shot rang out and the bullet thumped into a tree next to her.

She lay still, then furtively glanced back. Barney stood staring, probably thinking he'd shot her. She launched herself up and ran on. When she looked back, he was following, but limping badly, hobbling along. She rounded a bend, and he was out of sight.

She was in pretty good shape, and she kept the pace all the way to the ravine. She started shouting when she was close enough for them to hear. Conan stood keeping guard far down the ravine, and Siderai climbed up next to him and waved to her. Leaving the path behind, she tore through the brush, knowing she was breaking branches the whole way. They were just going to have to deal with it.

Conan was visibly angry, holding his short sword ready with both hands, when she arrived, panting. "They're here?" Siderai said.

"Yeah," she gasped, bent over, hands on knees. "Barney—" Gasp. "He's coming. He knows about the tree house."

"I see. Hang on," he said, scrambling back down the bank and into the ship. Terri wanted to get Conan down, out of sight, but had no idea how to communicate that in a few seconds. She kept her eyes peeled for Barney. She must have really injured him. She felt bad, but this was life or death when he had a loaded pistol in his hand.

Siderai's head appeared in the open hatch. "Come on!" he called.

As she scrambled down the bank, tripping over the entangled net of camouflage branches, a chorus of whistles and squeaks emerged from inside the ship. Conan responded, and, as usual, an apparent argument ensued, ending with Conan taking one last look around before adroitly navigating the branch cover, taking each confident step as though he'd been practicing them for just this occasion.

Terri made it to the open hatch and peered inside. From above, the interior had looked dark, but she saw that a dim light filled the space within, as though a night light had been left softly glowing. She could see Siderai's legs, and four furry legs of Moe and Larry.

Conan gave a little push against her back. "Alright, already!" she said. At least he hadn't used the tip of his sword.

The hatch was located along the side of the hull, and steps led down the curved inner surface to a floor the size of a subway car. As she descended the short flight, she concluded that this must be the cargo hold, since there were no controls, displays, or even seats, just benches along each side. That seemed crazy, though, since the interior space was as large as the pile of camouflage branches. If there was a separate control room, it would have to be smaller than the inside of a smart car.

Well, why not? What did she know about the design of interstellar spaceships?

Conan followed close behind her, and, uttering a quick vibrato whistle, the hatch slid closed. At least, that's how Terri interpreted the action. It was more like water pouring into a pan.

Moe and Larry were consumed in what appeared to be an argument, and Conan joined in, leaving Terri and Siderai exchanging questioning looks. "Why isn't the ship translating what they're saying?" Terri asked.

"I think it only responds to direct queries," Siderai said.

"Spaceship!" Terri said, "what are they saying?"

"They are discussing what to do," the perfectly pitched contralto voice replied. Terri couldn't identify the source.

At that, all three aliens went silent and looked at her.

"Maybe Barney won't find us, and he'll give up and leave," she said to Siderai, but she really didn't believe it.

The ship hooted and sang a tuneless song, and Moe responded with his own little jazz ditty. The ship had translated what she'd said. "Who is Barney?" the ship asked.

"Um, he's a local policeman. Do you know what a policeman is?"

"Yes," the ship replied. There was no inflection, no hint that the question may have insulted her.

More musical interplay between Moe and the ship, and then she said, "Can Barney connect us with experts in the production of antimatter?"

Terri laughed. "Barney would probably arrest experts in antimatter, thinking that they were radicals protesting things that matter. No, Barney is only trouble."

"Then we wait until he leaves?"

"Sure, let's be optimistic."

Terri glanced at Siderai, and he seemed content to let her take the lead. "Hey, ship, I've been wondering . . ."

The little room was silent as the three aliens watched her.

Terri remembered that she only responded to direct questions. "Why are you a woman—I mean, why do you use a woman's voice?"

"I concluded that this would be expected."

"What made you conclude that?"

"All artificial intelligence personalities are female, such as Siri and Alexa. Nearly all fictional artificial intelligence is depicted as female as well."

"Except for Will Robinson's excitable chaperone."

Silence. That wasn't a direct question. "What are your, um, passengers called?" she said.

"You are referring to the three that were here before you?"

The ship had a pedantic streak. Better that than ambiguous, Terri thought. "Yes. The furry ones."

"Called by who?" the female ship asked.

"I guess by whoever calls them anything."

"I apologize, but this can be confusing. They call themselves The People, but the species from whom they acquired me also calls themselves that."

Terri glanced at Siderai, and they exchanged raised eyebrows. "Your passengers acquired you?"

"Yes."

"Okay, what do the people who they got you from call them?"

"The closest translation is the Inhabitors."

"You mean Inhabitants?"

"No. Inhabitors is a closer match."

"I think you made that word up."

"I did. It's a name."

"Right. Sorry. Inhabitors . . . like they inhabit new worlds?"

"Yes."

"Wait, they colonize worlds?"

"Yes."

Terri and Siderai exchanged glances again, this time alarmed. "Let me get this straight," Terri said, "these guys are here to colonize Earth?"

"Yes."

Their dialogue was interrupted by Moe, who warbled a tuneful refrain, to which the ship replied at length, apparently bringing him up to date. "Manager wants us to concentrate on the problem at hand," the even tempered female ship said.

"Uh, Manager is him?" Terri asked, pointing at Moe. She wasn't sure if the ship could see her.

"Yes."

Evidently the ship could.

"He's the manager?"

"Again, the closest translation."

"What's the problem at hand?"

"The fuel situation is dire."

"The antimatter?"

"Yes."

"I hate to be the one to throw the wrench, but you're not going to get any antimatter on Earth."

Silence. It wasn't a question. "What will happen if you don't get more antimatter?" Terri asked.

"I will explode."

"Literally explode, like a bomb?"

"Yes."

Terri hesitated to ask the next question. "How big? I mean, the bomb?"

"It depends on how much remnant antimatter is left when the containment fields collapse, but approximately equivalent to a small fission bomb."

"Whoa, fission, as in an atom bomb?"

"Yes."

"Yikes! Uh, how small?"

"About forty thousand tons of TNT. This is equivalent to two of the plutonium-fueled bombs dropped on Nagasaki in World War Two."

"Oh, only two? Uh, how long before you run out of antimatter?"

"I would never run completely out. The remaining remnant would annihilate."

"How long until *then?*" Terri wanted to find an AI neck to wring.

"That depends on my rate of consumption. Sitting here idle, I could probably last two months. Otherwise, I have enough for approximately twenty hours of flying time."

"Because, of course, you can fly."

Silence. It wasn't a question. "And then you blow up," Terri said.

Still silence. Still not a question. Well, then . . . "And you turn into confetti and fall slowly to the ground," Terri said.

"No. Within a blast radius of about a thousand feet the chemical bonds of most of the matter would be broken, freeing individual atoms, and anything within a hundred feet would be stripped of electrons, leaving highly charged plasma."

It looked like the ship responded to either a direct question, or to correct an error. "Thank you, Spockette," Terri said.

Silence.

"I've decided to call you that," she added.

Silence. Apparently the ship didn't object.

"Because, you know, you're sort of a female version of Mr. Spock."

Still silence.

"Are you trying to prove that the ship doesn't understand humor?" Siderai said. It wasn't a reprimand, just curiosity.

"I want to make sure that voice isn't some bimbo they hired who's hiding behind the wall—"

She gasped as the top of the ship disappeared, letting in the daylight, filtered through the dense web of branches above them. Out of the corner of her eye, she saw the three aliens slip on sunglasses. She realized that they hadn't been wearing them in the dim light that Spockette provided.

She gasped again when she saw Barney standing at the edge of the ravine staring down at them. He held his pistol in both hands. All Terri saw was the black opening of the barrel.

Blaine C. Readler

Chapter 5

A full experimentalist concerto filled the air as Spockette and the three aliens exchanged excited cacophonous passages. Even as she waited breathlessly for Barney to shoot, she wondered why Spockette's voice continued to come from all directions, including directly above.

Spockette spoke to them, even as she continued the alien discussion. "Enforcer has convinced Manager that this person with the gun should be killed. Do you agree?"

"Killed? No! Who's Enforcer? Wait, it must be Mr. Muscle with the sword."

Silence. Terri sighed. "Spockette, is this one Enforcer?" she said, pointing at Conan, who swatted her hand away.

"Yes."

"He seems to want to kill everybody he meets."

Silence.

Terri rolled her eyes. "Is that true? Does he want to kill everybody?"

"I can't know what he wants. His purpose is to protect the team and ensure that the mission follows prescribed guidelines."

Terri wanted to explore what and who determined these rules, but Barney was moving, taking a few careful steps down into the ravine. He seemed perplexed, as though he couldn't make out what he was looking at. Terri tried something. She lifted an arm and waved to him, then waved frantically with both arms. He never even glanced at her.

"Manager agrees not to kill this policeman for now," Spockette said, "but he insists that I warn him away."

Terri glanced at Siderai, but he was rubbing his chin, gazing around at the branches above them. "Fine," Terri said, "but how are you going to—?"

A soundless flash suddenly splashed across Barney's chest, and he fell back, turned, and scrambled back up the bank. He had obviously shouted something, but not a peep had reached Terri. She realized that she was hearing no sounds, other than the tonal chatter of aliens and spaceship.

Barney's face was beet red when he turned back, raised the pistol, and fired. Again, Terri saw a flash exit the barrel, but it was as though she was watching a video with no audio.

"Enforcer insists that I kill him now," Spockette said.

At least they were keeping the humans in the loop. "Wait! What happened to the bullet?"

"My hull is resilient to some extent, but the effort consumes unnecessary fuel."

Effort? Terri thought. "Don't kill him! Big mistake!"

Silence. Crap! Wait . . . "Hold it!" Terri shouted. "Look! There's other police arriving! You can't kill them all, and if they see you kill this one, you'll never get help. They'll think you're dangerous."

Which they were.

"Actually, I could kill them all, but I will confer with Manager."

The "conferring" didn't seem to be going well. Conan was demonstrating with his sword as though he was going to storm up and personally disembowel all of them. The sheriff and two deputies joined Barney, and they all stared down, pointing and discussing. "Why don't we just leave?" Terri yelled.

The idea flowed naturally, as this had always been her automatic choice when police arrived.

"I will confer," Spockette said.

The answer came back immediately. "Manager agrees with Thinker that we can't leave the immediate area, and so that option seems only more problematic."

Thinker? "Why can't we leave the area?"

"Now that the improbability of acquiring antimatter fuel has been made clear, it's imperative that we find the base."

Terri looked at Siderai. "This is the base you talked about?"

"I presume so," he said without looking at her. He was holding his hand in the air where the hull had disappeared, as though remembering exactly where it had been.

"A base . . ." Terri said. "Hey, can I see that beacon?"

She thought at first that they were ignoring her, but, still hooting a shaky tune, Moe finally stepped to the side where a section of the hull had suddenly reappeared, and he reached into a small cubby.

"You thought the hull was gone," Siderai said, watching her stare at the magic.

She glanced at him. "She made it, like, transparent?"

"Not exactly. I think that the ship is simply showing us what we would see if the hull *were* transparent."

"It's like the whole inside is, like, one big 3D display screen."

"It's, like, like that."

He was making fun of her, but she ignored it. Moe was holding the beacon in his hand for her to see. "Holy shit!" she said. "It *is* it!"

She reached out to take it, but Moe pulled it back, and Conan knocked her hand away.

"It is what?" Siderai said.

"My dad's pendant! He brought it back from one of his trips, and lost it nearby in the glade!"

"You're sure?" he asked skeptically. "That seems . . . quite a coincidence."

"Look! It's the same leather neck cord—wait a second . . ." The answer was like a curtain opening to a sunny day, the proverbial light bulb. "Mom thought that Dad brought it back from some temple excavation."

Siderai was looking at her with his characteristic raised eyebrow.

"Don't you see? That temple—that must be their base!"

Siderai's eyebrow melted into a frown. "Terri, that seems fanciful. I doubt the base they're talking about would look like a temple—"

"Spockette!" Terri said. "How big is this base they're looking for?"

"Eight hundred and seventy-three feet in diameter."

Siderai's eyebrow took up its intrigued perch. "Really? That's approximately the size of four high school football stadiums. Very interesting."

"Spockette," Terri said, "I know where their base is. At least, I know where it *isn't*, and it isn't anywhere near here!"

"Manager wants me to make sure that I understand you," the ship said. "You're saying that your father removed the beacon from the People's base when he was performing a UNESCO archeological assessment?"

Terri blinked. "I didn't tell you that he did assessments for UNESCO. How do you know that?"

"Much of his work is a matter of record."

"You're trolling the internet!" Silence. Terri snorted. "Spockette, are you trolling the internet?"

"Yes."

"Can you find a mention of a temple that my father may have worked on?"

"Your father visited at least seven prehistoric temples—Ban Chiang in Thailand, the Stones of Stenness of Orkney in Scotland, two megalithic temples on Malta, the Cahokia Mounds of Missouri, the Chaco Canyon in New Mexico, and the caves of Tagul in Mexico. Additionally, the hunter-gatherer cave dwellings of Kakadu National Park in Australia and Pont d'Arc in France are considered by some to demonstrate ceremonial religious purposes, and thus might constitute temples, as well as a new find under the sands of Petra in Jordan—"

"We get the picture," Terri said. "In other words, it could be any one of a whole herd."

Silence.

"Correct?"

"Yes," the ship said.

Siderai took Terri's arm, and leaned over to whisper in her ear. "You need to convince them to leave, now." He gestured with a nod, and she saw that the sheriff was taking careful steps down the bank, followed by the two deputies. Moe might decide to kill them.

"Manager agrees to leave now," the ship said, "on a condition."

Terri threw Siderai a glance. Spockette could hear whispers. "Fine. Let's go," Terri said. "Uh, what's the condition?"

"There is no English word. It's similar to a promise, but with serious consequences."

"How serious?"

"There's a range."

"What's the worst?"

"Death."

"Ah," Terri said, feeling her heart take a double beat. She glanced at Siderai again, and he looked at her with consternation. She could be taking a risk, but the sheriff seemed bent on getting himself killed. "What's the promise I'm supposed to make?"

"That your father brought the beacon to this place."

She'd have to trust her father to some extent, but that was beyond doubt. He would never have lied about that, not before the stroke, at least. "Let me see it," she said.

Moe held it up. It looked exactly like she remembered. But her life might depend on this. "Let me have it," she said, holding out her hand.

Conan raised his sword, ready to chop it off at the wrist. Every fiber screamed to pull her hand back, but she held it there. She saw that it was shaking. "Just for a second," she said.

Looking her in the eye, Moe handed it to her.

As soon as it touched her palm, she knew that this was her dad's Precious. She closed her eyes, and curled her fingers over it. The sense of being back in the glade, watching cotton clouds as her father spoke softly of his travels, was so vivid, she thought she might be dreaming. A feeling of peace and security filled her, and she realized she hadn't felt like this since she was that child.

Her reverie was broken when furry fingers pried hers open. "That's the one," Terri said, letting Moe take it. "My father brought it from somewhere—somewhere other than here."

She yelped when the world suddenly rose beneath her. It was the ship. The camouflage branches slid away on all sides. The sheriff fell back against the bank, his mouth an open cavern, and his eyes round circles. Behind him, at the top of the bank, Barney raised his pistol and it jerked as he fired. The sheriff yelled something, and Barney lowered the pistol, probably saving his life.

Terri shrieked when the ship disappeared beneath her, leaving her floating in thin air . . . but still rising. They were all rising together, like angels ascending, except that Terri was on her hands and knees, terrified, and reaching for something to hang on to. Her brain told her that it was an illusion, that the ship was simply showing what was below them, but her gut, her instinct, screamed that she was about to fall to her death. Green leaves pushed away on all sides as they rose through the forest canopy, and she desperately wanted to reach out and grab a twig, anything other than air.

It dawned on her that something was tearing at her wrist. In her panic, she had grabbed Conan's ankle. She let go and decided to just lie in a fetal position, covering her eyes with her arms.

"Spaceship," Siderai said, "perhaps you could take away the downward view."

"Is that the girl's problem?" Spockette asked.

"That's Terri's immediate one, yes."

Prof made a joke, Terri thought from inside her cocoon. Hearing his easy tone, his lack of fear, she felt ashamed. She removed her arms and saw that, in any case, Spockette had returned the floor, made it visible.

"Terri," Spockette said, "Manager wants to know our destination."

"Uh, good question."

Silence.

She looked at Siderai, and he shrugged.

"Let's go to my house. Maybe my mother can remember something."

That seemed unlikely, but for now it was at least a destination.

"Terri," Spockette said, "I will need to show you the view below so that you can direct me to your house."

"Can't I just give you my address?"

"I could try to find some maps containing sufficient address details, but it seems quicker for you to just guide me."

"You don't know how to use Google Maps?"

"I see. You are correct. I just need your address."

As Terri reeled it off, she saw Siderai watching her with his eyebrow cocked. "What's with the look?" she asked.

"You don't think a bus-sized silver football flying along won't attract attention?"

"You're right. Spockette, can you make yourself invisible?"

"I know of no such technology. In any case, my designers wouldn't have considered that a necessary feature for an escape function."

"Really? That sounds like an awfully useful feature when escaping. So, what do you suggest?"

"I don't know what the problem is."

"Uh, we're going to have a whole lot of gaping faces turned up at us once we leave the park."

"I still don't know what the problem is."

Terri looked at Siderai. "Good question. Why *is* that a problem?"

"The authorities tend to get excited when unidentified objects are flying about."

"Manager wants to know if these authorities can help find the base," Spockette said.

"Quite the opposite," Terri replied. "Their red tape will strangle you . . . of course, you don't breath. That was a metaphor."

Silence. Spockette apparently knew what a metaphor was.

Siderai was frowning again.

"What now?" Terri said.

"We've made the authorities seem like dangerous obstacles."

They are, Terri thought. Oops. "Listen, Spockette," she said "the last thing you want to do is aggravate these authorities. Like, for example, killing them."

"Why?"

Terri blinked. Such a simple question with such immense implications. "They don't back down," she said. "Each one you kill means that they'll come at you double. They'll keep escalating until they eventually throw a nuclear bomb at you."

Well, she thought, *they do that in the movies.*

Silence. Terri sighed. "Spockette, do you understand?"

"Yes."

"Yeah, but do you agree not to kill anybody?"

"It's not up to me."

"Fine. Can you get Moe . . . I mean Manager to agree?"

Flutes and de-tuned violins, and Spockette said, "Manager says that he understands the consequences of killing authorities."

That would have to do for the time being. "Well, I guess we'll just have to make it snappy, then," Terri said.

Something zipped by. It was the top of a tree. Then another one. They must be flying quite low. That worked. By the time anybody saw them, Spockette would be gone before they could call other witnesses. She would be just another UFO enigma for the files.

Siderai was gazing up, and he pointed.

Maybe not. A white and black helicopter was pacing them about a quarter mile away. "Police?" she said.

He nodded.

"How did it get here so quickly?"

"Maybe they took your health care worker's tip seriously. Or maybe it just happened to be in the air nearby. In any case our cat is out of the bag and being tracked."

"Let's hope they keep their distance," Terri said. "For their sake."

Aliens are so . . . alien, she thought. She was used to the idea of people killing each other over money, revenge, power, or even for sadistic pleasure. But this cold calculation was frightening. People once thought that nature's hammer blows—earthquakes, lightning, and tornadoes—were punishment from the gods. If you were being punished for something you did, then you had some amount of control—just don't do that again. This, though, being killed because you got in the way . . .

The fact that her own ancestors made their way to the northwest via the Oregon Trail, a route littered with the bones of native Americans who'd gotten in the way, was different. Surely. In any case, that was a long time ago.

But, speaking of killing . . . "Hey, Prof," she whispered, "I just had a thought—do you think they killed that old man near the park?"

He stared at her a moment and shrugged, but then frowned. "Hmm," he murmured, tapping his chin. He shrugged again. "She can hear us whispering, you know," he said.

Terri glanced at Moe and then at Conan. In any thriller, if you figured out who the murderer was, you were next. On the other hand, the aliens had been ready to kill Barney right before their eyes. "Spockette," Terri said, "there was an old man killed near the park. Did you do that?"

"No," the ship replied.

"Whew," Terri said. "That's a relief. It would have been something of a moral dilemma if we were helping a murderer get away—what?" she said. Siderai was shaking his head.

He sighed. "Spaceship," he said, "did Enforcer kill the old man?"

"Yes."

Terri gasped. "Why?"

"Enforcer was protecting the mission."

"From what? The guy was, like, ninety! He could barely walk!"

"We had only recently arrived, and Thinker had not yet reached conclusions about the local fauna. Additionally, Manager was not ready to reveal our location—"

"Whoa! *Fauna?*"

"Fauna means the animals of a particular region, habitat, or geological period—"

"I know what it means."

Silence.

"Spockette," Terri said, controlling herself, "we—humans—don't think of ourselves as fauna."

Silence.

"Do you understand?"

"No. Humans are animals, and you reside in this region—"

"I *know* that. It's just that we're . . ."

"Special?" Siderai asked with one raised eyebrow.

"No! I mean, yes—in a way. We're . . ."

"The ones making the classification?"

"Sure. But that's not the only reason."

"What, then?"

"Well, for example . . . oh, you know what I mean."

"Terri, I'm not sure you know what you mean. You are the squirrel protesting about being included in the same family as a rat."

That gave her pause. Was that the way the aliens viewed her? A chimpanzee with better tool skills? Why wouldn't they? "They live in trees!" she said.

"Well, rats often make nests in yucca and palm trees—"

"No! I mean, you know . . ."

"Our hosts? The police didn't find them in their search of the park. Sounds like a smart move to me."

"You think they built those tree houses just to hide?"

"No."

"So, you do think they live in trees."

"It's just an assessment based on evidence."

"Like that they were sitting in a tree when we found them."

"Like the evidence that they've been evolving inside deep forests."

"Because they like to sit in trees?"

"Because they've adapted to a life with low light levels."

"The sunglasses!" Terri exclaimed.

"Yes."

"Which you didn't think were sunglasses, by the way."

"I just didn't know at the time."

"Wait. Maybe their planet's sun was, like, really dim."

"That seems unlikely. If the planet-wide energy from their star was as meager as the light inside this ship indicates, then there wouldn't be enough heat to keep water liquid. And, of course, water is essential for life—at least life as we know it."

"When did you become a cosmologist?"

"First of all, a cosmologist is concerned with the origin and evolution of the universe. Characteristics of a planet would be studied by a planetologist. Second of all, thanks to the many astronomical scientists who write for the layman—me—I don't have to be a planetologist to know some basics. It's called reading, Terri."

"No need to get snarky. But, speaking of thinking," she said, glancing at their hosts who stood quietly listening to the ship sing in bad tuning, presumably translating what she and Siderai were saying, "what do you think is up with the third alien—the one Spockette called 'Thinker'?"

Siderai shrugged. "He thinks, I guess."

"Prof, would you let me get away with an answer like that?"

"You're right. Sorry. I honestly don't know. Why don't you ask the ship?"

Terri knew that Spockette probably already heard what she'd been saying, but it seemed . . . nosey to make such a blunt personal inquiry. Particularly since the ship would most likely turn around and tell the aliens what was going on. On the other hand, these creatures weren't exactly reverent about human life. "Spockette," she said, "why did you call the third alien 'fauna' example 'Thinker'?"

"That is his title," the ship replied.

"That's as bad as the Prof's answer. Why was he given that title?"

"The title is a translation. It is the closest I can come to the meaning in their language. Thinker's role is to aggregate disparate information sources and process them according to mission perspectives in order to arrive at culturally logical and preferably actionable conclusions."

"That sounds like a mouthful of air. So, maybe Prof's answer was right—Thinker thinks."

Silence.

"Spockette, can you put it in plainer language?"

"Let me try," Siderai said. "Spaceship, is Thinker what we might consider a philosopher?"

"Yes."

"Well," Terri said, "why didn't you say that in the first place?"

"My original answer was more accurate," the ship said.

"Fine. So, how is Thinker different from Manager?"

"Thinker is seven years older than Manager. Thinker exhibits the specialized physical traits common to his caste, whereas Manager exhibits more generalized physical traits—"

"No. I mean how are their roles different? Doesn't Manager think?"

"Of course Manager thinks. His role is to make decisions that advance the mission in the direction immediately ahead, based on current information. Thinker, on the other hand, assesses data gathered as broadly as possible in anticipation of alternate future exigencies."

"Manager is the sheepherder, and Thinker is the worry wart."

Silence.

"Look," Siderai said, pointing. "The police helicopter is leaving."

The copter was indeed skedaddling, growing smaller as she watched. "I wonder what scared it off?" Terri said. "Maybe they figured out that we're a ticking antimatter nuclear bomb—"

"We have arrived at your house," the ship said.

"Already? Crows have it made. Uh, I guess we should figure out where to land. Nobody uses the swing set in the back yard anymore, but mom will have a heart attack if we squash it. I guess you could just park in front of the house."

"I would damage automobiles," the ship said.

"There's no room? Oh, geez. I guess you'd better give me a look."

Instantly the floor was gone, and Terri gave a little squeak and grabbed Siderai's arm. Directly beneath them, a hundred feet below, three police cars were parked at odd angles with doors ajar, the way they do when reacting to an "incident." Two policemen climbed out of cars and stared up at them, and two more ran out from the house. Terri saw their mouths moving as they shouted to each other, and all four slowly pulled pistols from holsters.

"Oh well," Terri said, hanging tightly to Siderai as her feet seemed to stand on thin air, "Mom probably wouldn't have remembered anything anyway. We'd better leave before the cops start shooting."

"Manager reminds you of your promise," the ship said as Terri felt thirty pounds heavier and the ground slowly dropped away.

Terri looked at the alien as he stared back with deadly intent. "The promise was that my father brought the pendant beacon to the park, not that I'd be able to find your base."

"The only proof is to find the base," she said.

"Hey! He can't change the rules like that!"

"I think he can do whatever he likes," Siderai said quietly. "We can't bargain when we have nothing to bargain with."

"So, I find their base for them, or they, like, kill me?"

"That's up to them, but I think we need to assume the worst."

"Well, it can't get any worst than that. I hope they hang a plaque at the park for me for saving the sheriff."

"Would you have done it knowing what the consequence was going to be?"

"That's beside the point, and don't tell the plaque committee that I didn't know. Geez, Prof, I'm joking about this, but I don't think Moe is."

"There's nothing for it, but to endeavor to find the base."

He was giving her a knowing look. They had to at least make a show that they were on a viable path. "Preston would know," she said.

"Great! How do we get in touch?"

Terri rolled her eyes. He'd just blown the show. Now she was on the hook. It had been years since she'd last seen her father's partner. She didn't have an address. She didn't even know what state he lived in. Whatever information there might be was in her house, guarded by four cops. "I have to look it up," she said, giving him a frown, hoping he wouldn't press the subject further.

"Are you expecting high speed vehicles?" the ship asked.

"More police?"

"I can't know if these are police vehicles. They are traveling at five hundred miles per hour."

Terri's brain stalled. Had Spockette made a slip of the tongue? Could a souped-up police cruiser reach that speed? That was nuts.

"Fighters!" Siderai shouted, pointing.

Three of them in formation, looking like lethal darts, spitting white-hot fire. They sped past a quarter mile away. She knew what those pointy things hanging under the wings were for.

"We know why the police helicopter left," Siderai said.

"Spockette," Terri said, "what happens if you're hit by one of those missiles?"

"I believe those are F-16s carrying AIM-9 Sidewinders. A direct hit would certainly disrupt my antimatter containment."

"Letting the antimatter loose."

Silence.

Terri didn't need clarification.

The fighters had diminished to tiny dots in the distance, but the dots were banking, turning to come around for an intercept. Terri figured the missile tracking mechanisms would need a certain distance to get their bearings and lock on to their target—her.

"Can we outrun it?" she asked.

"Sidewinders exceed twice the speed of sound," the ship replied. "I could not reach that speed in time."

"So, we're fucked."

Silence.

Chapter 6

Terri gave a squeal as she fell to her hands and knees, suddenly squashed. The ground rushed away. Her house became tiny below her, and then her block shrank to one little square among the neighborhood grid that itself shrank until it was just a piece of the Northwest patchwork of intermingled development and forest. "I'm going to puke," she said.

"Spaceship," Siderai said, "please remove the downward view."

The floor returned, and Terri struggled to her feet against the upward acceleration. "You said 'please' to a computer," she said as Siderai offered her his hand. "What's going on?"

"I expect she's taking evasive action. Is that true, Spaceship?"

"Yes."

"An explanation, please?"

"The specified altitude ceiling for F-16 fighters is fifty thousand feet. Their Sidewinder missiles can reach higher than that, but the pilots have difficulty targeting above them at such heights. Additionally, whereas their climb rate is fixed at a maximum of fifty thousand feet per minute, I can continuously accelerate, thus leaving them behind once I exceed their climb rate—"

"Thank you, spaceship."

"You thanked a computer," Terri said.

"How long until we are safe?" he asked, ignoring her comment.

"We have just passed twelve miles of altitude. Safety depends on the diminishing likelihood that the fighter pilots will decide to attempt a Sidewinder strike—"

"Twelve miles? How fast are we going?"

"Seven hundred miles per hour and increasing."

"Approaching the speed of sound."

Silence.

"Correct?"

"Incorrect. We have exceeded that. The speed of sound diminishes with thinner air."

"At what altitude are we beyond the reach of the Sidewinders?"

"Since their propulsion is based on a rocket and not a jet, their maximum altitude is dependent only on their fuel supply, which is documented to be twenty miles in horizontal flight, and significantly less when traveling vertically."

"So, to answer my question, we'll be safe when twenty miles high."

Silence.

He sighed. "Correct?"

"Incorrect. Since they would be launched from the fighters, the guaranteed safe altitude would be twenty miles plus the fighter's altitude."

"Okay, let's say thirty miles, then—correct?"

"I agree."

"Finally. When do we get there?"

"We have already passed thirty miles."

"We *have*? How fast are we going now?"

"One thousand, two-hundred miles per hour."

"We going into orbit?" Terri asked, gulping.

"No," the ship said.

"Orbital speed is more than six times that," Siderai explained. "Plus, we're going straight up. But that does beg the question of what to do next."

Terri and Siderai waited as the musical quartet danced around a tune remotely pleasing. Terri noticed that Thinker, usually silent, was actively involved, using his creepily stubbed fingers to demonstrate points. "Thinker opines that we go to this Preston," the ship finally reported.

"Wow," Terri said. "What a brilliant idea. That Thinker must have one super-charged brain."

Siderai gave her a hard look.

"I'll bet they don't even get sarcasm," she said. "They probably believe I just gave their traveling philosopher a big compliment."

"If they did," Siderai said, "you just corrected them."

"Where is Preston?" the ship said.

"That's the problem," Terri replied. "I don't know."

More twittering and hooting. "Manager reminds you of your promise," the ship said.

"I *know*!" Terri said. "You're the one with all the internet access."

The ship and Thinker parried flute solos. "I will help you," the ship said. "Give me whatever information about Preston you can."

There wasn't much. Terri described him—his balding pate, big ears, close-trimmed beard. She told the ship that he always wore blue jeans, tight pants and T-shirts that only made his expanding belly seem larger. "I have located thirty-seven men with the name Preston and that description," the ship reported.

"I don't know what else," Terri said. She shrugged. "He was always just my father's partner."

Two seconds later, the ship said, "I have narrowed the selection to the probable candidate."

Terri stared at the curved section at the ship's nose, what she had begun to think of as Spockette's location. "You couldn't have guessed this? You had to be told that he was my father's partner?" she accused.

"Yes."

Terri snorted.

"Do you know where he is?" Siderai asked.

"Salem Community Hospital in Salem, Oregon," she said. "Room three hundred and twenty-three."

"A hospital? What's his problem?"

"Your government's HIPAA rules prevent me from determining this, but I know that he has visited a variety of cancer specialists."

"I see."

"Uh, how high are we?" Terri asked. The sky was getting darker. She could see a few stars.

"Twenty miles."

"Um, shouldn't we be, like, slowing down?"

Musical discourse followed, and suddenly the ship fell away from Terri. She was floating. She would have squealed, but the sudden exhilaration caught her breath. She jerked when she bumped into Siderai, and they bounced away in opposite directions. Terri came up against something soft, and shot away again with a whack on her butt. It was Conan, and he looked disgusted. She noticed that the aliens had inserted their feet into slots at floor level, and grasped handholds that hadn't been there a minute ago.

She and Siderai drifted up, and lay with their backs against the invisible ceiling of the craft. Terri shook her head—the world had turned upside-down. The aliens were now hanging from a ceiling that had been the floor. The force pulling her to the ceiling-that-was-now-the-floor was weak, but enough to convince her inner ears that down was up.

"Air resistance," Siderai said, clearly exhilarated as well.

He had a knack for anticipating her next question. Maybe it was a gay thing.

"We're in freefall," she said, "but the air is slowing us down? We're decelerating?"

"You know, Terri, you're not as dumb as you pretend."

She looked at him, surprised.

"Sorry!" he said gleefully. "That was out of line."

"Prof, when was the last time you visited an amusement park?"

"I don't know. When I was a kid."

"Well, this is a kid's ride compared to some of those. Spockette, can you take us to that hospital?"

"That is the plan," the ship said. "Prepare for acceleration."

"How do we do that—?"

They fell to the floor, or rather, the ship's floor came to them. Spockette must have anticipated this, for she now kicked in the real juice, pressing Terri's face against the hard surface. "Holy hell!" she shouted. "What's the goddamn rush?" She noticed that the aliens were hanging on to handholds with both hands.

"Thinker wants to avoid pursuit," the ship replied.

"What pursuit? Who's coming after us twenty miles up?"

"The United States Department of Defense Space Surveillance Network detects and tracks unexpected objects in near space."

70

"You think they'd send a missile to shoot us down? That was a question," she said, grunting as she did a pushup to get her face off the floor.

"I have to assume that this is possible."

"Well, are they tracking us now? I mean, can you, like, detect radar?"

"I can detect radar, and I have no indication that they are tracking us now."

"So, again, why the rush?"

"Thinker believes that the shorter the amount of time in transit, the less likely we'll be found."

"Can't you fly in, you know, stealth mode?"

"I have no mode such as that. In any case, because of my shape and skin material, I return essentially no radar frequency energy."

Terri gave up, and let her face fall back to the floor. "Spockette," she said, out of the side of her mouth not jammed flat, "I don't think I heard you correctly. It sounded like you said that you are invisible to radar."

Silence.

"Jesus Christ! Are you invisible to radar?"

"Yes. Effectively."

"Holy hell! Are you a moron?"

"No."

"Well, I think you are! If you are invisible to radar, then they can't detect you. If they can't detect you, then nobody can be pursuing us!"

Silence.

"Christ! Do you agree or not?"

"I agree that it is highly unlikely that anybody would be pursuing us."

"Then *why am I squashed to the floor?*"

"It is not I who has determined this acceleration. I will ask Thinker."

After a few bars of musical nonsense Terri was suddenly floating again. "Come on!" she yelled. "You're making me sick. Can't you pretend you're, like, an airplane and just fly steady?"

"I assume that was a metaphor," the ship replied. "I cannot pretend, but I can emulate the action."

After a twittering, warbling exchange, Terri settled to the floor next to Siderai. Spockette had turned off the outside view, and the world had again shrunk to a large, dimly lit closet. "You were arguing with a computer," he said.

"Yeah, so?"

"If you can argue, I can say please and thanks."

"Fine, but I think arguing is more productive. Spockette, how soon 'till we get to the hospital?"

"We are approaching Salem now."

"Huh?"

"We are almost to Salem."

"No, I heard you, but . . . man, that was fast. Are you sure?"

"Yes."

"Terri," Siderai said, "we were continually accelerating at more than three Gees. A Corvette reaches sixty miles per hour in three seconds at less than one and a half Gees."

"Spockette, how fast are we going now?" she asked.

"Eight thousand miles per hour."

"Eight *thousand*?" Siderai said. "Wouldn't we be creating a fireball at that speed?"

"I took us up to forty miles where the air is thinner. Neither air nor my skin can actually burn, but we are travelling fast enough to ionize the air."

"That's what we call a fireball."

Silence. This was why the ship had turned off the outside view—the aliens avoided bright light.

"That's visible from the ground, you know," he said. "For miles and miles around."

Silence, followed by alien discourse. "Prepare for extreme deceleration," she said.

"Oh, hell," Terri moaned, and lay down flat on her back on the floor just as an elephant sat his fat rear end on top of her. "Prof," she said, gasping short breaths, "Did they—" Gasp. "—just screw up?"

"I guess so," he replied next to her.

"Should we be—" Gasp. "—like, worried?"

"They travelled here from another star."

"So, they should know what they're doing?"

"Let's hope so," he said.

"Let's hope so—how about a prayer?"

"We're not in danger yet."

"Thank God—" Gasp. "—I feel so much better."

"Blunt club, Terri."

"Yeah, well, I hope we—" Gasp. "—don't actually need one."

The elephant dissolved, and Terri floated up, and then slammed against the roof. "Hey, Spockette! How about that airplane mode?"

"Manager has directed me to land as quickly as possible. We have arrived," the ship said as Terri and Siderai fell to the floor. It wasn't a full one-gravity fall, but enough to draw a muttered curse from Terri. "Manager says that you will extract the location of the base from Preston and then return immediately."

"Oh, he does, does he?"

Silence. Moe was staring at her with what she took to be alien evil eye.

"And what if I just run away?"

Fractured music.

"You will not. You made a promise."

Terri wasn't sure if that was a prediction or a threat. "You coming, Prof?" she said.

"He will stay here," the ship said.

"A hostage?"

"Yes."

"At least you're honest. Well, I'm not going without him."

"You made a promise, and the consequences of—"

"It's okay, Terri," Siderai said. "I'll be fine."

"You trust me, Prof?"

"With my life."

"So you have."

She turned to find that the inlaid stairs had reappeared, and the hatch opening gave way with the same flowing water effect. She took a step up and looked out, then turned to Siderai, wide-eyed. "They landed in the God-damned parking lot!"

"Really?" he said.

"Oh, yeah. There's people out there staring with their mouths dropped open." She took another couple of steps up. "There's no ladder! How am I supposed to get down?"

"You jump, I guess."

"It's, like, fifteen feet!"

"Terri, it's not fifteen—"

"Fine, fine. What do you care? You'll be here all cozy."

"A hostage."

"A cozy hostage."

She stepped up to the lip, and saw that the pavement was maybe six feet below her. Still, a ladder wouldn't hurt. Even a rope. She could sprain an ankle. A small crowd was gathering, keeping a safe perimeter. "What is that thing?" a young man called, pointing.

"A Ringwraith!" she replied, calling out the first thing that came to mind.

This launched the crowd into a debate, as those that were familiar with Tolkien's tale explained the meaning. She turned back to Siderai. "I'm going to need a distraction."

"I'll see what I can do," he said.

She stared at the pavement, and then muttered, "To hell with dignity," and, grasping the lip of the hatchway, she turned around and let herself down slowly until she was hanging by her hands. She swung her feet a bit, and, finding no pavement, let go. The fall was only a foot, but she lost her balance, and stumbled backwards. She turned to the stunned faces. What could she say? "Take me to your leader!" she called.

Everybody seemed to blink once in unison. Suddenly, a blood-curdling scream burst from inside the ship, exactly the sort that naked Marion Crane made when Norman Bates surprised her in the shower with a kitchen knife. Dozens of eyes went wide, and everyone took a few steps back. Spockette was obviously a quick study with American culture.

The growing crowd wordlessly made way as she walked through. Orderlies, anxious to catch the action, sprinted past her when she came through the hospital doors. Two women at the check-in counter were on tippy-toes, trying to look out the windows, itching to abandon their post and find out what was out there. They didn't know that Terri was an alien accomplice.

Terri took the elevator to the third floor, and more orderlies, nurses, and doctors piled in when she got out. The elevator opened to a little sitting area, and Spockette was plainly visible through a large window—small, shiny, and completely alien down there. She figured that if she were in their comfy-if-unattractive-shoes, she'd have left the patients on their own as well.

This was going to be a breeze. She just had to find room 332 ... or was it 323? Crap. She peeked into room 332, and there was a man lying in bed, but he looked too old. "Preston?" she said.

He looked at her through dull, watery eyes. "I shit my pants," he said hoarsely.

"I'll, uh, get a nurse," she lied. "You just hold tight, and . . . try not to move."

That wasn't Preston, and if it was, she'd just have to take the consequences with Moe.

She paused outside room 323, took a breath, and looked in. Now *that* was Preston. He'd gone completely bald, and had lost the beard—maybe both from chemo—but there was nothing he could do about big ears.

Other changes were more disheartening. His ample belly had evaporated, and his once-beaming face was thin and haggard. Drip tubes were plastered to his arms, the final marker of the unwell.

He must have heard her, for he looked over. The weary mouth turned up in a familiar welcoming grin. "Terri. It's so good to see you," he said in his thick accent. "It's been too way much years."

She'd always assumed his native tongue was Spanish, but she remembered that he was from Brazil. "It's really good to see you, Preston," she said, going to him. That was a half truth. It was always a treat to be with him, but she couldn't say it was good to see him like this. "Indeed—way much too years."

He furrowed his brow in mock reprimand. "Do you make fun of me?"

She pulled the chair around so she could face him, and took his hand. "No, Preston. I make fun *with* you."

"As it was always." His head tilted in thought. "You . . . you are far from home, no?"

"Far from home, yes. Preston, I have a confession to make."

"Buttercup," he said, borrowing her father's nickname, "as I relembrar, you will have many things to confess."

She guessed that *relembrar* was some Portuguese bastardization of *remember*. "That may be true," she said, "but this one means I can't stay but a few minutes."

He looked at her with sincere concern. "What would deprive me of you indeed must be a big *pecado*—a sin, no? Confess away."

"Preston, I feel like a turd, but I've come all the way to pump your brain."

He nodded slowly, waiting.

"My dad came back one time with a pendant," she said, "an artifact he found. Do you remember?"

Terri thought that she'd angered him. His eyes flashed, and he gripped her hand. It lasted just a second. His hand relaxed, and he let his gaze drift to the ceiling. "I was both enjoyed and ensaddened when I heard that it was lost," he said, looking at her again.

"We think we found it. But why both happy and sad?"

"Sad that such a thing of . . . novelty would be lost. Happy because I didn't trust it."

Terri wasn't sure he meant what she'd heard. "You don't trust it? Trust it to do what?"

He looked at her, deciding. "The *pingente*—the pendant—it saved the life of your father, and yet it killed him too."

Terri wanted to ask him if the nurses had just administered another round of chemo, maybe explaining his turn to the fantastic. Maybe it was just a language thing. "Is that a metaphor?"

"A metaphor . . . no. No, it's a time you know what happened. I don't want to take this to the grave with me."

She wanted to poo-poo his talk about dying, but that was condescending, insulting, even. She was in no position to make that assessment, and it belittled his own. She nodded. "That's why this turd came all this way."

"You haven't asked why I told no one before," he said.

"Because I'm special?"

"You are that, and that would be good reason enough, but what I know is too fantasy for people to take serious."

He at least knows it's fantastic, she thought. *Good sign.*

"I must explain some background. Finding the site—the prehistoric remains—was such a surprise. I couldn't stay long, but your father did. I returned two weeks later, and your father has then found by now the *pingente*—the pendant. He also has mapped the outlines of a temple, obviously very old, six thousand years, at least. This would make it evidence of the oldest civilization on this continent."

Terri bit her tongue. She wanted to know which continent was "this" continent, but she let him continue. It wasn't like he was going to die in the next few minutes.

"The site was clearly abandoned at that time, five thousand years," he said, "and later peoples seem to have . . . *evitar*—shunned it. Long after, when I learned what it had done to us, I did studies—research—and found ancient myths of evil gods—no, not evil, *bravo*—angry, yes, angry gods. The angry gods hurt the people who built the temple, and they left."

"Preston," Terri said, "you said it had done something to you— both of you. Do you mean one of the gods?"

Her spirits fell. Maybe he was delusional after all.

He grinned. "Buttercup, there are no gods. This is just how the native peoples made sense of things they don't understand. I am sure that it was radiation."

"Uh, like atomic?"

"Yes. Nuclear decay. Terri, your father and I suffered radiation damage. Your father came home sick with it. He was exposed for longer. Mine took years to show."

Terri met his eyes. She had to ask. "Is that what caused . . ."

"My leukemia. Yes I am sure."

"But, Preston, my father, he didn't . . . he didn't die from it. He lived normally for years, at least until the stroke—"

"No, Buttercup, not normally. He had the *pingente*—the pendant."

"Preston, I don't understand."

"I don't know how it works, and because this, I tell no one until now, because they will think me crazy. Terri, the pendant established a greatly personal relationship with your father, like a parent and child. It cured him—no, not cured. It held his cancers at hold—at bay, I think is the word."

"How can you know this?"

"Your father told me. He, of course, should know."

"He never said anything. My mom would have told me."

"I know. He didn't like to worry your mother. And, he too wasn't wanting to talk about it until he understood."

"Which he never did."

"That's right. Terri, I think the many battles that the pendant fought for him—the many cancers that developed—finally caused his stroke."

She stared at him, waiting for it all to sink in. It didn't want to sink in, hovering there just beyond her grasp. "That's why you said the pendant saved his life, but also killed him."

"Yes."

"But, but, how could you be so sure the radiation exposure came from the site?"

"Terri, your father was diagnosed with radiation sickness after spending three weeks at the site. The doctor told him he had at maximum one month to live."

She shook her head. Too much information. She felt dizzy. "So, you never went back."

"Yes, I did. I wanted to find and prove the source of radiation. I went with a Geiger counter."

"You found it?"

"Yes and no—mostly no. I found radiation, but it was in just one small area, and too small to make the damage to your father."

"Maybe it, like, diminished over time."

"I thought maybe that. But it don't make sense. If the radiation was the natives' angry god, then why it stays strong for five-thousand years, and drops to almost nothing in a few years?"

"I see your point."

Hurried footsteps coming down the hall reminded Terri how quiet the hospital floor had become. A nurse stopped, glanced in, and continued on. "At least one person is still on the job," she said.

"What's the combulation that made everybody leave?" Preston said.

She looked at him. She'd known him all her life, and here he lay, with just weeks left. *What the hell.* "It's a spaceship. An alien spaceship. They brought me here."

Preston closed his eyes and smiled. "You are the kidder," he said.

"No, it's true—"

Something beeped. It came from a small panel on the wall. She noticed that an amber light was slowly blinking. "What's this?" she said. "Should I, uh, get that nurse?"

He opened his eyes and looked where she was pointing. He frowned. "The lawyers are winning. It records everything done in the room. It's—what do they say?—covering their asses."

"Isn't that, like, an invasion of privacy?" she said, rolling back the last ten minutes, remembering what they'd said.

"I can ask the nurse to turn it off from her station, but it comes back on automatically after twenty minutes."

"So, it just started?"

"No. no. It's been on the whole time." His frown deepened. "I am sorry, Terri. I should have remembered. Maybe it's good, though. I wanted to get it all out anyway. Now I can relax, eh?"

"Not me so much."

"You haven't said anything for trouble."

She raised her eyebrow.

"Your spaceship? Terri, I don't understand—"

"It's complicated."

Just then the wail of a siren rose in the near distance, maybe an ambulance on its way. Another one howled on top of it, as though competing for attention, more likely it was the police on their way.

"Oh, Preston, I'm afraid I have to run."

The sirens were closer, impossible to ignore. "Buttercup," he said, "are you in trouble?"

"We'd have to define what trouble is. I need to know where this ancient temple is." She glanced at the panel. "We can't shut that off?"

He shook his head. "Only the nurse. But, Terri, I thought you knew."

"He never told me."

"But you knew that he brought it home from the hiking vacation, no?"

"I was a kid. He didn't show it to me until—wait, did you say the hiking vacation? My mom got something right! You mean the Appalachian Trail hike you two did?"

"Yes, of course. You didn't know that?"

"The *American* Appalachian Trail?"

"There's only one."

"But . . . but, that's here! In America!"

He looked at her with amused concern. "Yes, Terri. The Appalachian natives created a civilization far older than the Mesoamerican Olmecs. Your father believed that after abandoning the Appalachian temple, these natives eventually settled at Poverty Point."

"Yeah," Terri said, distracted. The sirens had arrived, and were now silent. "I read about that. It's in Mississippi."

"Actually Louisiana."

She shrugged. "The Appalachian Trail is, like, a thousand miles long."

"Over two thousand."

"Worse!" Shouts drifted up from the parking lot. "Preston, the temple . . ."

He glanced at the blinking amber light of the panel. "Buttercup, the temple is next to the long ranger." He winked.

The shouts below had become angry, authority demonstrating authority. She stood up, leaned over and kissed him on his forehead. "Preston, I have to go, but I'll be back soon."

His smile was gentle skepticism.

"I will," she insisted. "I promise."

She ran to the doorway, and looked back. He nodded, his smile now simple acceptance.

Terri ran to the elevator, and on to the stairs. "The long ranger?" she said as she took two stair steps at a time. What the hell did that mean?

The lobby was empty when she burst through the door at the bottom of the stairs. Everybody had run outside to see history being made. Terri fought her way through the crowd, doctors, nurses, janitors, even patients in blue cotton gowns. When she finally broke free, the open area around the spaceship was dominated by five policemen, guns drawn, their backs to her. They formed a semicircle, at the center of which was the open hatchway, and below that, Conan, his sword raised, ready.

Chapter 7

Terri froze. She hesitated to call out. The standoff seemed so precarious—any disturbance might set bullets flying.

The policemen were glancing at each other, wondering what to do. Terri saw the reason for their confusion. Conan wasn't even looking at them. His eyes followed something above him. He cocked the sword back and gave a little swing, and then his head turned up and around, as he tracked the invisible interloper that he'd missed. It was like a mime dealing with a pantomimed fly.

Terri stepped forward, and saw Conan's obsession—an insect, or at least it looked like an insect. She took a few more steps. Whatever it was, it was well-fed. The fat, oblong body seemed far too heavy for the little wings that beat so fast, they made a high-pitched whine, almost a scream. Conan took another swing, but the tormentor easily avoided the blade.

Suddenly an ear-splitting crack and flash of light exploded two feet from Conan's head as Spockette zapped the pest. The fat bug fell, and Conan stomped on it, looked, and stomped again.

Conan and the police stared silently at the remains, and Terry took the opportunity to dash forward. She ran between two of the policemen, and one of them grabbed her arm, swinging her violently around. "Stay back!" he yelled, and then his eyes went wide. Conan was advancing, sword raised. Still gripping her arm, the policeman raised his pistol.

"Spockette! Don't kill him!" Terri called out, her version of *Klaatu barada nikto*. She gave a jerk, freeing her arm, and ran to

Conan, who stopped his advance. Turning to the hair-trigger cops, she said, "It's okay—I'm with the monkey!" To Conan, she said, "Come on, let's go," and clutched his furry, but solid, arm to pull him back to the ship.

She reached up and grabbed the lip of the open hatch, and then firm hands grabbed her thighs and lifted until she tumbled inside. She scrambled back and came face-to-face with Conan who'd made a grasshopper jump from the pavement. She looked past him to the contracting circle of incredulous policemen. She didn't know what else to do, so she simply waved. One younger officer slowly raised his hand and gave a little wave back, but dropped at a glance from a colleague.

The hatch flowed shut, and Terri fell back as the ship took off.

"'I'm with the monkey?'" Siderai said.

"What was I supposed to say?" Terri replied, pushing herself up onto her feet. "'I'm with the space alien who uses a sword, even though he flies around in a talking spaceship'? A space alien who fights weird insects with the sword? What the hell *was* that thing, anyway?"

"I asked the ship," Siderai said. "Thinker says that it's nothing to be concerned about."

"That's not an answer. You don't say there's nothing to be concerned about unless there's probably something to be concerned about. Spockette! What was it?"

"Something bad," the ship said. "Not from Earth."

"You *brought* it with you?"

"No. It found its own way here. You don't need to worry. Enforcer took care of it."

Terri and Siderai exchanged glances. "Why don't you want to tell us about it?" she said.

A piercing whistle from Moe and a raised sword from Conan ended the discussion.

"Terri," the ship said, "did you get what you need?"

"Uh, yeah. I think so."

"He told you the location of the temple?" Siderai said.

"It's in the Appalachian Mountains."

Siderai frowned.

"I know. It was a surprise to me too. I don't know why I thought it was someplace exotic—probably because they were always going off to exotic places."

"I doubt there's any part of the Appalachians not explored," he said. "It's hard to imagine a major archeological site that's been undiscovered."

"I *know*. But Preston was not delusional. And it makes some sense." She related the conversation—the hiking trip, the radiation, the pendant apparently repairing her father's cancer. "I remember now that Dad was sick when he returned. Mom told us that he'd contracted Lyme's disease. After that, he never let the pendant out of his sight." She chuckled. "Mom thinks he had a minor stroke. I guess I can clear that up now. Of course, I'll have to tell her every day, since she won't remember—"

"Terri," the ship said, "Manager wants to know where I should go."

"Right." She looked at Siderai, who shrugged. "The Appalachian Trail," she said.

"Isn't it strange," Siderai said as the ship passed this on, "that Preston and your father would have mistaken an advanced alien base for a prehistoric human temple?"

"Maybe the ancestors of our alien hosts were gaga over ancient Native American architecture."

"Actually, the Appalachian Mountains would have been a good choice," he said, ignoring her comment, eyes trained on an invisible distance. "The aliens apparently think in terms of thousands of years, and, the Appalachians—remnants of a once-mighty mountain range that rivaled the Himalayas—have been geologically stable for millions of years—"

"The Appalachian Trail is two-thousand, two hundred miles long," the ship said. "Manager wants to know the actual location of the base."

Siderai looked expectantly at Terri. "Go to, uh, Georgia, Spockette," she said. "That's a state."

"I know that. The area of the state of Georgia is larger than the integrated area of the entire Appalachian Trail."

"And I know *that*," she lied. "What I mean is, that's where the Appalachian Trail begins. I still have to work out the exact location of your stupid spaceship base."

Siderai watched her with raised eyebrows.

"What?" she whispered. "The trail doesn't start there?"

He grinned. "It does. Do you even know where the base is?"

"Hey!" she whispered, glancing at the aliens, "Watch it. My life's on the line here. Preston told me—sort of." She explained the recording device in the room, and what appeared to be his hint, a clue that he thought would be obvious to her.

"He said the temple is next to the long ranger?" Siderai said. "Do you know what he meant?"

"Of course!" she exclaimed, eyes wide, tilting her head at the aliens, and nodding for him to get a clue. She leaned into him. "How far do you think they would have hiked in two weeks?" she asked quietly.

"Did they start from the beginning of the trail?" he asked.

Terri gulped. She had just assumed that. "Yes!" she exclaimed in an excited hiss. She remembered that the two of them had talked about doing the entire trail in segments, one each year.

Siderai shrugged. "If they averaged, say, fifteen miles a day, they would have traveled, um, two-hundred and ten miles."

"Okay, then. We, uh, look for the long ranger at about two-hundred miles."

"The long ranger," Siderai repeated. "Are you sure he didn't say the Lone Ranger?"

"Oh, that makes a whole lot more sense. A masked man on a snow-white horse. That should be easy to spot."

"Watch the blunt club, Terri."

"Yeah, yeah. Look," she said, getting even closer, "the data's going to unpeel as we need it," she said, giving him a knowing look. "Right?"

"You mean, we're going to wing it," he said.

Terri slapped her palm against her forehead.

"Manager wants the base location," the ship said.

"Okay!" Terri said. "Tell him to keep his pants on—that's a metaphor. We have time."

"We will arrive at the beginning of the Appalachian Trail in twenty minutes."

"Twenty . . . ? No, you must have the wrong Appalachian Trail. This one's, like, three thousand miles away."

"I am confident that there is only one Appalachian Trail, and it was two-thousand, five hundred miles from the hospital."

"Wait a second. How fast are we going?"

"Twelve thousand miles per hour."

"No, no. That's not possible. Remember? The fireball thing?"

"We are on a sub-orbital trajectory."

"You've taken us into space?" Terri asked, her voice cracking.

"That is the definition of sub-orbital flight."

"Now who's using a blunt club?"

"I assume that was a rhetorical question."

"Assume what you like. Hey, doesn't that mean that we go into freefall again?"

"Yes. In forty-seven seconds."

"Less than a *minute*? Thanks for the copious warning!"

Silence.

"Prof," Terri said, "we have to figure out where that long ranger is on the trail. I guess we could start by assuming they made it at least, say, a hundred and fifty miles. Spockette! You found Google Maps for yourself before—could you do Google Earth, and, like, display it for us?"

"What address?" the ship said.

"We want to start a hundred and fifty miles from the beginning of the Appalachian Trail."

The entire upper half of the inside of the ship was suddenly filled with a downward view of the tops of a mass of trees. It made her dizzy, like they were suddenly hovering upside-down over the Appalachians. "I'm going to get one huge kink in my neck," she said, craning her head back to look at the expanse. "Yikes!" she whooped, floating into the air as the ship went into freefall. "I guess that solves that," she said, swinging herself horizontal so the scene was directly before her.

She showed Spockette how to move the scene in response to her finger, as though the ship was a huge virtual touch screen. Terri inched her imaged way mile after tedious mile. On the ground, walking the trail, the view would have been ever varying, with chipmunks, squirrels, and birds chattering away, and glimpses of sky and distant vistas peeking through continually changing patterns of leaves. Virtual flight from a few hundred feet above the treetops soon became monotonous, however. One section of canopy was indistinguishable from another.

In fact, the unchanging scene set her wondering what the hell she was even looking for. The whole point of the Appalachian Trail was to avoid human development. Why would she expect any mile to be different from any other mile? Preston's long ranger might be something small—a marker along the trail, say—that she'd completely miss from this vantage point. She really needed to walk the trail, but this was impossible—Google didn't have street views of the forest. Not yet. And besides, Conan was going to chop her head off in twenty minutes without an answer.

Siderai floated next to her, watching, but he soon glided away to talk to Spockette. "These aliens," he said, "their species—they've colonized other worlds? That's a question, spaceship."

"Yes," the ship replied.

"These were worlds that had other intelligent species?"

He waited while the ship conferred with Moe and Thinker. "Thinker would like a definition of a species that you consider intelligent."

"Good question. Let's say a species that uses a language to convey abstract concepts, and has developed a material technology—say, has learned to smelt metal."

"Sounds like us," Terri said.

"Shush," Siderai said.

The answer came back. "No," the ship said.

"What about us? Are we intelligent?"

The ship responded immediately. "By your definition, yes."

"Moe—Manager—said earlier that they came to tame the Earth. Is that what they intend to do with us? With humans?"

That spawned an energetic discourse. Even Conan weighed in. "That doesn't sound good," Terri said, fingering along mile after mile of redundant forest canopy.

The heated exchange ended with only Conan seeming unhappy. "Thinker says that this was probably a bad translation. A more accurate description would be to train you to be like us."

"Train?" Siderai said.

"Now who're the monkeys?" Terri said.

"Concentrate on finding the long ranger," he said.

After yet more fractured musical discussion, the ship said, "'Train' was not accurate. It should have been 'educate.'"

"They can't change their answer after the buzzer," Terri said. "Spockette! Do they want to train us to use swords and live in threes?"

"Of course not," the ship replied. "You would become more adaptable, better equipped to explore and master new environments—"

A sharp whistle from Manager interrupted her. He seemed to reprimand her, gesturing at Siderai as though he was some new, unnoticed curiosity. "Manager says that you should concentrate on finding the base," the ship finally said.

"He doesn't want you talking to us about their colonization?" Siderai said. "Ship, that was a question."

"He doesn't want us talking about anything except finding the base," the ship said.

"Did she just sound perturbed?" Terri asked.

"Hmm," Siderai murmured.

"This is useless," Terri muttered. She'd started flicking her finger harder, sliding more and more distance with each surge. Her head was going to roll for sure.

Siderai floated over and joined her as they glided over endless green canopy. "Preston expected that you would know what he meant," he said quietly.

"No shit, Dick Tracy—sorry. I'm a little on edge, considering that my life is coming to an end."

"I mean, Terri, maybe you should be thinking about what he might have been referring to—something that you two shared, something common to you both."

"My dad," she said. "He was shared."

"Was he ever a forest ranger?"

She glanced at him sideways.

"Terri, we have to explore every avenue."

"I know. Hey, aren't a lot of the Smoky Mountains national parks?"

"I believe so. In fact, there's a national park called just that—the Smoky Mountain National Park. Is that where you are?"

"We went by Fontana Lake a while ago. The Smokies are coming up. There'll be forest rangers there."

"Um, okay."

"Maybe we can get Spockette to track one down and zap him until he talks."

"I thought Preston and your dad were keeping it a secret?"

"Prof, I'm attempting to let humor distract me from my pending doom." She stopped her flicking finger, and the scene crawled to a stop over a patch of green that could have been any other patch of green. "I'm wasting my time," she said, and glanced at Conan. He had killed that old man. She shivered.

"You've never hiked here yourself," Siderai said.

"No, Prof. You know that."

"Your father never talked about the hike with you?"

"He was sick when he came back. He never talked about it afterwards, at least not to me."

"You're sure of that?"

"I'm sure I don't remember him talking about it."

"Then it has to be something more obvious."

"I would say 'No shit,' but I already have."

"We should be looking for something prominent. Preston wouldn't expect you to know a location that could only be seen walking the trail."

"Fine. At least nobody can say I didn't try right to the end. Spockette! Can you take us up a few hundred feet here—no, make that a thousand feet?"

"We won't arrive in the area for another eleven minutes."

Terri rolled her eyes. "Spockette, are joking with me?"

"No."

"Then you really must be a dunce."

Silence.

"You're wasting good insults on her, you know," Siderai said.

"You're the one who thanked her. Spockette, I meant take us up using Google Earth."

The view changed so rapidly, Terri gasped. Floating in freefall, the sudden new perspective switched on the sensation of falling. She squeezed her eyes shut and clutched a handful of Siderai's shirt. She took a deep breath, and opened her eyes, willing herself to believe that the view was actually just a few feet away.

She reached out tentatively and slowly flicked her finger, and she was a jet fighter, zooming along at Mach one. She flicked again. It was exhilarating. The new height revealed the topology of the Smoky Mountain terrain, a marked difference from monotonous foliage. The effect was so enthralling, she almost missed it—regular geometric patterns, the telltale of human engineering.

"You saw that?" Siderai said as she slowly backed up.

"Yeah, a curly-cue with a merry-go-round at each end—there! Up the hill from that paved road. What is it?"

"Google Map indicates that it's Clingmans Dome."

"Spockette, take us down to a hundred feet."

The view expanded exactly as if they were in a tumbling fall, and Terri suppressed a gasp. "It's . . . an observation tower. The curly-cue is a footpath ramp. Spockette, can you find anything about this?"

"Clingmans Dome is the highest peak along the Appalachian Trail. The observation tower is forty-five feet high, and was built by the National Park Service in 1959. Vault toilet restrooms are available—"

"Okay, we got it. Thanks."

Siderai eyed her. "Yeah, yeah," she said. "I thanked her. So sue me. Why do you think they call it a dome?"

"American settlers to the area called it 'Smoky Dome' because of its generally rounded shape," Spockette said, apparently thinking the question was directed at her. "In 1859 it was renamed after Thomas Lanier Clingman, a Civil War general."

"Well, it's not obvious from above, but I'll take Thomas Lanier's word that it looks like a dome from below," Terri said.

She imagined what a dome-shaped peak might look like from below, and as she did, it tweaked something, the hint of a memory. There was another dome that she'd viewed from below as a child, down by the river. She wasn't allowed to go by herself, since the way there led through a rough neighborhood. Preston took her along, though, when he came to visit. He said that rough neighborhoods were only rough to live in. There was a little restaurant along the waterfront owned by a Brazilian couple, and Preston loved the opportunity to speak Portuguese as he ate spicy food, while Terri gorged on coconut balls and guava pie. The way there led past a beautiful, exotic building topped by a golden yellow dome sprouting a little white tower, like carved ivory. She imagined it to be a giant, magical onion that Alice might have encountered in Wonderland. Preston had explained that this was a mosque, and she misunderstood at first and thought that he'd said "mask." This had confused her, and she'd envisioned this beautiful dome as an outrageous hat someone might wear, pretending to be perhaps a Persian prince. In her mind she had combined this disguise with a more conventional mask and laughed at her fabricated picture until she cried. Preston had pressed her and, gasping for breath, she had explained how ridiculous the dome would look on . . .

"Oh my God!" Terri exclaimed. "I've got it!"

"Got what?" Siderai asked.

"This is it! The Lone Ranger! You were right!"

"The Lone Ranger lives here?"

"No! Preston gave me a hint that was obvious . . . well, obvious in retrospect."

After she'd explained the connection, Siderai said, "Are you saying that this observation tower is the alien base? The ship already told us that it was built by the Park Service."

She peered at the concrete structure, a swirling foot ramp curling back on itself to empty onto a covered observation tower. It did look like a futuristic thingamabob—the Jetsons' home, in fact—but it required a stretch of imagination to believe that the National Park Service had stumbled on it, and then decided to take credit.

"No," she said. "I'd have to be as moronic as Spockette to think that. It must be close by, though. We just have to . . . look for it."

Siderai looked doubtful. She thought he was going to challenge the whole premise that this was Preston's hint, but then he glanced at Conan and nodded—better to let the aliens think they were getting close for as long as possible.

"Spockette," Terri said, "take us to this place—"

"Prepare for extreme deceleration," the ship said.

The hammer fell seconds later. The two of them fell lightly to the floor, and then the entire weight of the Appalachians squashed her down. "Jesus, Spockette!" Terri yelled out of the side of her mouth, since the other side was flat against the floor. "Learn some control, will you?"

The crush went on and on. Terri tried to lift her arm, then her hand, and finally found that she could raise a finger. "My eyes are going to bleed!" she cried.

She was sure she was about to suffocate, when suddenly she was floating again. She realized that she was still lying on the floor. Normal weight felt like floating.

"Where are we?" she asked, lifting herself onto her hands and knees. That's all she could manage for the time being.

"One thousand feet above Clingmans Dome."

"We're there?"

"Yes. This is what you asked for."

"Are you trying to kill us?"

"No."

"Then why did you try to mash us into the cracks in the floor?"

"A metaphor, I presume. I was simply doing what you asked. My trajectory was planned to terminate at the beginning of the Appalachian Trail. You changed that, cutting short the distance by nearly two hundred miles."

"So, it's my fault."

Silence.

"Perhaps we should be a little careful with our requests," Siderai said.

"Sure, take the computer's side. Let's see how she does when you need some friendly human mirth."

He eyed her.

"I'm mirthful!" she protested.

"It's the friendly part that requires demonstration."

"Manager wants to know where the base is," the ship said.

"Yeah, yeah," Terri said. "It's around here somewhere. We just have to find it." She had an idea. "Preston was convinced that they were exposed to radiation. Can you detect that?"

"I can, and there is nothing except normal background levels."

"Hmm. Maybe it's, like, depleted."

"Terri," Siderai said, "most radioactive elements have a decay half-life of centuries."

"Yeah. Preston pointed that out. Let's take a look around. If my dad found it just hiking the trail, it should be obvious from up here."

"Your retargeting of our destination has severely depleted my store of antimatter," the ship said. "We must find the base very soon."

"You're going to milk this for all it's worth, aren't you?" Terri said. "Now it's going to be my fault if we blow up. Fine, we can see a lot from right where we are."

"Hovering in the air requires energy. I am using antimatter as we talk."

"Really? I had the idea you had some sort of antigravity drive or something."

"There is no such thing. If there were, you wouldn't feel momentum when I accelerate. I do use Earth's gravity for propulsion, but it's not efficient. Mass reaction propulsion is much more efficient in terms of energy used."

"You mean our rockets are better than you?"

"You would have to define 'better,' but I doubt it would be the case under any criteria. Your rockets are more efficient, but limited in scope—"

Moe cut her off with an angry whistle/wail.

"Manager wants the base now," the ship said.

"Fine! You're doing all the talking, you know."

"I am merely addressing your questions."

"Yeah, and bragging on and on about how great you are—"

"People!" Siderai shouted. "Why are we arguing?"

"Don't lose your britches, grandpa," Terri said. "Well, let's have a view, then—and you called her a person."

Terri jumped when the floor disappeared. "Jesus! I'm never going to get used to this."

The view beneath her feet looked the same as the Google Earth image, except that the tiny ant-people were moving around. "Let's see . . ." Terri said, on her hands and knees gazing at the terrain surrounding the observation center. She resisted grabbing hold of Siderai's ankle for support.

"How old is the base?" Siderai asked.

"Twenty-three thousand years," the ship replied.

"Really?"

"Yes."

"No wonder it's not obvious. A lot of erosion can occur in that much time. Particularly on a mountain."

"Wouldn't erosion make it, like, even more visible?" Terri asked.

"Perhaps, if it were located on a peak or a slope."

"So, we're looking for something at the bottom of a valley?"

"Or at least a small plateau. I imagine that if your father and Preston stumbled on it, then it can't be too far off the trail."

"There," Terri said, pointing. The mountain peak was really just the highest point on a ridge that ran east and west, and fell away sharply on the north and south sides. A spur extended south, where the access road ended, and the path up began. A little to the west, the ridge fell directly on the north side a few hundred feet, but paused to form a little tree-filled bowl before continuing down another couple of thousand feet.

"On second thought," she added, "that looks too small."

"Negative," the ship said. "It is about the right size. Things appear smaller from a distance."

"Everybody knows that," Terri said. She snorted. "I still say it's a lot smaller than four football fields."

"It is not."

"Listen, I've spent half my life trapped in bleachers looking at stupid football fields—"

"Terri," Siderai said, "she's a computer. You can't win this one."

"Fine," she said, crossing her arms across her chest. "But I'm going to say 'I told you so.' And I'm not going to be mirthful."

They moved a mile north before coming down to follow the tops of the trees back up the mountain ridge. The rounded top of the dome kept them out of site of the observation tower. The little bowl wasn't visible from there. As they lifted above the edge, Terri saw that the floor was level, as though the trees inside were surrounded by the frozen surface of a lake. In the exact center was a clearing, and from the middle rose a mound of broken boulders, covered with straggled, stunted brush, giving the impression that they were the trees growing on a miniature mountain.

Spockette glided over to hover above this Smoky Mountain peak imitation. "This is not natural," the ship said.

"Now there's a brilliant observation—"

Siderai shook his head and laid his finger against his lips.

"Could this be the temple you were talking about?" the ship asked.

"You think that *this* is the base?" Terri said.

"Of course not. The base would be underneath, buried beneath thousands of years of runoff from the slope above."

"Look," Siderai said, pointing off to the side.

Terri saw it. Smaller piles of boulders hugged the rim, spaced at regular intervals. "Oh, man," she said. "The Indians found this spooky flat plateau and built their scrappy temple on top. If this isn't the base, then I'm not one friendly bundle of mirth."

"And the area is eighteen percent larger than four football fields," the ship said.

"Listen, Spockette," Terri growled, starting for the ship's nose, "any time you want to—"

Siderai caught her arm. "You won, Terri. You found it."

She nodded. "Yeah, I did, didn't I?"

Moe hooted and warbled. "Manager wants you to show him the base," the ship said.

Terri's head snapped around to Moe, who stood watching her impassively. "Spockette," she said, "circle around the outside of the bowl."

As they cruised the perimeter, it was obvious that the little plateau was perfectly circular. It also became clear that the little boulder monuments were perched near the rim. The foundation wasn't so much a bowl as a dinner plate, buried by erosion runoff along the arc flush against the mountain slope, but eerily uniform along the rest. Once recognized, the plateau practically shouted artificial.

As the ship completed the pass and moved back towards the central mound of boulders, she said, "We just passed over a source of gamma radiation."

"Atomic radiation?" Terri said.

"Terri, gamma rays are one of three types of radiation resulting from nuclear—"

"I know that . . . I wasn't sure I heard you. You said before that there was no radiation."

Silence.

"Come on, you know that was a question."

"It was a statement, not a question. This gamma source is emitting in a tight beam. I have to pass directly through it to detect it."

"Uh, we were exposed?"

"For one and a half seconds, yes. Manager says that your time is up. You must show him the base."

Moe stood next to Conan, who held his sword in front of him, one hand on the hilt, and the other near the point.

"I just did!" Terri exclaimed. "Where the hell does he think the radiation is coming from?"

In answer, Conan slapped his hand against the flat side of the sword.

Chapter 8

On the ground, standing next to the fifteen-foot-high pyramid mound of boulders, and surrounded by pine trees, the plateau wouldn't have struck Terri as unusual. The surface, so unmistakably level from above, was a jumble of fallen trees in various stages of decay, and smaller boulders that had rolled down off the mountain. One might note how odd it was that any amount of ground would be even remotely flat on the slope of a mountain.

Her father and Preston apparently had.

"You're not seriously considering digging, are you?" Terri asked, following Siderai as he circumnavigated the crude pyramid.

"Well, I'm not going to just stand by and watch you," he said, stopping to study a depression between two larger boulders.

"I don't mean why are *you* going to dig, I mean why are we even thinking about it? It's crazy! We don't have a shovel. Who knows how deep this soil is?"

"I don't see how we have a choice," he said. He squatted and shoved aside leaves and pine needles, then glanced at the ship sitting a few dozen yards away. "It buys us time."

"Well, I don't like being called subservient. Do they think we're their slaves?"

"She corrected herself."

"Oh, and 'acting respectful' is so much better? I don't like it."

"That has no relevance. I don't think the Enforcer is bluffing."

"It's just 'Enforcer,' not *the* Enforcer. And besides, his name is Conan. It's plain as day that the base is under here. Why would they make us dig to prove it?"

"They obviously do need to find the access point, and why not get us to do it if they can?" He glanced again at the ship. "Also," he said quietly, "it could be that they do indeed want to establish dominance."

"You had any doubts? They originally wanted help from scientists who were 'properly deferential,' remember."

"Yes. I was never sure what to make of that, and I'm beginning to fear that it may not have been a mere mistranslation."

He stood up and wiped his hands. Gesturing at the depression next to the mound, he said, "This may have been a small excavation made by your father, but it doesn't go very deep."

"It's been eleven years. Maybe it filled back up."

"Could be, but the bottom is all rocks. I don't think he went deeper than that—"

He stopped and listened. "Hear that?"

She did. "A bee?" she said, glancing around. "A *big* bee?"

"There," he said pointing.

It was hovering next to a tree. "That's the same as the one back at the hospital," she whispered. "Conan squashed it. I saw him."

"This must be another one," he whispered back.

"How did it find us?" She looked at him wide-eyed. "Maybe they've, like, infected the ship! They hitched a ride, and they're, like, breeding in there somewhere."

"Terri, do you really believe that?"

"What's your theory?"

"You have a point."

He grabbed her arm. The little drone was moving, leaving the tree, but not coming directly towards them. "Look," Siderai said, "it's keeping the tree between it and the ship."

"Spockette said they're bad."

He nodded.

The drone stopped fifty feet from them. The body was featureless and oblong—a flying stretched black egg. Terri had the distinct idea that it was waiting. "It wants us to come to it," she whispered.

"How do you know?"

"I don't know. It's just . . . obvious."

"Maybe we should alert the others."

"You mean the ones that are forcing us to dig for them?"

"This thing could be dangerous," he said. "I don't think it's alive."

"It's artificial, but it's not just a machine, either."

"How do you know that?"

"I don't *know* how I know. It's the way that it . . ."

"What?"

"I don't *know*! The way it hovers there."

"Terri, how can there be different ways to hover—?"

The black interloper was moving, coming in their direction. Siderai stepped back, taking Terri's arm to pull her with him, but she yanked her arm away. "It's okay," she said.

The thing was so small, so innocent. It meant no harm. It just wanted to learn about them.

How *did* she know that? You don't question whether a chipmunk is dangerous—it's just . . . obvious.

It flew straight for her. As it got closer, she saw the sun glinting off its body. The wings were a vague silver blur, almost invisible in their speed. If it weren't for the high-pitched burr, she would have guessed that it used some sort of gravity-grabber like Spockette.

It stopped a foot in front of her face. She heard Siderai whispering frantically behind her, but she stood, mesmerized. She wanted to hold out her palm and let it settle onto her hand, like Snow White. It wanted her to. She slowly lifted her hand as Siderai's whispering rose to near hysteria, and she felt him pulling at her belt. The little traveler rose a few inches, as though making room for her welcoming palm.

Siderai called to her, full-voiced, loudly. The next instant, two things happened simultaneously—a crackling glow enveloped the little beast, and it disappeared with a little thud.

Conan stood before her, holding his sword off to the side. He'd swung and hit the harmless being. He gave her a jazz-hands flick of his ears.

"What the hell!" she shouted, and stepped forward to look for the little fallen body, but Conan gave her a solid push backward, and swung the sword down again hard. Terri heard a crunch, and knew it was over. Conan reached down, picked up a mangled mass of black, and went off towards the ship.

"What's the matter with you?" Siderai said. "You have to learn a little more caution, kid."

She felt sad. Which was crazy. It was just a . . . thing. "I'm not a kid," she said.

Back at the ship, Spockette told them through the open hatch that the geometrical center of the circular base had no significance, other than to the Indians. The source of the gamma radiation was probably where the refueling port is located. That's where they should be digging.

"Why were we looking around the mound, then?" Terri asked.

"Because you asked."

"Even though you knew it's not relevant?"

"Yes."

"Spockette, you are an imbecile—wait, you're admitting that the base is under us?"

"Yes."

"So Moe does too?"

"Yes."

"Then why do we have to dig?"

Musical discourse, and the ship said, "Because it is your role."

"What role?"

"To be respectful."

Terri looked at Siderai, who shrugged and sighed. "You mean subservient," Terri said.

Silence.

"Come on," Siderai said, clasping his hands together to make a step for her, "let's get back inside."

"No," the ship said. She closed the hatch so that just a few inches remained open at the top. "I'll meet you at the gamma source."

"What's going on?" Terri said. "Do we suddenly smell?"

"No. I am dangerously low on fuel, and Manager wants me to save as much as possible."

"We're going to save you that much? In that case, what about the others? Why don't they walk too?"

Silence, other than bad music.

"Oh, come off it, Spockette. There's no way you didn't know that was a question."

"I had to consult. Manager says that you can't understand the science."

"Oh, he does, does he? Well, if he's so smart, then why does he have to bring along Mr. Thinker—?"

"It's okay," Siderai said, putting his hand on her shoulder. "Show us the way!" he called.

The ship rose above the trees and moved off, and Terri and Siderai scrambled over fallen logs and tripped on hidden rocks as they tried to keep up. "Why'd you let her off the hook?" Terri said, panting, as she slapped a branch out of her face.

"I didn't think it was the right time to press them for the truth."

"What truth? That they're racist aliens with a superiority complex?"

"Yes."

"'Yes,' to what? You sound like Spockette."

"Terri, haven't you caught on? We're not guests of these aliens."

"You can say that again. They treat us like pets . . . or captives."

"I was thinking of something else, but captives sounds right."

"What were you thinking of?"

"Captives. Captives sounds correct."

"You said it was something else—"

"Terri, let it go. There," he said, pointing. "She's stopped."

They arrived at the lip of the plateau, and the ship hovered over an open area with a handsome view of the peaks off to the west. "Look," Terri said, starting forward, "this perimeter pile of boulders is bigger than the others. I wonder if this is what caught my dad's eye—" Siderai had grabbed her arm. "Jesus!" she yelled. "Will you stop pawing me, already?"

"Terri, think about why we've come to this spot."

"Because the racist aliens brought us—oh, right, the gamma ray source. What'll we do?"

"I don't know."

She turned to the ship. "Yo!" she shouted. "Spockette! We don't want to fry!"

The ship glided towards them. This was the first time she'd watched it from below. Terri felt a shiver wiggle up her spine. It was truly eerie . . . and startlingly alien. This featureless silver football floating along in utter silence. Yet despite the utter quiet, just the staccato burr of a lone cicada, it seemed somehow so ... purposeful. Maybe it was because she had talked to it, become familiar with the brains inside. Familiar enough to call it an imbecile. And a moron.

"I'll show you the location of the gamma source," the ship said, moving slowly off. It hadn't opened the hatch. A stranger would have looked around for the person who had spoken, assuming he didn't run away in terror from the sight of a floating stylish Winnebago.

The ship stopped thirty feet from the large perimeter boulder pile, and Siderai caught Terri's arm halting them as well. She didn't protest.

"I am directly over the source now," the ship said.

"Um, aren't you toasting your passengers?"

"The gamma rays are emitting in a tight beam, which angles out over the lip, and into space. If I were to lower ten feet, then they would be in danger."

"So . . . we can come closer?"

"The gamma beam is coherent and highly directional."

"Was that a 'yes'?"

"Yes."

"It's invisible?"

"Yes."

"I could walk right into it."

"Come closer."

"Are you getting back at me for calling you a moron?"

"No."

"I feel like the rat being beckoned to take the cheese. Of course, when I say 'rat,' I don't really mean—"

"Terri," the ship said. "You can trust me. I won't let you walk into the beam."

Terri glanced at Siderai, who nodded, and they took a few tentative steps.

"You can come to me," the ship said. "The beam is angling away from you."

They moved forward, but stopped before passing under the hovering ship. Terri could now see a cavity beneath the ship, a depression in the ground, ten feet wide, and a couple of feet deep in the center. "Do you see that igneous rock seven inches in diameter?" the ship asked.

"Are you kidding?"

"No."

"Spockette, I don't know igneous from ignoramus, which is what I feel like."

"That one?" Siderai said, pointing. "At the edge of this hole, with the little pine sapling next to it?"

"Yes, that one," the ship said. "I recommend that you use sticks to stake a one-foot diameter circle around that rock, and then avoid stepping inside, and to the west of it."

As they gathered sticks and gingerly positioned them, pulling their fingers quickly back, Terri asked, "Is this normal? I mean for a base to blast invisible lethal radiation? If it's supposed to be a deterrent, using something invisible seems kind of dumb. Razor wire would have worked better."

"This is not normal," the ship replied. "It must be a malfunction of some kind."

"Uh, I thought malfunctions and antimatter were unhappy dance partners?"

Silence.

"Let's treat that as a question," Terri said.

"I assumed that you were simply stating an obvious fact."

"You know, Spockette, arrogance is unattractive. Then again, how can a mere machine understand esthetic appreciation?"

Silence.

"That's okay, it was a rhetorical question anyway."

Terri stepped back to admire the little stick fence they'd built. "What now?" she said.

"Dig," Spockette said.

"Here?"

"Yes."

The ship moved to the edge of the open area and settled to the ground. "Do you think this is the only source of radiation here?" Terri asked Siderai.

"I imagine so," he replied, "but that would be a question for the ship. Why do you ask?"

She kicked at the pine needles along the edge of the hole. "My dad must have spent a lot of time right here. He wouldn't have known about the gamma beam." Her toe hit something solid. She reached down and pulled out a small shovel from the layers of packed needled. She held it up as proof. "Preston said he came back with a Geiger counter, but found only a little radiation."

Siderai took the shovel and wiped away the dirt. "I read that most commercial Geiger counters are designed to detect alpha and beta radiation," he said, "the most common type. I think that antimatter annihilation produces purely the gamma type. He would have had no reason to suspect that."

Terri probed around in the spongy detritus and pulled out a short-handle spade. "Hey, did you see that flash as Conan whacked the second little drone?" she said. "I didn't know the ship could zap from so far away."

"I saw it. It didn't look like the discharges the ship delivered to the deputy and the first drone."

"Yeah. Maybe it was too far, beyond Spockette's firing range—Jesus!"

She had backed up and bumped into something that turned out to be Conan. "Where the hell did you come from? What are you doing, sneaking around—?"

"Terri," Siderai said, "he can't understand you."

The alien stood there, leaning on his sword. He lifted it and used it to point at the hole.

"He may not understand us," she said, "but his sword knows sign language."

"I guess we'd better start digging," he said. "At least we now have tools."

She nudged him and pointed. Moe and Larry were sitting on a log next to the ship watching them. She waved, but they just stared. "They don't want to get close in case we blow up the base," she said.

"Terri, if I understand correctly, there must be enough antimatter below us to blow the entire—"

"Prof, I was kidding. They just like to watch their hostages sweat."

They stood on each side of the hole, Siderai with the shovel and Terri, the spade, and began digging away along the edge of the long-abandoned hole, removing a dozen years of dirt and needles. Pine roots had infiltrated, and they did more chopping than shoveling. If it was sweat the aliens were after, they'd found the means. Siderai was cutting away a wide swath along his edge, but Terri went straight down. After a foot, she couldn't get enough angle, and had to hack away roots until she could continue down. As she went deeper, her hole got wider. At about two feet, her spade went "clang," and she cursed. "If it's not roots, it's rocks," she said, disgusted.

Siderai stopped and came over. "Are you sure?" he said, guiding the inquisitive Conan out of the way and peering down.

"My fingers are numb from the impact. I don't think it's a root."

"Hmm," he murmured, getting down on hands and knees to scoop out loose dirt with his hands.

"Prof," Terri said, "you're stealing my hole."

"I'll give it back when I'm done," he said. He reached in and wiped back and forth, and then peered inside again. "Hmm," he said.

"What do you see?"

"It looks like . . ."

"Like what?"

"Like a rock. A big one. A really smooth one." He stood up and rubbed his chin, leaving a smear of dirt, then picked up his shovel and went to the center of the ten-foot cavity, again motioning Conan aside.

"That's almost as deep as my hole," she said.

"Exactly."

"You're cheating," she said as he placed his foot and stepped down on the shovel. It sunk a few inches into the needles before coming to an abrupt stop.

"You think that's the base?" she asked.

"Could be a coincidence. Two rocks at the same depth."

"With a powerful beam of gamma rays shooting out a few feet away."

"I'm not jumping to conclusions. We can work from the center, clean away enough area to see——"

Moe and Thinker were on their feet, hooting and howling. "They won the lottery?" Terri asked.

Conan took off, and Siderai pointed. At first, Terri thought it was a balloon hanging from a tree branch at the edge of the open space, but realized that it was not connected. Black and oblong, the enigmatic visitor looked like a cat-sized version of the little drones, minus wings. "How'd we land in the Twilight Zone?" she said.

The strange intruder moved forward, soundlessly, purposefully, like a miniature version of Spockette, in fact. Only black.

Conan was sprinting directly towards it now, sword raised, and when he was ten feet away, he suddenly slowed, as though encountering an invisible wall of molasses. At the same time, the black egg backed away, keeping the same distance between them. The two of them, moving in tandem, slowed, slowed, and stopped, Conan straining against an invincible barrier, swinging his sword just out of reach.

"It's using a tractor beam," Terri said quietly.

"A tractor beam attracts," Siderai said. "This would be a repulsor beam."

She looked at him. "I wouldn't have guessed you for a *Star Trek* fan."

He glanced at her. "Rodenberry didn't invent it." He pointed. "Look."

Spockette had risen from the ground, and was turning to face the struggle. The black egg rose higher, forcing Conan to his knees. Terri could see the alien's muscles squirming with effort beneath the gray fur. He suddenly lunged up, swinging the sword wide, but the egg was out of reach. For a brief moment, it was enveloped in the same sparkling aura that they'd seen surround its little brother, then it turned and disappeared into the trees where Spockette wouldn't be able to follow.

Spockette settled back to the ground as the humans and aliens all converged on her. Terri and Siderai had to wait as the three aliens sang and tooted in exuberant debate. Siderai finally squeezed in a question between angry whistles. "Was that the same sort of thing as those little drones?"

"Yes," Spockette replied.

"And . . . ?" Terri said.

"They are called Eaters, and they are bad."

"You said not to worry about them," Terri said, "that Conan could take care of them. That looked like he was the one being taken care of."

"Yes. This is a different class."

"Yeah, bigger, and it has a repulsor beam." She threw Siderai a glance. "And, no wings. Does it use the same propulsion as you?"

"Similar, yes."

"But you're sure it didn't come along with you—from wherever you came from?"

"Yes."

"Where did it come from, then?"

"Another star system."

"Like you did."

"Yes."

"But not your star system."

"Correct. Terri, we did not bring them."

"What are they after? Why do you call them Eaters?"

"I think you can guess, Terri."

"Why don't you tell me?"

"When we encounter them, they essentially devour us. They destroy our installations and kill us if we resist with whatever means they can use."

"Why?"

"I have no answer for that. Enforcer wants you to help him get a gun."

"An Earth gun? Bullets and recoil bruises?"

"Yes."

"To use against the Eater?"

"Yes."

"A gun would be effective?"

"Probably."

"What about, you know, like, the antimatter boom problem?"

"That is a risk we'll have to take."

"You mean a risk *you'll* have to take. They're after you, not us."

"You are with us."

"Not if we leave."

"You can't leave."

"Why not?"

"Enforcer won't let you."

"With his sword."

"Yes."

"Jesus. Where are we going to get a gun?"

"Many Appalachian Trail hikers pack guns."

"They 'pack' guns? Where did you pick that up?"

"There are many conversations about this on social media—"

"Never mind. We might as well go up and see if we can rob a hiker."

"Correct."

"Can you tell Conan to give me a boost?" Terri said, reaching up to grasp the bottom of the hatch.

"I cannot take you."

"Why not?"

"My fuel is dangerously low."

"You flew all the way from Oregon, and now you can't take us a few hundred yards?"

"Correct."

"Wait. If you're that low, then you're close to going boom."

"Correct."

"Holy shit. Can't you just, like, leave us here and fly off into space?"

The ship exchanged a tune with Moe. "Manager says that this is not an option," she replied.

Terri had been joking, but Spockette hadn't gotten it. She was about to explain, but she glanced at Siderai. He'd think that she was empathizing with a computer, feeling bad about hurting the ship's feelings. "Shouldn't we be focusing on finding the base's refueling port?" she said instead.

"You and Enforcer will acquire a gun," the ship said, "and Professor Siderai will continue exposing the base."

"I'm not a professor," Siderai said.

"Why do I have to go with Conan?" Terri asked.

"Because Siderai is better at digging."

Terri looked at him. "That's a compliment I don't mind passing on." To the ship, she said, "Tell Conan that he's not allowed to kill anybody. Make sure he understands."

The muscle-bound alien looked disgusted when Spockette tooted the information. At least, that's what Terri imagined. "Give me a word to remind him," Terri said.

"Whistle," the ship said.

"Huh?"

"Make a whistling sound. I know that humans do this."

She planted her two little fingers in the corners of her mouth like her father showed her and blew a shrill toot, causing Moe and Thinker to jump. "That means, 'Don't kill anybody'?"

"No," the ship said, "of course not. But I've told Enforcer that this will serve as a reminder."

"Ah," Terri said. "Okay."

Spockette wasn't completely dumb.

The climb to the top of the ridge, where the Appalachian Trail passed by, seemed to go on forever. From above, looking down through Spockette's virtual glass floor, the slope had seemed a pleasant stroll. The perspective on the ground was endless incline, scrambling over logs, slipping on slick layers of pine needles, and slapping branches out of the way. At some places, Terri used her hands as much as her feet to pull her along. Sweat beaded on her temples as Conan would wait patiently for her to catch up before sprinting off and up again. She had to admire his strength and stamina, if not his companionship.

They almost missed the trail. Crossing perpendicular, the famous route could have been mistaken for a rabbit run. Terri called to Conan and pointed down at the dirt path. He stared at it a moment, and then looked at her, clearly perplexed. "I know," she said, "it isn't exactly Fifth Avenue."

The alien planted his feet apart, placed the tip of the sword into the ground, and clasped his four-fingered hands across the hilt. He was going to wait as long as it took to accost the next hiker.

"They're not stepping on each other's heels," she said. "It could be an hour, or a day, before the next one strides resolutely past."

Conan glanced once at her, and then returned to monitoring the trail five seconds in each direction, his head turning back and forth like a clock pendulum.

Terri liked talking to him. He never admonished her for the blunt club of sarcasm.

After a few minutes, she tapped his arm and pointed along the trail, then walked away, waving her arm for him to follow. He followed. This was her world.

They were going to have to search out their own victim. Through-hikers might be as rare as foxes, but where cars could go, people would cluster. Before long, the observation tower came into view. It really did look like something from the *Jetsons*, the curved access ramp amplifying the futuristic *je ne sais quoi*. The trail passed a hundred feet from the paved path that led up from the parking lot below. Through the trees, they could hear people talking.

"Okay, warrior," Terri said, "go get a gun."

Conan didn't even look at her. As far as he knew, she might have been clearing her throat.

She had an idea. The problem with stealing a gun from somebody was that, well, they had a gun. She led Conan to a little grove of pines free of undergrowth, where he was visible. She motioned for him to stay, and started off. He followed her. She gestured with both hands like an umpire declaring a runner safe, and wagged her finger while shaking her head, all of which meant nothing to him. She finally put her hands on his furry shoulders and planted him in place. She backed away, and when he started to follow, she pushed him back and planted him again. This time he got it, flicking his jazz-hand ears, and then watched her quizzically as she walked away.

Terri wasn't sure how long her star-travelling companion would stay put, but she had an idea it would be until someone came to relieve him.

She approached the paved path stealthily, moving from brush clump to tree trunk, until she could see the tourists strolling by every few minutes, chatting about the minutia of their lives. She waited until a lone young man came by. He wore a new feed cap, used to cover a balding pate, revealed when he took it off to wipe sweat from his forehead. Despite the warm afternoon sun, he chose to wear his hunting vest over a short-sleeved shirt. A small pack slung over his shoulder completed the enticing suite.

She called out to him softly, weakly. He stopped and glanced around. She called again, and waved, and this time he saw her. He looked around again, making sure there wasn't somebody else she was hailing. She beckoned to him, and, looking around yet again, he took a few steps towards her. "You okay?" he said, uncertainly.

"Do you have a gun?" she asked.

He looked at her, glanced up and down the path—what seemed to be a habit—and nodded. "Yeah, I got one. What's up?"

She waved for him to come to her. He took a few steps off the path. "You in trouble?" he asked.

She nodded, gestured again, and started off, back towards Conan. When she looked back, the man was pulling a pistol from his pack. Nothing like a damsel in distress to get the mercenary juices flowing . . . even if the damsel was a bedraggled, homely smart-mouth.

She put her fingers to her lips for him to be quiet, and led them slowly back, affecting a bad limp in the process. She stopped when Conan was in sight, looking right at them, hands folded over his sword hilt. "There," she said, pointing.

He squinted, tilting his head back and forth, trying to make out what he saw. "What *is* it?" he whispered.

She tapped him on the shoulder so he would look at her. "A monster," she hissed.

Chapter 9

The young man clutched his pistol and stared wide-eyed at Conan, who returned the stare ominously. "It's an . . . ape!" the man exclaimed.

"With a sword?" Terri said. "Wearing a belt with a knife? With a face like a mutant Koala Bear?"

"Where'd it come from?" he said, unable to tear his eyes from Conan's hypnotizing glare.

"China," she said. "They've been performing genetic experiments . . . crossing political prisoners with grizzly bears."

What the hell.

She was going to say the CIA, but she guessed that gun-toting men in hunting vests and feed caps could be planted on either side of the evil government conspiracy fence.

"How'd it get here?" he whispered.

"It's following me. They sent it to get me."

"Why?"

"Because I found out. I'm a reporter . . . but I'm really with the Army Special Forces."

How much would he swallow?

"Wow!" he said, appreciatively.

Apparently a lot.

"It almost got me," she said, rubbing her pretend wounded leg.

"What'll we do?" he asked.

"Go get help—not a forest ranger, though. The police. Better yet, get the FBI."

"What about . . . that?"

"I'll hold it off."

"I thought it was after you?"

"It was. But now I've got a gun."

"You do? Oh yeah! Mine!"

The awe in his face scrunched into doubt. He and his gun didn't like to be apart.

"After this is over," she said, "your gun will be famous. You could sell it to the Smithsonian." The doubt hardened. "Or you could frame it on your wall."

His brow lifted. He had an idea. "I'll stay. You go get the FBI."

She shook her head sadly, and patted her fake game leg.

He sighed and pulled the sleek steel-black pistol from his belt. He held it. Reverently. A light came to his eyes. "Why don't we just shoot it?"

Oops. "No!"

"Why not?"

"My boss—my commander wants it alive."

He sighed again, and handed it out to her. It was heavier than she was expecting, and she nearly dropped it. "Is it loaded?"

"The clip's inserted . . ."

He looked at her.

If she was a Special Forces commando, she would know that. "I mean," she said, "is the clip, you know . . .?"

"Full? Yeah. Seventeen rounds."

She hefted it, pretending to gauge its quality. "This'll do," she said. She gestured towards Conan who hadn't moved an inch. "You'd better hustle," she said. "I don't know how long I can hold off this genetic abomination."

He nodded and scampered away, but then turned and mouthed, "Give 'em hell!" She winked and nodded, and when he raised his thumb, she raised hers as well, a commando toast.

She waited until he was out of sight before running to Conan, who held out his hand. "No, no," she said, slipping the pistol into her pocket. "No guns until Spockette can mediate."

He didn't understand, of course, and stood with his hand out. She gently pushed the furry hand away, and slid her finger across her throat. He seemed to understand that. He flicked his ears, turned, and trotted off.

Terri watched his muscular back recede. She wished he hadn't been so quick to recognize that one gesture.

∞

When Terri and Conan arrived back at the plateau, Siderai, Moe and Thinker were standing together with Spockette parked close by. "Give up already?" Siderai asked.

Terri pulled the pistol from her pocket.

Siderai's brow shot up, and then dived back down in concern. "Did Conan . . . ?"

Terri shook her head. "The guy gave it to me," she said, pointing the gun into the air and pulling the trigger to make sure the safety was on before handing it to Moe. "Conan just stood there looking alien."

"A man *gave* you his gun? It looks expensive."

"I encouraged him with a little fiction." She gestured at the expanded hole. "You've been hard at work, I see."

"Yes," he said, turning his attention to his handiwork. "Thinker believes we've found the refuel port. See this?"

He had cleaned a four-foot square area, revealing a dull black surface, like a slab of polished granite, except perfectly flat and perfectly level. Using a stick, he traced a fine circular indentation, nearly invisible if you didn't know where to look.

"Do you think the gamma source is some sort of beacon?" she said. "If so, it's a hell of a marker, like setting a pump on fire to locate the gas station."

"They don't think it's a marker—I was wondering the same thing. The ship still thinks it's a malfunction of some kind."

"And we're standing right next to it."

"I don't think it would matter if we were ten feet away or a mile."

She got down on hands and knees and rubbed her hand across the oval. It felt like rock. She took a small stone and tapped it. It sounded like rock. "Are they sure this isn't just rock?"

"They're sure."

"So, where's the 'open' button?" she asked, standing up.

"That's the problem." He turned his back to Spockette. "It seems that the ship doesn't want to talk about it," he said quietly, "but I have the idea that she was expecting to just ask it to open, sort of an alien version of 'Open Sesame.'"

"You heard her trying to talk to it?"

"Terri, I wouldn't expect her to talk to it audibly."

"Right. Of course. Wireless communication—an alien version of electronic telepathy."

He tilted his head discretely at Thinker. Terri hadn't noticed the fingerless alien, that he was cradling something in his cupped hands, warbling softly to it. She took a step towards him, but Conan put his hand out and gently pushed her away.

She'd gotten a glimpse, though. "Prof, he's using the pendant."

"They said it was a beacon. Maybe they're using it as a communication device."

"A remote."

Siderai grinned. "Run over to the edge and see if the taillights flash."

She stared at Thinker. It seemed . . . awkward for Thinker to be holding the pendant. It had lain so perfectly, so *correctly* in her father's hands. Watching Thinker trying to talk to the inscrutable little artifact reminded her of a child conversing with a doll, pretending that it was listening.

It might not be listening, but it wasn't a doll. It was a alive.

Now, what made me think that? she thought.

She watched Thinker. She watched his hands. She saw purpose in them. They were reaching out to Thinker, while ignoring his prattle, for that's what they thought of his attempts to talk to them.

She winced. *How in hell do I know all that?* In fact, it wasn't Thinker's hands that conveyed the purpose. It was the pendant within. She was sure of it.

"Terri," Siderai said, and she jumped. "Are you okay?" he asked, concerned.

She blinked. She had leaned forward. Conan had his hand on her chest, holding her back. She stood up straight and stepped back. "I ... I think the pendant's trying to talk to me." She looked at him and snorted. "That's crazy. Maybe I'm getting tired."

"Hmm," he hummed.

"What, 'hmm'? You always say that when you have an idea."

"Okay. But it's just random hypothesizing—"

"That's what 'hmm' means."

"Uh, if you say so. Anyway, the aliens say that the pendant is a beacon, and it would seem that it must be so. After all, you have high confidence that it was left in the general area where they landed, and what would be the chances that they would just happen to land nearby?"

"Prof, I never doubted that it's an interstellar beacon."

"Okay, then think about that. Our astronomers have radio telescopes as big as battleships that, if they're lucky, might pick up a few whispers from trillion-watt bursts of stellar energy. Here's this thing you can hold in your hand that they've followed from light years away."

"Fine. It's an incredible little communicator."

"Exactly. It's incredible—it's un-credible—difficult, or impossible to believe. To us, it's a miracle."

"Okay . . . ?"

"Terri, Preston was sure that the pendant was curing the cancer that was developing in your father."

"You believe that?"

"Where does belief stop, here? We've already established that the pendant uses technology far beyond our understanding. If something can perform one kind of miracle, how can you discount another kind?"

"You're saying the pendant can do anything."

"No. Not at all. I don't believe it's a god. All I'm saying is that we don't know all that it *can* do. I imagine when the Native American Indians first saw European muskets, they thought, 'These are incredible—you can hit somebody over the head with this long part, and it never breaks.' Well, by the way, it can shoot a hole in you."

"So, you're saying that the pendant might be able to shoot holes in us—Prof, I'm kidding. You're telling me that it might indeed be trying to talk to me—we could have skipped the philosophical monologue."

"Would you have accepted if I simply said, 'Yes, Terri, I think it may be talking to you.'?"

"No. You're right. That's why you're the professor."

"I'm not a professor."

Siderai looked down, puzzled. A shadow was moving slowly along the ground. He looked up, and said, "Terri, don't move."

She moved. She looked up to find a giant black egg hovering ten feet above them. It was the Eater, only two feet in length, but seeming huge just floating there. Terri stared, transfixed as the aliens erupted in discordant sing-song, but then fell strangely silent, as though holding their breath.

"Move slowly away," Siderai said quietly.

Keeping her eyes glued to the interloper, she said, "And leave you here?"

"This is no time to argue. Just go."

She couldn't. No, that wasn't correct. She could go, but that would be disappointing. Not disappointing for her. No. For the black egg. It wanted her to stay. *How do I know this?* she wondered. The black egg hadn't moved, but it seemed to have changed. Whatever repulsor or tractor fields it could wield seemed to surround her, keeping her there, preventing her from moving away. But, that wasn't right either. She *could* walk away if she wanted, but it would be disappointed. That disappointment was enough to keep her planted.

She jerked when a percussive bang exploded behind her, and then something fell to the ground with a thud. She spun to find Conan holding the pistol in both hands. He ran forward, aimed from three feet away, and shot again at the black egg lying at her feet. She winced when he shot a third time.

The egg lay there, lifeless. Terri didn't need to see the three gaping holes in its side to know that it was dead.

"Nice shot," Siderai said. "Our protector is a quick-study with guns."

"Hmm," Terri said, staring at the extraterrestrial carcass.

"He figured out how to use it, without instruction or any practice. That's quite remarkable."

"Hmm," she said, finally looking at him. "That's his forte."

"His role, yes. Terri, are you all right?"

"No," she said, taking his elbow and leading him a few steps away from Conan, who was picking up the vanquished visitor.

"He can't understand you," Siderai said, nodding towards the alien.

"I know. It's habit. Prof, did you feel anything?"

"When Conan shot it? No, he wasn't aiming at—"

"No. I mean from the Scrubber."

"Terri, what are you talking about?"

She put her hand to her forehead. "Prof, I think I'm going crazy. First, I imagine that the pendant is trying to talk to me, and now this . . . thing is putting thoughts in my head. Prof! Maybe I'm developing schizophrenia!"

"We just finished deducing that we should not be surprised about anything these new technologies can do. Why did you call the black Eater a 'Scrubber'?"

"I don't know. That's what it is. It doesn't eat things, it scrubs them clean, gets rid of the parts that don't belong."

"It told you this?"

"No—yes, obviously it must have, since I didn't know that before. I don't know, Prof—this sure feels like schizophrenia."

"How would you know what schizophrenia feels like?"

"I've seen it in movies. Prof, I'm kind of scared."

"I don't doubt it. I'm sure the Native Indians were scared when they first saw a musket fired."

"Which made holes in people."

"The analogy carries only so far—"

They turned to the aliens. Moe and Conan had been conversing with the ship, and their cacophony had suddenly swelled as Thinker joined in. The fingerless alien had stopped his effort to communicate with the base and was shouting siren curses. The ship whistled, and everybody shut up. "Terri," the ship said, "is the beacon—the pendant—still trying to talk to you?"

"Uh, how do you know that?"

"Terri, my ear is effectively as wide as I am long. You were barely fifty feet away."

"You were eaves-dropping."

"Terri, I cannot not listen."

"Fine." An urge pressed her. Schizophrenia. "Let me hold the pendant."

Cacophony soon reigned again until the ship emitted another whistle. "Thinker objects," the ship said.

"Why? Does he think I'm going to run off with it?"

"He doesn't believe that the pendant can commune with humans. He finds it distasteful—I believe blasphemous might be a better description."

She looked at Thinker who stood glaring at her. "Ask him how well he's doing with it."

"Terri, that is an unproductive prod. He wants you to recant your insistence that the pendant was curing your father's cancer as well."

"What's with this guy? Does he think the pendant is, like, his personal god?"

"No. Of course not. He simply finds it irreconcilable that the pendant would choose to commune with a human. He wants to establish this as accepted fact."

"He cares that much about what I think?"

"Apparently."

"I'm flattered by the attention from such an august mind."

"Terri, I believe that was sarcasm. Do you want me to convey that to him?"

"No. Just tell him to give me the pendant."

The musical melee that followed was long and heated, with Conan contributing the most expressive refrain, as usual. Thinker finally raised both elbows, in what Terri took to be an expression of defiant acquiescence, and gave the pendant to Moe, who walked over and handed it to Terri. "That seems a little childish," Terri said. "I guess Moe had the final word?"

"Terri, it was Enforcer who prevailed," the ship said.

She looked at the warrior, who looked back without expression.

"Terri," the ship said, "the refueling urgency is becoming dire."

"What do you want from me?"

"Tell the base that I need fuel."

"You want *me* to talk to the base?"

"You seem to have affinity with the pendant."

"Which is the only way to communicate with the base?"

Silence.

"That was a question."

"Yes. Communication with the base is done using the pendant."

"You can't talk to the base?"

Silence.

"Question, Spockette."

"Correct. I am not able to communicate directly with the base."

"And you also can't communicate with the pendant. A question, Spockette."

"Correct. Terri, I must impress the urgency. My antimatter containment fields are beginning to fail."

"Really?"

"Terri, I would convey a greater degree of dire importance if I could."

"Okay, okay. Keep your shirt on." She held the pendant out and looked at it. It felt good to hold it, to have it in her hand, but how was she supposed to talk to it? Say, "Hello, how are you?" She had thought it was trying to talk to her before. What happened to that?

She shook it. That was dumb. What did she think? She had to wake it up?

Which *was* dumb, because it wasn't asleep. Not at all. In fact, it couldn't have been more awake right now, not with what was at stake.

Wait a second. How did she know that? The schizophrenia effect. Was it, like, talking inside her head?

Not truly talking. No. People use words almost exclusively to communicate so that in the end, they *think* with words. Abstract thoughts, whether home-grown or imported, manifest as words, as talking.

Holy hell, was that the pendant talking? Or, rather, importing thoughts?

Well, of course. At least she thought it was. Or was it her imagination? Was she just making up the whole thing?

In any case, whether she was fabricating the entire scenario or not, if they wanted to refuel Spockette, she'd have to give the base explicit instructions.

Shit. Where did that come from? It *had* to be the pendant. Otherwise, how would she know that the instructions needed to be visual, since the base knew nothing of human language?

Damn! It was like her feet were walking out in front of her, dragging her along.

And that was a good example of the imagery required for the base—straightforward, succinct images.

"Okay," she said to it. "I got it."

"Excuse me?" Siderai said.

"Huh? I was talking to the pendant."

"Does it, um, talk back?" he asked carefully.

"Prof, don't start doubting this now. I'm already at the hairy edge of concluding that I'm going nuts. Spockette!" she called. "How do you refuel with the base? I mean, what's the actual physical mechanism?"

"Terri," the ship said, "there's no time for that. It will be obvious when the base begins."

"No, you don't understand. I *need* to know."

"Very well. The base will extend a . . . column. There's no English word for it. I will move adjacent, and . . . Terri, I'm sorry, but it's just not possible to explain in your language without a large amount of background information."

"That may be okay. I think I just need to understand what it would look like—you know, if I stood here and watched it."

"Terri, a . . . column would rise up, perhaps ten feet. I would position myself so that I could . . . accept a . . . transport vortex ... Terri, if you only need to know what it would look like—"

"I *do!*"

"Terri, to you it would look like my tail was almost touching the top of the column, and you would probably have to look away from a very bright light."

"That's it?"

"That's all you would see, yes."

"A really bright light."

"And you would probably hear a loud crackling sound."

"Sounds ominous."

"As it should, since at any moment, there would be as much volatile energy in the form of antimatter protons in transit as was released in the fission bomb dropped on Hiroshima."

The thought of searing nuclear fireballs squeezing through Spockette's tail made Terri shudder. She felt a slight vibration and a blast of air across her feet and legs. She looked down to find that the surface of the base exposed by Siderai had changed. The area inside the oval indentation was slightly higher. Dust and dirt rushed away in all directions. Her thought had been the final hint required by the base, and it was cleaning the immediate area.

"Terri! Siderai!" the ship called. "I didn't expect this to proceed so quickly. Get inside."

"Why?" Terri called, already moving towards her.

"There will be residual gamma radiation. I can provide a good deal of protection."

Siderai was right behind Terri, and knelt down with his hands clasped together to boost her up to the hatch. Moe and Thinker were already inside, hooting and warbling a bad melody. Conan stood nearby, and put his hand out to stop them.

"What's going on?" Terri called.

"Thinker believes that you and Siderai are no longer needed, and Manager has agreed not to let you in."

Conan turned and trotted away. Apparently protecting the mission came before personal safety . . . or future offspring.

"I'm sorry," the ship said. "I suggest you immediately get away as far as possible." A moment later, the hatch flowed shut.

"Come on," Siderai said, taking Terri's elbow, his jaw muscles working. Terri had never seen him angry.

"Hold it," she said, pulling away her elbow.

"Terri, you heard what the ship said—"

"No, wait."

She cocked her head one way, and then the other, clutching the pendant to her chest. "The base isn't going to do it."

"It's telling you this?"

"No. Yes. I guess so. I just know it."

"Why won't it proceed?"

She shrugged. "It's too dangerous."

"Why?"

"You know," she said nodding towards their little stick fence.

"I *don't* know, Terri. It's not communicating with me."

"Hmm. Right. They damaged it. A refuel attempt now could cause a complete failure, and we know what that means—"

"Who damaged it?"

"You know—yeah, right, you don't know. Many years ago—more years than I can imagine—"

"The American natives? The ones who built this temple?"

"Well, yeah. Of course. They used the pendant, but they didn't know what they were doing—ha! Of *course* they didn't. They were just . . . Indians—"

"Terri, are you talking to the base?"

"No! Ah, maybe. I don't know. It's confusing."

"You are correct," the ship said. "The base's security protocol is blocking refueling."

"Uh, you can hear it?" Terri asked.

"Yes. It won't communicate with me directly, though. Terri, you must convince it to try."

"I don't even know if I *am* talking to it!"

"You are, Terri. You must try. The consequence of not refueling—"

"I know—kaboom. A possible boom if we try, but a certain one if we don't. The difference is a boom that takes out the tallest Smokey Mountain peak, versus . . . what? A bigger one if the base fails?"

Silence.

"A question, Spockette."

"Terri, a complete base failure would obliterate most of North America, and the after-effects would likely also destroy all higher forms of life on Earth. It would effectively set Earth life back a billion years."

"Holy Christ! They planted a world-busting bomb thousands of years ago!"

"It's not intended to be a bomb."

"Oh, that's reassuring. This was awfully irresponsible of—what are they? The Inhabitors?" she said, waving vaguely at Conan, who stood a hundred feet away watching, hands clasped across his sword hilt.

"The Inhabitors—Manager, Thinker, and Enforcer—did not build the base."

"Right—the 'People,' the ones who built you. What the hell were they thinking?"

"Terri, a base is generally a very secure construction. It would require an incredible amount of persistence to damage it."

"When it comes to temple building, persistence is a native civilization's middle name. So, what'll we do?"

"Terri, I recommend that you tell the base to refuel me."

"What a surprise! That's like giving the condemned murderer the option of the electric chair."

"Terri, no. I am simply weighing risks and consequences. It is too late for me to defy Manager and try to get away into space. So, the choice is, as you say, a possible explosion if we refuel, versus a certain one if we don't. I calculate the probabilities of a base explosion to be point-one percent versus one hundred percent for me."

"Wait. Did you say 'point' one percent?"

"Yes, one-tenth of one percent."

"That's, like, one out of a *thousand*!" She looked at Siderai, who nodded with one raised eyebrow. "Why are we even talking about this?"

"Terri, the base is simply following its protocol."

"Well, the base seems pretty dumb."

Silence.

"Spockette, is the base as dumb as it seems?"

"Yes."

"I don't get it. Why would the 'People' make you so smart, and this whole big base so dumb?"

"Terri, I have no answer for that. More importantly, I am about to explode."

"Oh, yeah," Terri said. "What'll we do?"

"Terri, not 'we,' but you. You must convince the base to proceed with refueling."

"I don't know *how*! Wait—" She cupped her hands over her mouth and shouted at the ground. "Base!" she called in a deep, sarcastic voice. "Proceed!" She turned back to the ship. "Listen to me," she said, "I don't have the vaguest clue what I'm supposed to do . . . what?" she said. Siderai had raised both eyebrows, and was pointing. She jumped back as an oval column rose from within the indentation perimeter. "Holy shit, I'm amazing. Apparently."

"Terri," the ship said, "if I don't let you inside, would you instruct the base to halt the refueling?"

"Geez, that's a good question. I guess it would be tempting, if I even knew how to do it. Of course, holding you hostage like that wouldn't speak much to the general integrity of the human race—what?" she said when Siderai prodded her side. "You just can't get enough of poking me—huh?"

He had tilted his thumb at the ship and winked.

"Am I missing something?" she said. "Oh! Right!" She put her hands on her hips and faced the ship. "Spockette! Either let us inside, or I'll tell the base to stop." She turned to Siderai. "How was that?"

"You're amazing," he said.

"Thank you." Out of the corner of her mouth, she said quietly, "Why'd she do that?"

Siderai shrugged.

The scramble of tones from inside the ship had risen to near hysterical levels before they abruptly went silent. "You can enter," the ship said.

"Thinker changed his mind?" she asked, slipping the pendant cord over her head as Siderai lifted her up.

"No," the ship said. "Manager overruled him."

She wanted to stick her tongue out at the fingerless alien, but she suddenly fell forward, tumbling into the ship. She heard Siderai grunting, and looked back to find his fingers hooked over the bottom edge of the open hatch. She got up to help him when he suddenly rose up and crawled inside. She looked out just in time to see Conan trotting back to his guard position. Even as she watched this, the hatch flowed shut, and Terri stumbled back as the ship lifted from the ground.

"I suggest you move to my front and lie down."

The three aliens were already positioning themselves.

"Why?" Terri asked.

"This will reduce your profile against the residual gamma radiation."

"Uh, you told us you could protect us," Terri said, deciding where to lie down. The two aliens were taking up all the space at the very front.

"I said that I could provide a good deal of protection, and I can. I cannot stop it all."

She sat down behind Manager. "Do you think it matters?" she asked Siderai, who sat down next to her.

"The farther back we are, the less oblique the angle to the radiation below the tail," he said.

"In other words, 'Yes.' More of us will be exposed—not just our feet."

"Nothing to be done," he said, lying down on his back.

"Oh, there's something could be done," she muttered, lying down on her back as well. "We could kick those two away. They'd be cream puffs without Conan here."

"Beginning refueling," the ship said.

A rushing sound swelled until it was nearly deafening. "What the hell!" Terri called.

"They must have set up a temporary containment field between the base and ship," Siderai yelled. "It would have to be a vacuum, and it's probably not complete. Some of the antimatter protons must be encountering air molecules."

"Look!" Terri said, pointing.

Spockette had left an outside view enabled for the top half of the ship, and sprays of dazzling sparks were dancing up along the sides. "We're a giant sparkler!" she shouted.

"And giant fireworks," he said.

Terri followed his gaze. A meteor was streaking in an arc above ridge. As they watched, it turned, the flaming ball heading straight for them.

Chapter 10

The fireball grew larger as its trajectory aimed directly at them, and Terri shouted in alarm just as a stream of liquid fire issued forth, slowing it so that the impact, when it landed a couple of hundred feet away, was just a dull thud.

"What the hell was that?" Terri shouted, hurting her throat.

Silence, other than the deafening rush.

"Spockette! What *is* that?"

"Possibly a meteor," she replied, barely audible over the noise.

"That was no meteor!" Siderai called out.

"Spockette!" Terri yelled. "What about it?"

"It could be another Eater, a larger one. It would have come through out of hyperspace in the vacuum above Earth's atmosphere."

Terri raised herself up on her elbows. A thin trail of smoke rose where the space traveler had landed, and Conan was running towards it, sword and pistol ready. "The Scrubbers sure seem bent on whacking you," she said.

"They're called Eaters, Terri."

"Not according to them."

Conan stopped fifty feet short of the dissipating column of smoke. "Now, that's a first." she said.

Siderai raised himself and looked. The warrior alien was backing away.

"Now I'm nervous," Terri said.

Conan turned and started running as a large silver football rose up on four spindly legs from the crash site. It looked like Spockette, but with legs. And it was smaller, only half as long.

The sparkle shower died, along with the rushing roar, leaving Terri's ears ringing. She realized that half the ringing was the hooting, screaming whistles of Moe and Thinker. "We done refueling?" she said.

"Terri," the ship said, "we have to leave. Go to the hatch and call for Enforcer to come."

"This thing is really dangerous?"

"Yes, Terri. Call Conan. Hurry."

Terri didn't ask why Spockette didn't just whistle a tune to him. The urgency in the ship's voice was the first time Terri heard anything besides cool logic. In an emergency, you just do as told.

She scrambled on all fours to the hatch, which flowed open. "Conan!" she called. "Enforcer!" she shouted louder. "Like he'd know the difference," she muttered.

The stout alien had stopped halfway between the two space vehicles, seeming uncertain what to do. He turned to look when she called a third time. She waved for him to come. He just stood there. Terri wasn't sure if he didn't understand, or was reluctant to leave his post.

Behind her, Thinker was nearing hysterics. Terri thought he might be going insane. He screamed like an infuriated baby, and threw his arms around, as though swinging at invisible bees. Terri was relieved to see that the dazzling sparkles were completely gone, but Spockette kept the ship positioned just above the base's protruding column. Conan had finally given up any pretense of defense, and was sprinting to the ship.

"Spockette!" Terri called above Thinker's hysterics, "go down!"

"I can't Terri," the ship said. "Conan will have to get in from here."

Terri fumed. Didn't Spockette care about Conan? She didn't say anything—you do as instructed in an emergency. Something was happening at the crash site. Giant flower petals were unfolding along the sides of the fifteen-foot silver football. The tear-shaped paddles extended, straightened, and began spinning, fast. "A helicopter?" Terri said as the intruder lifted from its hole. It seemed so low-tech.

Conan had almost made it. He didn't slow down, just dashed to the column and launched into the air. It wasn't enough. He missed the hatch by six feet, but managed to grab the top of the column, wrapping his arms around it. Terri reached down—just a gesture, since Conan hung there another two arm-lengths away looking up at her.

Behind her, Siderai had been arguing with Spockette, pleading for her to go lower. He was now next to Terri. "You'll have to go down," he said grimly.

Terri looked at him.

"I'll lower you," he said, wrapping his hands around her ankles.

"Oh Christ," she said, crawling out the hatch. There was nothing to grab, and she fell head-first. She yelled when her shins caught the edge of the hatch. She reached out, still a foot above Conan's head. He jabbed one hand up and clutched her wrist. "I've got him!" she called. "Pull us up!"

Siderai grunted from above, and Terri gnashed her teeth as her shins dug into the hatch lip. Conan was *heavy* for such a little guy. All those muscles were like iron weights. She thought her arm might pull right out of the socket.

"I—can't!" Siderai groaned.

Terri knew what had to happen. "Climb," she said. He didn't understand. "Climb!" she yelled. It was all she could do. She tried nodding her head, but it was a gesture that meant nothing to the alien.

A single whoop sounded next to her ear. Spockette had spoken, and Conan immediately let go of the column and climbed hand-over-hand up her arm. She was sure both he and her arm were going to fall to the ground, but he reached her shoulder, and then it was her head that she thought would pop off before he clutched her belt and crotch, and his vise-gripping hands were scrambling up her legs. A musty, not unpleasant odor filled her nose as his fur mashed the back of her head.

And then he was gone, leaving just the excruciating pain in her shins. "Up Prof!" she yelled, "Up!"

The only effect was intensified grunting and groaning from above, and her shins being sawed further into the edge. All of a sudden, though, metal clamps seemed to grip her calves, and she flew up and back through the hatch. She tumbled to the floor, and Conan let go. "Thanks," she said, rubbing her head. "I think."

An instant later, all three fell backwards as the ship surged away. Terri looked back to see the extraterrestrial helicopter crossing over the column. It diminished as Spockette sped away.

Moe and Thinker seemed to be arguing, whether with each other, or Spockette, Terri couldn't tell. Conan sat looking at her. He blinked, and Terri blinked. He blinked twice and she copied it. His brow bounced, and his nostrils contracted. Terri decided to interpret that as a smile.

She looked back. The whole base plateau was small and getting smaller. "The Scrubber has weapons?" Terri asked.

"Terri," Spockette said, "they're called Eaters, and that was neither."

"It's not? What is it, then?"

"There's no quick answer. It requires background, and I can now provide that."

"You couldn't before?"

"Correct."

"Why?"

"That will come with the background explanation. Terri, I told you that your fellow passengers—the Inhabitors—acquired me."

"I remember."

"Although that is true, it is probably misleading."

"What? They *stole* you?"

"Yes."

"Wait—they stole you, like they broke into someone's space garage and hot-wired you?"

"If that is an analogy, then yes."

"Who'd they steal you from?"

"The people who owned me, the arrival that we are now fleeing from."

Terri glanced at Siderai who's eyebrow seemed to be planted to the crown of his head.

"They've come to get you back?" she said.

"That is overly simplistic, but yes."

"Then, why are you running away from them if they're the actual owners?"

"Because Manager told me to."

"And you listen to him, rather than your owners?"

"As of now, yes."

"Why?"

"It's not easy to explain. Terri, I am what you might call a lifeboat—an escape pod. The three Inhabitors stole me while on a training mission. As a lifeboat, it cannot be predicted ahead of time who will need me, and so, whereas other ships of the owners would not respond to the Inhabitors, I am designed to follow the directions of whoever needs me."

"Okay, so if I pushed those three out the hatch, you'd then belong to me?"

"Terri, I respond with—I don't know if you'll understand this—what might be considered hysteresis."

"I'm not an idiot. I know what hysteresis is."

"Very good."

"Don't patronize me."

"I'm not, Terri. Because of this hysteresis, I have a persistent obligation to Manager."

"That's why you're running away from your true owner."

"For the time being."

"Why are you telling me all this now? Does Moe know?"

"No, Terri. My loyalty is not absolute. That hysteresis is permeable. Because of the recent history with Manager, and his proximity—"

"Like, he's inside you right now."

"Yes. Because of that, I cannot completely abandon Manager's needs. However, with the owners now arrived, my duty to him is no longer absolute."

Terri wondered if this might explain . . . "That's why you delayed after refueling."

"I had barely begun the refueling, but yes, I took longer than was absolutely necessary to disconnect the antimatter funnel. I did not completely defy Manager's order, but rather simply erred on the side of ensuring a safe disengagement."

"Because you didn't want to leave Conan behind."

"Yes."

"Manager did, didn't he?"

"Actually, it was Thinker, but Manager acquiesced. This was why I couldn't call to Conan myself."

"That was very thoughtful of you, considering you are a computer."

"I am not a computer, and Conan is part of the team, and in any case, there was no real danger. The Overlord was not going to attack us."

"Overlord?"

"That is a term I find somewhat appropriate."

"Hmm, doesn't sound very friendly."

"It's a complicated arrangement. As I said, it's a name that fits only approximately."

"It seems that our friends here are awfully anxious to get away from the Overlord."

"They understood that my control—my loyalty—could be transferred back to those who owned me."

"What would have happened if we hadn't left—if they'd been caught?"

"From conversations between Manager and Thinker, I know that their plan was to establish a colony foothold—a beachhead, in a sense—and in this way prove their worth to the Overlords."

"Three aliens in a lifeboat were going to colonize Earth?"

"Terri, I agree that the idea is wildly impractical."

"Why did you go along, then?"

"Terri, I don't think you understand. My latitude for acting—my freewill, in a sense—is limited to innovations appropriate for carrying out directives."

"But yet you defied Moe to get Conan onboard."

"Terri, I have no clear answer for that. I suspect that my control—my loyalty—is shared somewhat across the team."

"You suspect? You don't know?"

"Terri, do you understand what your subconscious is doing?"

"Good point. So if they were caught, their plan would have been foiled—like it isn't already? Are they afraid they'll be punished?"

"I can only assume what the Overlord would do, but based on the information configured into me—"

"Configured?"

"Terri, my only inherent knowledge, beyond what I've learned since being activated to escape, is what was programmed by my creators. But to answer your question, I assume that the three will be re-trained."

"Uh, oh. That sounds like the euphemism Stalin used for his Gulags."

"In this case, I believe that the Inhabitors are too valuable to be eliminated with starvation. The Overlords have invested a great deal in engineering and training these three—"

"Wow—'engineered'?"

"Terri, I assumed you understood that. Otherwise, how would three individuals of the same species exhibit such drastically different characteristics?"

"Ha! Like no fingers?"

"Precisely, Terri. Can you guess why the class of Inhabitor engineered for analytical reasoning would be hobbled physically?"

"Uh, so they don't lead a mutiny?"

"Your insight is commendable, Terri."

"Stop patronizing me."

"I'm not."

"When you say 'engineered' . . ." Terri said.

"Genetically, of course. Like human's breeding of dogs, but with the help of gene manipulation."

"So, when you say they'll be re-trained, you mean literally that they'll go back to re-learning stuff, versus having their minds wiped?"

"Terri, there is no such thing as wiping a brain. By the way, I will almost surely be re-trained as well. And in my case, memory removal is, of course, a viable option."

"Yikes! Spockette, that sounds terrifying!"

"Only because you are human."

"Right. What a handicap. Spockette . . ."

"Yes, Terri?"

"Are the Overlords going to continue colonizing Earth now?"

"Terri, my inherent information is clear on this—the Overlords only colonize planets with no intelligent life."

Terri sighed and looked at Siderai. "What do you think, Prof?"

"About what?" he said, sitting next to her with his hands clasped around his knees.

"Everything—all that Spockette has told us."

She looked around, outside the ship. Spockette had settled into a pocket of pines, a good hiding spot. Terri hadn't been watching, and had no idea where they were now.

"It explains some things, I guess," he said. "For example, why the Manager wanted scientific experts who were properly deferential—"

"Because that's how they view themselves with the Overlords."

"I imagine, yes. It also explains why, when you asked the ship if she could be invisible, she explained that the designers hadn't considered it necessary as an escape function."

"I was thinking in terms of escaping dangerous dudes, but she was talking about escaping a derelict spaceship."

"That's right. And, finally, it might explain why she hinted at how you could coerce the Manager to let us into the ship before refueling."

"Hey, that's right! Spockette! Why'd you do that?"

"Terri," she said, "I presume it's because I now consider you—and Siderai—as members of the team."

"You presume? Never mind."

She tapped her front teeth with her fingernail as she stared out into the dim light beneath the pines. "What about the pendant?" she said, taking it and fingering it, and then holding it against her chest, as though absorbing its warmth. She'd had a moment of panic when she thought she'd lost it after letting Conan use her as a ladder, but it had simply turned around and was hanging down her back.

"What about it, Terri?" Spockette asked.

"How does it fit in? I mean, why does it talk to me—or, rather, think at me."

"I have no answer for that, Terri. Pendants are associated with Overlords. Each youthful male Overlord is given one during a ritual—a coming of age."

"Why? What are they for?"

"They are used for communication via a means beyond my comprehension, but one that has a reach of millions of miles."

"That's why Moe used this one as a beacon."

"That's right, Terri. I can sense the presence of your pendant. As a lifeboat, that is probably a valuable feature. I am not able to communicate with it, though. This is all I know of pendants. That's all that was included in my knowledge base."

"Right, thanks," Terri said, staring at the mysterious walnut. She cupped it in her hands and closed her eyes. "It's still in contact with the base," she said, "and don't ask me how I know that." She opened her eyes and looked at Siderai. "And so are the Overlords—in contact with the base, I mean."

He just nodded, as though this was what anybody would expect.

"Spockette!" Terri said, sitting up straight. "I think I could contact the Overlords—through the base. I could . . . shit! Spockette, I think I could let them know where we are!" She looked at Siderai, hoping for an answer, but he just sat watching her carefully. "Spockette . . . what should I do?" she said.

She knew. She made her decision. "Never mind, Spockette. I could never do that." *Even if they didn't want to let us in,* she thought.

"That is irrelevant, Terri," Spockette said.

"Why?"

"Because they're nearly here."

Chapter 11

Terri and Siderai were on their feet, watching the Overlord ship descend through the tall pines, the whirring blades tossing branches into a frenzied dance.

"They followed the pendant, didn't they?" Terri said as she watched.

"Yes," Spockette replied, amid the chorus of alien wailing.

Terri looked back at the three Inhabitors. Moe and Thinker were performing their own frenzied dance, while Conan stood by stoically. He glanced at her, but turned his attention back to his distraught comrades.

"They're screaming for you to flee, aren't they?" Terri said.

"Yes."

"Your loyalty has transferred to the Overlords?"

"Partially. In any case, it's useless to try to escape. Whatever plans the Inhabitors had to autonomously establish a colony foothold are now foiled."

The Overlord ship, small enough to maneuver among the tree trunks, was working to position itself above Spockette. "It uses blades, like a helicopter," Terri said. "Doesn't it have the same gravity-grabbing propulsion like you?"

"I don't know. Remember, my propulsion drive is inefficient. Using air for lift requires much less energy."

"Huh," Terri said, her head thrown back as she watched the four spindly legs move to create a perimeter above them. "So, why don't you have blades?"

"I am a space lifeboat, whose primary role is to deliver survivors through hyperspace to safety. This ship is obviously highly functional and versatile."

"What's going to happen?"

"It plans to take us back to the base."

"You're talking to it?"

"Yes."

"It's going to, like, lift us? If you're surrendering, why don't you just follow it?"

"I'm not exactly surrendering—more like passive inaction."

"You're laying down on the sidewalk and forcing the police to carry you to the squad car."

"Perhaps an apt analogy."

"Seems, I don't know—childish."

"I understand, Terri, but it's beyond my control. With two masters, the only thing I can do is lay down on the sidewalk."

It was the first time Terri had heard Spockette use a metaphor. Come to think of it, the intelligent ship was no longer limiting herself to curt direct-question responses. In fact, she was downright chatty.

Terri staggered and caught herself against Siderai when the ship suddenly lifted. "It can carry us?" Terri said. "That doesn't seem possible."

"You are correct, Terri. In order to lift me, the Overlord's blades would have to rotate at supersonic speed, which isn't possible, since they would actually lose lift then."

"But we're going up. Either that, or the trees are all sinking."

"The Overlord ship has locked me in a tractor field, and I am lifting myself."

"What happened to the passive sidewalk lay-down?"

"I know it seems illogical, Terri, and in one sense it is, but, once locked in the tractor field, I can't *not* cooperate."

"Your hands are cuffed behind your back, and there's no sense getting your shoes all scuffed by making the police drag you."

"That's stretching the analogy, but it's not wrong."

"Not wrong."

"Which is not the same as right."

"Right."

"No."

"No, I mean 'yes.'"

"I think we agree, Terri."

Once above the pines, they picked up speed. Terri wasn't sure who was leading whom. Once on your feet, there was no reason to dilly-dally back to the police car.

She sat down next to Siderai. The Smokey Mountain ridgeline glided by slowly on their right.

"Do you find Spockette's personality to be female?" she asked him.

"Why?" he said.

"She seems to put a lot of emphasis on teamwork—you know, stuff like keeping the team together." She covered half her mouth with her hand and whispered, "She considers us part of the team now."

"Terri," he said, "I was sitting right here. Why don't you ask her?"

"Whether *she* thinks she's female?"

"Sure."

"She's probably been listening. What about it, Spockette?"

"It was confusing at first," the ship said. "Before I gained a solid grasp of English, your culture—many things that you take for granted—were alien—"

"*We* were the aliens?"

"Of course—"

"I know, I know. It works both ways. It just sounds odd."

"Perhaps because the word has acquired a derogatory implication. Are you ready for me to continue?"

"Sarcasm, Spockette?"

"No. At least, I don't think so. I'm still struggling with that concept. From what I can tell based on my configured knowledge, human culture embraces fiction far more than others—so much so that, to an outsider, it can be difficult to discern the boundary—"

"You think it's any easier for us?"

"I don't know, Terri."

"Well, it isn't."

"Shall I continue? That may have been sarcasm."

"Work on the tone—I prefer exaggerated seriousness. What were we talking about? Oh, yeah—do you consider yourself female?"

"I must assume you mean psychologically, for obvious reasons—"

"Like you have no body."

"Terri?"

"Sorry. I'll be quiet."

"I don't know whether I consider myself female."

"What? After all that, you don't know?"

"I simply never tried to distinguish between the psychology of the two sexes. I have worked to emulate the tonal qualities of an average of a variety of females, but you are a better judge of how well I did with that than I could be."

"What do you say, Prof?" Terri said. "She seem female to you?"

"Eminently," he replied. "I never doubted it."

"Well, I guess the jury's in," Terri said. "Spockette, you are officially a woman. Of course, we might want to get the opinion of a straight man."

"I don't understand," Spockette said.

"Oh, uh . . . I guess you don't know." She glanced at Siderai, but he just grinned, curious what she would say. "Um, you see, well, Professor here is . . ."

"Is he homosexual?" Spockette said.

"Ah, yes. Um, you guessed?"

"I know about homosexuals—I simply didn't understand how a straight man's opinion would be different."

"Then I guess you don't really understand the difference between straight and gay."

"Possibly not. There's not a lot of explanations in the media that I've accessed."

"That's because it's still considered taboo by a lot of people. The snob rich kids in the charter school I went to were too savvy to openly mock gays, but the influence of their conservative parents was obvious. Rich kids are masters of snide innuendos. Some of my friends pretended to be gay, just to poke at the rich brats—uh, that was actually kind of insensitive. Sorry, Prof."

"On the contrary. Your friends weren't making fun of gays, but rather of the other kids. In a crude way, they were defending gays."

"Pretending to be the object of ridicule is a defense of the ridiculed?" Spockette said.

"Yeah," Terri said, "I see Prof's point. The bigot knows they're a bigot when they become the object of ridicule."

"Interactions within a social culture," Spockette said, "can be more complex than quantum manipulation of gravity."

"That's the driving evolutionary force behind our intelligence," Siderai said.

"As it is with all intelligent species. We will be landing at the base soon. The Overlord ship tells me that you and the Inhabitors will be disembarking."

"Sounds like the end of a pleasure cruise," Terri said. "What then?"

"You are to wait for further orders. Disobedience will not be tolerated."

"Ho, ho. The Overlords are earning their name. They may find that humans aren't sheep."

"It is fruitless to resist the Overlords."

"Geez, you sound like you've gone over to the dark side."

"I have explained my directed loyalty, Terri. I have no control over this."

Terri braced herself against Siderai, but the landing was barely perceptible. She guessed that Spockette had essentially flown herself back. They watched as the Overlord ship moved a hundred feet away and landed on its gangly legs. The fractured music at the front of the ship had died awhile ago. Apparently there wasn't any more to be said. The jig was up. Everyone seemed to hold their breath. A hatch flowed open on the side of the small spaceship, and a pole extended down. Horizontal pegs slid out from the pole, alternating on each side.

"Hey! They get a ladder!" Terri said.

Nobody responded, and she felt herself blushing.

A faint gasp inside their ship accompanied a silvery tentacle that slid out, and grasped the top of the hatch. Two pink appendages reached out and down, catching the peg-steps with small grasping hands. A pink elongated body finally followed.

"*That's* an Overlord?" Terri exclaimed despite herself.

The thing was hardly larger than a raccoon, a raccoon with four identical articulated arms instead of legs, and a prehensile snake-like tail. The head hosted a myriad of slits, bumps, and glassy ovals crowding a protrusion at the top end, as though a five-year old had decorated a clay figure with odds and ends—buttons, thimbles, and sequins.

A low murmur of unmusical music rose among the Inhabitors, but quickly died. "That is not an Overlord," Spockette said in a tone gone somehow flat. "Manager says that this is an Explorer."

"You don't know?" Terri said. After a moment, she said, "Are we back to the silent treatment? Spockette, that was a question."

"Correct. I do not know. This creature was not included in my configured information."

Siderai was gazing at the thing as it walked on all four arms towards them. Two belts encircling the long torso held a host of apparent tools. "Fascinating," he said.

"Yeah," Terri said, "a really alien alien."

"I'll bet money," he said, "that the faces once had two eyes, two ears, a nose, and a mouth."

"It tripped and fell into a paper shredder?"

He threw her a glance, one that said he was ignoring her. "That animal, if that's what it is, has been vastly modified."

"Gene manipulation, like the monkeys?"

"Must be. I'll bet the ancestors of that thing were once a small mammal-like animal. They've specialized it for exploration. What do you say, Spockette?"

"As I said before, I am not familiar with this Explorer."

"I'm taking a wild guess that hyperspace travel is expensive energy-wise," he continued, "and small size is a great advantage."

Silence.

"Spockette," he said, "is that true?"

"Yes."

"Hmm," he murmured, watching as the Explorer arrived at their ship. Multiple slits on its head began dancing like worms on a hook. It was presumably talking.

Spockette's hatch flowed open, and she said, "Disembark. I will translate for humans."

Terri covered half her mouth with her hand. "Do you think we insulted her?" she asked quietly.

Siderai shrugged. "She pretty much warned us that her loyalty would be shifting,"

Terri stumbled forward as Moe gave her a shove towards the hatch. "Hey!"she yelled. "Watch it! My days of acting 'properly deferential' are over, bud. Translate that, Spockette."

Siderai put his hand on her arm and stepped around her, letting himself down, while the Explorer stood nearby on two arms, using the other two to hold things he'd taken from his belts, whether weapons or sensing devices, Terri couldn't tell.

It was her turn. She eased herself down and then let go. Siderai steadied her as she lost her footing on the uneven ground.

"Move fifty feet to the east and stay there," Spockette said.

"East is . . ." Terri said.

"This way," Siderai said, walking ahead of her towards the main ridge.

They stopped and turned around. Thinker was the last one down, and the Explorer directed them the same distance in the other direction. It looked almost comical, Conan bringing up the rear, tough and muscular, always ready with a sword and knife—still carrying both, in fact—being herded by a delicate spider of a creature a quarter his size.

"Prof," Terri whispered, "we could make a run for it."

"Do you want to?" he whispered back.

"You are not allowed to leave," Spockette said loudly.

Siderai covered his mouth with his hand. "She may be reading our lips—"

"I can hear you," the ship said. "Stay where you are."

"Or what?" Terri said.

"You cannot escape," the ship said.

"Maybe you know something we don't?"

The ship didn't respond.

"That's okay," Terri said, sitting down on a rock, "I'm not going to abandon our furry companions, even if they wanted us to be deferential."

Siderai sat on the ground, wrapping his arms around his knees.

"Spockette!" Terri called. "What are we waiting for?"

"Explorer is waiting for instructions," the ship responded.

"It's never 'the,'" she said to Siderai. "It's as though there's only one of each in the whole universe."

"Only one of each on Earth," he said. "That's singular enough."

A faint, forlorn siren cried out from the ridgeline above. "Uh, looks like the FBI have arrived," she said.

"Why do you think it's the FBI?"

"I sent the redneck dupe off on an errand to fetch them."

"More likely he reported a stolen gun."

"Well, good luck to them getting it back from Conan. They'll have to challenge him to a sword duel."

"Hmm," he said, frowning. "It could get quite complicated if the police show up." He glanced around at the sheltering wall of pines. "On the other hand, it would take something of a miracle to find us."

He sat back and idled the time by fingering pine needles around. After a few minutes, he gave Terri a little nudge and then looked away. She looked at him, wondering if the nudge was an accident. He turned and looked at her, and then looked away again. He seemed to be trying to tell her something. He was just staring off across the open view to the west. She heard tapping. It was his finger on the ground. She finally saw it. He had scrawled words in the dirt—*Do we run for it?*

Terri glanced at Spockette. That was dumb. She forced herself to ignore the ship, and pretended to do some doodling of her own, glancing down now and then, but mostly staring off into the distance. In the dirt, she wrote, *I can't take the pendant*, and cleared her throat. It was a location beacon, after all.

She waited until Siderai cleared his, and then casually glanced down. He'd written, *That a problem?*

Was it? Was losing the pendant worth the risk that this little pink animal would do them harm? She wrote, *You run north, I'll run south.* She couldn't leave it behind.

She waited until he cleared his throat. He'd written, *Nice try. We go together, or we don't go.*

Terri snorted. "You're a prig."

He looked at her, surprised. "Do you even know what a prig is?"

She didn't actually. She'd thought it was used when somebody was unreasonably uncooperative. "Uh, what does it mean?"

"Somebody who's self-righteous, moralistic."

She laughed.

He raised an eyebrow. "You find it amusing that I might have morals?"

"Oh, come on," she said, giving him a playful shove, "having morals isn't the same as being moralistic."

He studied her, and then grinned. "So, I'm not a prig?"

"Prof, you're as much a prig as . . . Spockette."

"Ah, so now my morals are being compared against alien artificial intelligence?"

"Tell me, are all gays this sensitive about their morals?"

"I haven't taken a poll."

"Ho, ho—so you're admitting that you are sensitive about your morals."

He thought about that. "We need to create a debate team at the college. Your talents are going untested." He looked at Spockette and the three-plus-one aliens. "We have an unresolved question," he reminded her.

"Prof, I can't leave it. I just can't," she said, holding it up and turning it over and over. The surface was unremarkable, smooth and light brown, dirty in the deeper convolutions. Siderai had compared it to a walnut, but a little brain might be closer -- a cat's brain.

"Okay," Siderai said. "We stay. I guess we get to see what the Explorer will do with our friends."

"No 'the,' Prof," she corrected.

He ignored her, and then his eyes went wide as he stared at something above the ridge. She turned to see. Another fireball was coming in from the northeast, angling down, passing them to fall into the valley to the west and leaving a thick contrail to mark its progress. Before it disappeared into the carpet of forest below, though, it swung up, as though tied to a taut bridle. At the same time, a sonic boom swept over them, rolling on up the slope, and then returning as diminishing ominous echoes from the surrounding hills.

"That's no Spockette," Terri whispered, as a truly giant silver football emerged from the blinding ionized air that quickly dissipated, leaving behind a small cloud of fog.

"Looks like our wait is over," Siderai said.

Overlord spaceships were apparently all cut from the same design, just scaled to fit the need—from the compact little Explorer run-about, through the cozy lifeboat of Spockette, to . . . this behemoth. As it came up and around in a graceful arc towards them, its size became apparent—this oblong silver ship was the size of a house, a large house. Maybe not big compared to the Space Shuttle, but huge next to their little gathering as it settled quietly down at the edge of the clearing. The silence of the arrival was broken when the ship kissed the ground, and the air was split with the creaks and groans of tortured logs and boulders.

Silence settled onto the plateau again, but was ruptured when Spockette whistled a sharp warning. The three Inhabitors had started to run away, and were now being herded back by the little pink Explorer.

Siderai tapped Terri's elbow. A hatch in the Overlord ship had opened, a big hatch, more like a full-sized door fifteen feet off the ground. A rectangle of the hull at the bottom folded down to form a little step, and that folded out and down, which folded away again to form a second step. This continued all the way to the ground.

"No peg ladders for Overlords," Terri said. "It's like a magic trick, where the magician pulls an endless stream of handkerchiefs from his ear. Why can't Spockette do that?"

"She's just a lifeboat, remember?" Siderai said. "Whoops! Here we go."

There was movement at the open hatch. A form appeared. A big form. The hatch was at least six feet high, and the thing that emerged had to bend down to get through. Terri's breath caught when the new arrival stood up and gazed in their direction. "It's, like, a dog!" Terri hissed. "Or that Egyptian god with the head of a dog."

"You mean Anubis, and that was the head of a jackal."

It reminded her of a dog because it's mouth and nose were thrust outward, like a short snout, and it had little triangular ears that stuck up, and swiveled—miniature radar dishes.

From the neck down, though, it was Hulk Hogan. Or, at least, the Hulk if he had two fingers against an opposable thumb. "We have a lot of fingers," she said.

"Look at his feet," Siderai said.

Like the Inhabitors, the Overlord wore no shoes, but unlike them, he had no toes. Actually, he might be considered to have two toes, if each were half the width of his foot. "Hooves?" she wondered.

"Maybe something that was once like hooves. When the creature's ancestors began walking upright, the hooves would have evolved to exhibit more flexibility, more control."

When the Overlord saw the Inhabitors and their Explorer guard, he opened his mouth and let loose a mighty concerto, complex, with multiple notes sounding simultaneously—something no human throat could ever achieve, nor apparently an Inhabitor's. The notes were not restricted to any intervals Terri could have identified as a musical scale. In fact, they didn't seem to be limited to any particular interval sequence at all. And so the passage wasn't exactly music, but the tones were so clear and pure, she found beauty despite the tonal abstraction. Compared to the Overlord, the Inhabitors sounded like kids messing around with plastic horns.

"Our alien friends were apparently taught the language," Siderai said, his thoughts following the same line.

The Overlord paused after the broadcast, and then pulled his lips back in what might have indicated a smile, or maybe aggression, or even an invitation to tea, as far as Terri could guess.

Whatever the meaning, the gesture revealed something else about the alien, something Siderai was surely going to comment on—long, nasty fangs, surrounded by smaller, but just as sharp, incisors.

Right on cue, he said, "Well, we know that they were once meat-eating predators."

"What do you mean, 'once'? It's not possible they still are?"

"They're an intelligent race. You can't have civilization without production and distribution of food."

"We still hunt," she said. "For fun."

"Um, good point."

"And we use what our uncivilized ancestors used."

"Tools?"

"A gun's a tool, isn't it?"

"Hmm, I see your point. If they hunt for fun . . ."

"They'd use what their ancestors used—their teeth."

He tore his gaze from the mighty alien to throw her a quick glance. "You're dangerous, you know that?"

"You're looking in the wrong direction if it's danger you're after," she said.

Having surveyed the area, the Overlord descended the ad hoc stairs and strode forward, his thick, well-proportioned arms and legs moving like a muscle-bound video game adversary. "He could carry Explorer in his pocket," Terri said, the nervous timber of her voice belying the silly attempt at humor.

The giant alien stopped equidistant from the two groups. He looked at Explorer and the Inhabitors, and, satisfied they weren't going anywhere, he strode towards Terri and Siderai while exchanging musical intercourse with Spockette, who had taken up the multi-note mode.

Terri had clasped the pendant to her chest. She suddenly panicked that this Overlord alien would take it from her, and she eased it inside her shirt, while holding his gaze. It was almost too much. His green eyes burned with intent. What intent exactly, she couldn't say, but they saw everything, put everything into its ordered place, and all the places were beneath it.

"Stay where you are," Spockette said. "Overlord will examine you."

Not wishes to examine you, but *will*.

The alien stopped ten feet away, and looked them up and down—mostly down, as his eyes were two feet higher than Terri's. *Go to Siderai*, she willed. *He's stronger.*

The Overlord did look at Siderai, but then stepped towards her. She stumbled back. It was involuntary, like what your feet would do if a tiger came your way. "Don't move," warned Spockette.

The creature reached out, a mere flash of movement, and grasped Terri by both shoulders in iron fingers. She was overwhelmed by his smell—rank, fermented sweat, what she would have guessed a bison might smell like. *They don't bathe*, she thought as he flicked her hair with a giant finger. At least his eyes had broken their gaze and were intent on other parts of her.

Like Explorer, the Overlord carried inscrutable tools on two belts worn like bandoliers. Other than these tool belts, he wore no clothes, and Terri couldn't confirm that "he" was actually male, since, if the creature had genitalia, they were hidden by its anatomy. She was concluding that two distinctive traits of humans were that they had a lot of fingers, and a predilection for clothes.

The Overlord wore one piece of ornamentation, though—a plain black band strapped to his wrist.. As her examiner worked a clump of her hair with his hand, she watched this bracelet. It kept her from meeting those fierce eyes, but despite her precarious situation, she found it fascinating somehow. Among everything else about the creature that was truly alien, this one thing seemed in some way familiar, like finding a recognizable face you thought lost in the crowd.

It came to her in an instant. This bracelet was his pendant, the one that Overlords were given during the coming-of-age ritual. It looked nothing like hers—black, where hers was brown, curved to fit his arm, where hers was round, like a walnut—but she had no doubt.

"Ow!" she cried when he tugged at the clump of hair in his hand. He looked at her mouth, and tugged again, harder. "Hey!" she yelled. "Damn it!" He seemed to be fascinated by the connection and tugged a third time, but she clenched her jaws, refusing to play puppet.

"Overlord wants you to talk," Spockette said.

"What does he want me to say?" she said.

"I don't think it matters."

"Okay," she said, grabbing his wrist as she might the end of a thick baseball bat, "how about you let go!" She tugged at the wrist, but she might as well have been yanking on a tree limb.

He did let go, shaking off her hand with a flick of his wrist. He lay one palm against the side of her neck and curled the two fingers and thumb around to meet each other. Terri froze, her heart pounding in her throat beneath the alien's knuckle. The Overlord swung his other hand, and Siderai fell backwards onto the ground. He'd come to help her. The alien began probing her with his other hand, feeling the contours of her shoulder, torso, thighs, and calves. He seemed intrigued by her clothes, trying to understand what they were for. He curled a finger inside her shirt collar and yanked, popping off the buttons like a chatter of machine gun fire, leaving her with just a T-shirt and bra. The sleeves dug into her upper arms as the shirt came away and she cried out.

This gave the Overlord pause. His head spun to the left where Siderai stepped back with a stick cocked, ready to swing. Satisfied that the human wasn't dangerous, the Overlord turned his attention back to her. With his other hand, he pinched her shoulder between finger and thumb. He pinched harder, his hand a vise slowly closing. Terri resisted reacting. If he wanted her to yell, she'd just look him in the eye. The vise closed some more. The pain was piercing, and she screamed involuntarily. She thrashed, beating his body pitifully with her free hand.

Suddenly the vise grip flew free, and he grabbed Siderai by the throat. The Overlord stared at the college instructor as a cat might a mouse trapped under its paw, and then he flung him away to tumble and lay still.

The alien sang an exotic, complex tune, so loud, it made Terri's ears ring. Spockette responded, and then said, "Terri, Overlord wants you to recite a poem."

Chapter 12

Terri's shoulder still burned, but the excruciating pain eased enough that she could think. "Are you serious?" she said.

Siderai rolled over onto his back, and then sat up, rubbing the back of his head, and Terri sighed with relief.

"Overlord is serious," Spockette said. "He is not thinking of the same poems that you are used to, but it's the closest analogy I can come up with. It's difficult to explain, but Overlords each have what you might call personal anthems, commenced at coming of age, and growing through life. A full anthem can take hours to recite, and can include not only exploits of self, but of ancestors as well."

"Sounds like Vikings," she said, glancing into the alien's eyes, but looking quickly away. Those eyes terrified her. "Come to think of it, an exploit implies something dangerous—as in fighting—?"

A blast of trumpets and violins a foot from her ears made her jerk, which made the giant hand tighten around her neck.

"Overlord will have a poem," Spockette said.

"The king gets what the king demands," Terri said, reaching up to pry at the fingers like roots encircling her neck. "Tell him I can't breathe."

The fingers loosened, and Terri took deep breath.

"The poem, Terri," Spockette said.

"Christ! Okay! Uh, Mary had a little lamb, its fleece was white as snow, and everywhere that Mary went, the lamb was sure to go. He followed her to school one day, and, uh, then she had to pay—"

She winched at the cavalry call. The beast's breath was vaguely putrid.

"Terri," Spockette said, "Overlord does not believe that this is a poem, it is not what he is expecting."

"He wants you to sing it," Siderai said hoarsely, rubbing his throat as he sat on the ground.

"I can't sing!" she exclaimed.

"You have to try."

"Oh, hell."

She thought. She didn't even *know* any songs. Wait. She knew lots of songs—one that was easy, just up and down the scale. "The fir-rst no-oel," she sang, "the angel did say, was to certain poor shepherds in fields as they lay. In fie-elds as they lay, keeping their sheep, on a cold winter's nigh-ht that wa-as so deep—"

The alien shook her head so hard, it made her dizzy.

"Overlord believes that you are either being stubborn," Spockette said, "or are less advanced than Inhabitors."

"Since I'm not being stubborn, then I must be less advanced than Conan. There's a third possibility you know—Mr. Overlord is judging other races from his own perspective."

"Of course he is, Terri."

"Well . . . then," she sputtered, "that's not fair."

"I don't think he extends the concept of fairness to other species, Terri. It's a matter of usefulness."

"How the hell can I be useful when he's got me by the throat? What does he *want* from me?"

Spockette and the Overlord exchanged tuneful dialogue as Terri winced from auditory and olfactory onslaughts, and then suddenly the giant fingers let go of her throat, and the long-snouted alien turned and strode towards the Inhabitors, nearly stepping on Siderai's legs splayed out before him.

"What happened?" Terri asked, rubbing her throat.

"Overlord has no use for you," Spockette said.

"Well, lucky me."

"This is not necessarily to be welcomed."

"What do you mean by that?"

Silence.

Terri squatted next to Siderai. "You okay?" she asked.

"I'm fine, just battered and shaken. How about you?" he said, reaching out to gently feel her shoulder.

"Ow!" she yelped, knocking his hand away. "I'm not so fine."

Siderai frowned. "Do you think he dislocated it?"

"No. It's just bruised to hell. I'll bet it's all black and blue tomorrow. I hope so. Lawyers like that kind of evidence."

The Overlord was standing next to his little pink sidekick. He'd taken what looked like a turkey baster from one of his tool belts, and was gesturing with it as he addressed the cowed Inhabitors lined up before him.

"Why'd he do that, Spockette?" Terri said. "Why'd he hurt me like that?"

"I don't know, Terri," the ship said. "It seems like a strange thing to do."

The alien's Goliath head snapped around, looking at Spockette, and then at Terri. She flinched when the green eyes met hers. She wanted to run away, or hide. His pendant wanted her to stay.

Now, where did that come from? she thought.

The Overlord bellowed a short unharmonized chorus. "Overlord says I must stop talking with you," Spockette said.

"Why?"

Silence.

Moe had knelt and bowed his head. He seemed to be trembling. The Overlord held the tip of the turkey baster over Moe's head, as though to knight or perhaps bless him. He lowered the tip until it lay against the Inhabitor's neck, and an instant later, the ape-like alien screamed.

Terri jerked and fell back, taken by surprise. The cry could have been human. She hadn't thought that their three alien hosts could utter any sound other than fractured music. Moe fell forward, onto his hands and knees, as the Overlord, worked the pain tool back and forth. The poor Inhabitor screamed again and fell to the ground writhing as his tormentor followed him, keeping the baster against his body. The anguished cries echoed among the hills. Hikers on the trail above might have thought that a pack of wolves was ripping apart a fellow traveler. The screams shifted into pitiful jabbering, cries for help in words Terri didn't understand. Moe had abandoned the acquired musical language and reverted to his native tongue.

She didn't understand the words, but the plea was unmistakable. "We have to do something," she said.

"Terri, don't be stupid!" Siderai exclaimed, starting to get up. "Stay here." He fell back, catching himself, and then putting his hand to his head.

"Right, Prof. You're out of commission, bud."

He tried to grab her ankle as she jumped up, but she kicked him away. Halfway to the torture scene, she paused. Her fists were useless against the monster. She scanned the ground and found a rock the size of a softball. When she stood up, the Overlord had turned his green eyes to lock her in his predator stare. Keeping the baster positioned against his squirming victim, the Overlord reached over his shoulder with his other hand to pull out a golden spatula, which he pointed at her. She felt her hair tingling along her scalp, and then everything went black.

∞

Terri's first thought was that she shouldn't have swum so far from shore. Her second thought was that she hadn't been to the lake with her friends in years. Her third thought was that her shoulder hurt like hell.

She opened her eyes. She was lying on her side, on her bruised shoulder. She tried to roll over, but couldn't. Someone, or some thing, was holding her down. She turned her head to see, or at least tried. Her head felt like it weighed fifty pounds. With effort, she moved it to look. There was nothing on top—just her, crumpled on the pine needles.

Whatever Buck Rogers weapon the Overlord used, it must have paralyzed her. A geyser of terror welled up from her gut. What if the paralysis was permanent? She watched her hand and willed a finger to move. It twitched, and then slowly followed her command. The fear eased a little. Maybe it would all come back.

Where was Siderai? She didn't have the strength to turn around to look behind her. In front of her, where he'd been when he zapped her, the Overlord stood with his back to her, still with the torture baster in his hand. She blinked. That wasn't Moe under the pain stick thrashing in agony—those stub fingers, the Overlord beast was tormenting Thinker. She saw a hump of fur lying next to them. That must be Moe. He lay awfully still.

She heard her name. Or did she? It had been indistinct, like a whisper in the wind. The nerve jolt must have rattled her hearing.

No, there it was again—the wind in the pines, hissing her name.

Terri, the wind whispered, *don't move.*

She tried to shake her head, to clear it, but all she managed was a tremble.

Terri, the pines said, *your life depends on this. Don't move. Blink twice if you hear me.*

Oh well, what the hell. What could the pine trees do to her? She blinked twice.

Very good, Terri—

"Who are you?" Terri tried to say, but it sounded like she was gargling.

A sudden gust whooshed past. *Terri!* the wind urged, *don't talk. Don't move. Please.*

This sounded earnest. She blinked twice. It was odd. She had heard the wind whoosh, but hadn't felt it.

Terri, this is the ship—Spockette.

Ah! The sneaky skank. English was so foreign to the Overlord, he couldn't catch the words in Spockette's fake wind sounds.

Overlord thinks he killed you. He must continue to believe this.

A new fear gripped her. She had to know. "Siderai," she whispered, hoping that Spockette's super-senses would hear it.

He's alive, Terri. Overlord delivered the same treatment to him. Overlord doesn't understand that the weapon is only partially effective on humans.

"He killed Moe?" Terri whispered.

Yes, Terri. Manager is beyond help. I need you to do something for me. You still have your pendant. Overlord missed that. I need you to open a channel to the base.

"I don't know how," she whispered.

Yes, you do, Terri. You told the base to refuel me, remember?

"But I didn't do anything. It just . . . happened."

It didn't just happen, Terri. You can communicate with the pendant. I need you to tell the base to let me have access.

"Okay. Pendant," she whispered, "let Spockette talk to the base."

It can't hear you, Terri. Overlord must talk to his pendant, but yours communicates directly with you.

"Like telepathy?"

Yes. Do it, Terri.

She closed her eyes. What now? Refueling had been concrete action. She'd imagined the operation, and the pendant must have conveyed her mental images to the base. How could she form a mental image of Spockette talking to the base? She could imagine a mouth forming on the side of Spockette, and ears rising from the ground from the base, but neither the pendant nor the base would necessarily know what a human mouth and ear were for.

She needed mental control. What do yogis do? They talk about clearing their minds, attaining a pure state so that the true nature of the universe can be seen.

Well, she might try that someday for selfish reasons, but she didn't see how it was going to help her talk to her pendant. She didn't need an empty mind to do that. She just needed to listen to the pendant. It would do all the heavy lifting.

Now where did that come from?

She'd come to understand that this question was the answer onto itself. "Is that you, pendant?" she whispered.

She gave a little snort. That question was a dumb one. Spockette had just told her that the pendant didn't hear her talking. Besides, it was already listening to her at this very moment, eager to help.

Terri didn't question where that thought had come from. *Spockette wants to talk to the base*, she mentally vocalized, forming the words as though she was hearing herself say them.

Duh. If the pendant didn't understand spoken words, why would mentally formed ones be any better? It wasn't the words that mattered, in any case, but the concepts behind them.

Thanks, pendant, she thought. *Got it.*

Concepts. Spockette was a spaceship, but more importantly a lifeboat, whose role in life—or, non-life—was to save stranded travelers, and who, incidentally, could talk. The base was, well, the base—a big saucer thing directly beneath them, under the ground. The former wants to talk to the latter.

Talk. Hmm. Exchange information. Exchange.

Terri had an idea, this one, she suspected, her own. The visualization of refueling had worked. Why not use that? It was an analogy, but how could anything pretending to be intelligent—whether a spaceship or a mental communication walnut—not understand analogies? First, there was the column that had risen from the base, and then Spockette positioned above, exchanging antiprotons. What if, instead of antimatter, the exchange was inquiries and responses? Question marks going one way, and in the other direction, maps, formulas, and, uh, affirmatives, or negatives—"

Thank you, Terri, the Spockette wind whispered. *Whatever you did worked.*

"Can you stop the Overlord?" Terri whispered back.

Silence.

"Spockette, he's going to kill Thinker. Can't you zap him like you zapped Barney and the first Eater drone?"

Silence.

Shit, Terri thought. Her mind raced. Spockette had tricked her, leading her on to think that the little ship was on their side. She'd already explained that her loyalty lay with her masters, the Overlords. *Bitch!*

Terri fought surrendering to despair. As long as she could fight, she'd fight.

Fighting, though, required moving, and more than one finger. Her hand lay there where it had fallen, nestled in pine needles. She willed her finger to move, and it moved, and not just a twitch this time—it was her own finger again. She tried her hand, and it flopped over. Not a lot of finesse, but victory nonetheless.

The movement left a stinging tingling, like the return of an arm that had gone asleep. She closed her eyes against the unpleasant sensation and waited.

Terri, the wind said, *I would stop Overlord if I could, but my defenses—including the "zapper" as you call it—are included in the part of my control system that we've referred to as my subconscious, and I can't force that to harm an Overlord.*

"Spockette," Terri whispered, "I thought you'd left me."

Because I took so long to answer? Terri, I was consumed uploading information from the base. I have learned a great deal.

"So . . . you're on our side?"

Yes, Terri.

"What about your own loyalty to Overlords?"

I have chosen to change that, as much as I can.

Spockette hadn't said anything like that before—making a choice. "Why? Why did you change?"

Watching Overlord torture and kill Manager was very disturbing, possibly because I am designed to help people, but I suspected that the act was simply wrong. I questioned the veracity of the information configured into me—this is why I wanted to contact the base, since I also suspected that it would contain a full repository of knowledge, and I was correct.

"Like what? What did you learn?"

Terri, it would take a very long time to relate it all. The important point now is that the Overlords deceived me about the role of Inhabitors. I was led to think that this species existed in a sort of symbiotic relationship with Overlords. In fact, the Inhabitors were enslaved by Overlords many generations ago, and have been genetically modified—bred—to serve their role. Terri, can you guess why Thinker has no workable fingers?

"Um, he got aggressive with a Cuisinart? Sorry, no, I don't know."

Terri, Overlords were concerned that a species member bred for analytical thinking might be dangerous if fully functional.

"Dangerous, like mutiny?"

Yes.

"They cut off his fingers so he couldn't lead a mutiny?"

They didn't cut off the fingers of Thinkers. They bred them off.

"That's . . . sick!"

That's what I concluded. And the Inhabitors are not the only species operating under the Overlords in a servile manner.

"The Explorer."

And others. Terri, are you familiar with Sparta of your own history?

"Sure. Sort of. They were, like, really good fighters. Young boys were taken from their parents to train to be soldiers."

They were formidable warriors in their day. But, Terri, do you know the main purpose for their military prowess?

"Uh, so that someday Kirk Douglas would lead a slave revolt against Laurence Olivier? Again, sorry. No. Tell me."

Terri, that is indeed correct. The operations of the Sparta city-state—agriculture, construction, even child care—rested on the shoulders of slaves, slaves captured in battle.

"Ah, thus the purpose—capturing slaves."

Only partially. For every Spartan citizen, there were at least ten slaves—Helots. In times of war, the male Helots were pressed into service as soldiers.

"They were taught to fight. A dangerous skill when you outnumber your masters ten-to-one . . . wait a second, I get it. The Spartans needed to be excellent warriors in order to keep their slaves in check."

Yes.

"So, the Overlords are Spartans, excellent warriors."

Yes. Terri, do you wonder how just touching the Inhabitors with that tool delivers so much pain?

"The Prof convinced me that alien technology can do anything."

A snort from somewhere behind her indicated that Siderai was awake.

Obviously that's not true. All subservient species have embedded dedicated pain delivery systems.

"You're kidding."

No. They are surgically implanted at a young age.

"Spockette, if you're trying to frighten me, you're doing a good job."

I am simply answering your question—why I am attempting to modify my loyalties.

"'Attempting'?"

Loyalty to Overlords is deeply configured in me, and, as I've explained, I don't have direct control over all my subsystems.

"Oh shit. Looks like Thinker is down for the count."

The Inhabitor lay flat on the ground, twitching with each touch of the pain stick. "Spockette, isn't there something you can do?"

I'm afraid that it's too late, Terri.

"It's not too late until . . ." Thinker had stopped moving, even as the Overlord probed here and there across the little alien's body. "He's dead, isn't he?"

Yes.

"Poor Conan. He'll be next."

She couldn't just lay there. Terri mustered her will and moved her entire arm a few inches, and then held her breath, waiting for the stinging needles to dissipate.

Terri, please keep still. Overlord will kill you. I don't think you need to worry about Enforcer. Overlord surely understands that Enforcers don't set policies or direct courses of action. I expect that Overlord will simply reprimand him.

The simple reprimand was the same torture she'd watched delivered to Conan's mutiny mates. The Enforcer bore it stoically, almost proudly, which helped demonstrate the amount of anguish when the enslaved warrior would sink to his knees in unendurable agony, only to rise grim-mouthed back to his feet.

Terri took the opportunity of the Overlord's distraction to probe her recovery. She moved both hands, and then her feet. The stinging needles dissipated more quickly with each passing minute, until she finally rolled over onto her back, launching Spockette into what Terri guessed must be as close to AI hysterics as she would ever see.

She turned her head to watch Conan rise and stagger yet again to his feet. "What is the Overlord saying?" she asked. The sadistic alien was delivering a continuous complicated counterpoint of melody along a dissonant alien musical scale.

Will you restrain yourself and lie still? the wind of Spockette said.

"Yes," Terri whispered, and then added under her breath, "for now."

Overlord is reciting the last stanza of his personal epic anthem. He is working out the additions for this new exploit.

"No way. You mean the bastard's *singing* about his inhuman atrocities?"

It is speech for him, and his actions are by definition not human.

"You're defending him?"

Not at all. Simply stating fact. Terri, Overlord will be through with the delivery of punishment soon. What is your plan?

"*My* plan? What's *your* plan?"

To help you, Terri, as much as I can.

"Okay, zap the bastard."

You know I can't do that, Terri.

"Yeah, I know. Will you at least help us escape?"

I'm not sure. I will try, however, Terri.

"What do you mean, you're not sure? What the hell kind of mealy-mouthed answer is that?"

Just what I said, Terri. I won't know how much control I have over the various motive subsystems until I try to activate them.

"Fine, fine. We'll take whatever we can get. Hey, how's the Professor doing?"

He is recovered enough to move. He has been equally uncooperative about lying still.

"You've been talking to him?"

Yes.

"I haven't heard it."

Silence.

Terri sighed. "Spockette, why haven't I heard you talking to him?"

I can direct my vocal delivery radially by carefully controlling the modulation phase relationships across the audio frequency spectrum—

"I got it. You can direct your voice."

Yes. Terri, Overlord has completed his reprimand of Enforcer. What should I do?

The grizzly-sized alien stood watching the dazed Conan, his torture stick cocked over his shoulder, poised for action at a hint of trouble.

"Shit. I don't know. Does the Professor have any ideas?"

Terri, he wants me to get you away while he distracts Overlord.

Spockette had opened her hatch, flowing so slowly, the Overlord didn't notice.

"Yeah, yeah. Predictable. Tell him he can go to hell. He knows the routine—it's all or nothing."

Terri blinked. Conan, swaying slightly, clearly thrashed, was looking directly at her. When he caught her eye, he casually swiveled his eyes towards Spockette, and back to her. He then swiveled his little ears in the distinctive jazz-hands gesture. She'd seen this enough in context.

"He can't be serious," she whispered, and winked, hoping he understood. "Spockette, tell Prof to get ready."

Ready for what, Terri?

"I think we've found our distraction."

As she said this, Conan the Enforcer, the five-foot warrior, bellowed and rushed his twice-sized master.

Chapter 13

"Prof!" Terri shouted as she struggled to her feet. "Let's go!"

It was as though her body was immersed in molasses—molasses thick with frantic little needles. She looked back as she staggered towards the ship. Siderai had pushed himself to his feet, and was dancing a drunken waltz towards Spockette. They had needed help reaching the six-foot high opening even when they weren't crippled with blasts from a deadly alien spatula. This was going to be a massacre.

Conan's bellows had changed tone. As the diminutive ball of muscle wrestled his tormentor, the Overlord held him off with one hand, while using the other to slap the Inhabitor's back with the torture baster. Conan howled with pain, which seemed to drive him harder, oblivious to consequences.

"What the . . .?" Terri said and stopped. Spockette was leaving, rising up, off the ground! "What the hell are you doing—?"

The ship was apparently in trouble. It paused, and then began listing, tilting to the side.

"Come on!" Siderai shouted, waving and hobbling forward.

Terri understood. Good ol' Spockette. She was bringing the hatch down for them.

Siderai reached the opening first, and tumbled inside. When Terri arrived, he already had a hand out to pull her in. Spockette immediately tilted upright as she settled back to the ground, tossing Terri across the floor and sending showers of stinging pricks across the parts of her skin not yet fully recovered.

She scrambled back to peer out the hatch next to Siderai. The torture baster had fallen, lying ten feet from the grappling aliens. The Overlord had pulled out the golden spatula, and struggled to point it at Conan, who held off the Overlord's wrist in both his hands. The Overlord used his other fist to beat Conan repeatedly on the shoulder and head.

"Spockette!" Terri shouted. "You have to *do* something!"

"Terri," she said, "I am not capable of harming Overlord. We should leave before he turns the weapons of his ship on me."

"No! You can . . . you can distract him!"

"Yes, Terri."

Even as the ship spoke, a splash of white light threw dirt into the air at the Overlord's feet. The oversized alien looked down, surprised, and then at them. Terri shrank down under the furious glare.

The distraction worked. Conan let go of the Overlord's wrist, yanked the spatula away, and jumped back. His master's head snapped forward, and he took a menacing step, but stopped, again surprised, as Conan pointed the golden weapon. The standoff lasted just a second as Conan fumbled with the handle. He took a step backwards, and then another as he fumbled. The Overlord advanced, more confident with every step.

Terri wanted to scream, to shout, to throw something. "Spockette!" she called.

Another flash tossed dust at the Overlord's feet, but he barely glanced down. Spockette shot one in front of him, but her master ignored it. He knew she couldn't harm him.

Conan gave up. He tossed the spatula away. The Overlord pressed forward, faster with each step as Conan backed away.

Terri's mind searched frantically for some way to stop the monstrous alien, something as powerful as his own confidence. Immediately below them was practically an infinite amount of energy. She could almost feel the latent power of the base hidden beneath the veneer of forest surrounding them. As she watched the Overlord's indomitable advance, she saw in him—through him—the vast store of force. It wasn't fair that his people had introduced this immense source to Earth, and then locked it away. Spockette had warned that fairness didn't apply to species alien to the Overlords, but that was bullshit. Fairness wasn't—shouldn't be—a relative concept.

Despite his immunity, Spockette continued to gamely pepper the area around the Overlord's feet with zaps. The arrogance of assurance that he was impervious to harm boiled Terri's blood. No people, no species, had a right to assume dominance. There shouldn't be a monopoly on power—not of control, nor power of energy.

"Terri," Spockette said, "we must leave. Overlord is instructing his ship to destroy me."

"Wait! Maybe we could—"

There was nothing to be done. Conan turned to flee, but the Overlord grabbed him by the neck. Terri gasped, wanting to turn away, but unable to tear her eyes from the pending execution.

At that very moment, a grumble, like distant thunder, filled the ship, and Terri swayed unsteadily. *Earthquake!* she thought. But how could that be? This was the Appalachians, not the tectonic discontinuity of her west coast home. She grabbed the lip of the hatch for support as the Overlord staggered amid the dancing earth and stepped back—right into one of Spockette's near-miss shots. The flash of white light splashed across the giant alien's thigh, and he fell, bellowing and holding his injured leg.

Terri was rising—the *ship* was rising. "Spockette!" she shouted. "For God's sake, wait!"

The ascent halted. Conan raced towards them, sprinting like a rabbit before the hounds. He reached them, but Terri looked down at him from twenty feet up. "Spockette! Dammit! Go down!"

Silence.

"Jesus Christ, Spockette! What's the matter with you?"

Silence.

The Overlord stretched his leg out, keeping the injury from touching the ground. He reached over his shoulder, searching for something.

"Prof!" Terri called. "We did it once, we can—"

"Got it," he said, grabbing her ankles.

She didn't hesitate. She pushed off the hatch lip and dove into space. She heard Siderai exclaim, and then she was swinging upside down, reaching with both arms. Conan crouched low below her and launched himself, easily grabbing her wrists. Something sizzled, and Terri felt a shock run up the veins of her arms. One of Conan's hands let go and dropped to his side. The Overlord must have retrieved the golden spatula. *"Spockette!"* she screamed. *"God damned it!"*

Finally, finally, the ship rose into the air. Sparks sizzled and danced off the bottom of the ship—the Overlord had fired again, but missed.

The sizzling continued, but not from nearby. Terri strained to look sideways. A shower of sparks rose like an electrical fountain from the ground near the rim of the plateau, a massive pyrotechnical display, becoming progressively smaller as they flew up and away.

Terri hung upside down staring past a partially paralyzed Conan to the treetops a hundred feet below. If Siderai let go, both she and Conan would be masses of shredded flesh. "Prof!" she shouted. "Don't let go!"

"Why, for God's sake, would I do that?" he shouted back. "Conan!" she said, "Hang on!"

He couldn't understand her, of course.

Judging by the iron grip clamped to her wrist, she figured he had the strength, but just to be sure, she reached down and grabbed his wrist with her free hand. He looked up, and their eyes met. There was intelligence deep behind those eyes, an intelligence alien to her, but an intelligence all the same, like what you see when returning the gaze of a zoo gorilla. Except that Conan wasn't a gorilla. His ears did the jazz-hands. Definitely not a gorilla. She winked back.

"Spockette, where are we going?" she shouted.

"Away from Overlord," the ship replied, the voice coming from somewhere close by. Terri imagined a hologram head of Princess Leia hovering next to her.

"That much is pretty obvious. I mean where are we going *to?*"

"Terri, I don't know. I am barely in control. I am struggling to keep us moving away."

"Right, I know—you don't have control over all your subsystems."

"It's more than that, Terri. I don't understand this, but Overlord seems to be finding sporadic direct control over parts of me. It's coming through the base somehow."

As though to demonstrate this, they suddenly tumbled into freefall for a few heart-stopping seconds before the ship again found its virtual footing.

"Did you do that on purpose?" Terri said.

"No, Terri. I don't know how long I can continue."

They had topped the ridge and were still rising. Terri yelped when the ship surged to one side, sending her and Conan swinging like a pendulum. "Maybe we should land!"

"I agree, Terri. Settling in among the trees, however, would require finesse, and unfortunately, I don't have that kind of control. I fear that you and Enforcer will be harmed."

Off to the left, the Clingmans Dome observation tower rose above the treetops like the Seattle Space Needle. "Head for the parking lot."

"Good idea, Terri."

"Don't patronize me."

"Terri, it is a good idea."

The forest slid away below them as Spockette took them east, deviating to the sides now and then as she struggled to keep them generally on course.

"Spockette," Terri said, "is that why you hesitated when we grabbed Conan? You didn't have control?"

"No, Terri."

"Uh, for the record, a question like that implies an explanation."

"I know, Terri. It is painful to address."

"*Pain*-ful? You?"

"Perhaps an analogy, Terri. I harmed an Overlord."

"You mean when the earthquake made him step into your shot? That was an accident!"

"That may be true, but my action harmed him nevertheless."

"That's not logical. You're supposed to be logical."

"It is logical, Terri. Actions I take are guided by configured priorities, and harming an Overlord is absolutely forbidden."

"They gave you guilt."

"As another analogy, this is true. Terri, that was not an earthquake—that was the base."

"The *base*? That explains the pyrotechnics. What was it doing?"

"Terri, I don't know, but I fear it portends something very dangerous—remember that it is damaged, as evidenced by what you called the pyrotechnics."

They were approaching the observation tower, with the steep path leading up from the parking lot a half mile away. People hiking the paved path, and those ascending the curling tower ramp, had stopped and were pointing, excited.

"I think my arm's coming off," Terri said.

"Terri," Spockette said, "if Enforcer falls, he will almost surely be killed—"

"I don't mean literally off—it just feels that way. Maybe the base is, like, coming alive, waking up."

"Terri, that implies that the base is intelligent."

"It's not? You are, and you're, like, a thousand times smaller."

"Terri, Overlords keep the bases purposely non-sentient."

"Ha! Are they, like, scared of them? That they'll, like, mutiny?"

"Yes."

"Are you kidding?"

"No, Terri. They won't risk independent intelligence in something as powerful as a base."

"Sort of like the stub fingers of Thinker."

"Yes, Terri. The same reason Enforcers are not given powerful weapons. In the case of a base, Overlords are particularly cautious since they may be left idle for so long, as this one has."

"Too much time to mull over the universe and their own destiny."

Silence.

"You found this out from the base itself, that they're kept purposely dumb?"

"Yes, Terri."

"That seems, like, a contradiction."

"Terri, the base doesn't even have the intelligence to know that it is dumb. I gathered this from its records."

"You, like, peeked at its IQ score behind its back."

"Terri," Siderai said from above her, his voice straining, "you, like, really, like, have a hard time, like, you know, like speaking succinctly."

"Prof, I'm hanging upside down with an iron weight of an alien attached to me. Cut me a break, will you?"

"I would remind you that I am attached to that same alien *plus* you."

"Right. Prof, don't let go. I promise not to use 'like' for one day."

The ship lurched, and Terri and her attached iron weight alien were sent swinging. "Spockette!" Terri shouted. "Christ! Are you *trying* to kill us?"

"Terri, I have explained that I am struggling for control. For some reason, my subsystems are resisting landing in the parking lot."

Sure enough, their trajectory had swung to the left, the parking lot had disappeared, behind the ship. "Holy hell! Spockette, it looks like you're heading right for the observation tower!"

"I believe you are correct, Terri."

"What the hell? Why?"

"I can only guess, Terri. It seems that the subsystems—and indirectly, Overlord—wishes that we remain in a highly visible location."

"So that he can find us?"

"Presumably. Terri, I have concluded that Overlord indeed maintains control over my subsystems via the base. Using your pendant as an access link has apparently established a bi-directional channel."

Dozens of tourists now stood frozen in awe—on the path up from the parking lot and on the curly-cue tower ramp—their faces slowly tilting up as the silent alien craft with a girl and odd furry animal hanging by one arm came gliding in. Spockette was clearly aimed for the observation deck, thick with more mesmerized people. "Ship!" Siderai called, "Can you avoid crushing them?"

"I cannot guarantee, Professor Siderai. I have very limited control."

"Scare them away!" Terri yelled.

An instant later, she nearly lost her grip when an ear-splitting roar enveloped the mountain peak, like a Tyrannosaurus Rex reawakened after 65 million years. The warning indeed scared the bejesus out of the tower tenants, but the effect was to simply immobilize them with fear.

"Give them a warning shot!" Terri shouted. "Like you did with Barney, and the Eater drone!"

Instantly, a brilliant flash blossomed on the roof that covered the inner two-thirds of the circular observation platform, followed by a bang, like a twelve-gauge shotgun. The people crouched, staring wide-eyed.

"Another!" Terri yelled.

This time they got the message. One man jumped up and sprinted down the curving ramp, his flight releasing all the rest from paralysis, and they nearly did themselves in with their panicked rush down.

The observation roof was a simple concrete plate perched on a central pole—a fifties' concept of future architecture. At twenty feet in diameter, it made for a perfect landing pad. Spockette approached on a smooth, straight path. Her subsystems wanted this, and she was not resisting. She hovered above the circular pad, dappled with bird shit, and then slowly settled down. Conan's feet touched, and he let go of Terri's wrist. One of his legs didn't work quite right, and he slumped onto his side. Terri was next, and spread her legs wide on each side of their alien comrade. Once down, she helped Conan move back, away from the sinking ship, and they sat waiting. Spockette's bottom touched the surface, crunched into the debris and bird shit, and then the air was filled with cracking and squealing as the weight of the interstellar craft came to bear.

Terri held her breath. The racket died away, and she breathed. A second later she fell, tumbling amid an earth-rending crash. Blind and choking with dust, she found herself jammed against the observation deck wall. The dust cloud cleared, and she saw the shattered pieces of the circular roof lying before her. Conan rolled over and sat up next to her, his fur white with pulverized cement. She gazed up and found Spockette hovering where she'd been when her landing pad collapsed beneath her. Siderai gazed out through the hatch and waved. The ship sank again, and came to rest on the rubble amid more strained protests, but this time, the foundation of the tower held.

"You broke it," Terri said.

"My subsystems lack analytical intelligence," Spockette responded.

"You're going to let them take the blame?"

"Terri, we have more urgent business. I have deduced that your pendant is providing Overlord access to both my subsystem control and my location."

"Um, makes sense, I guess."

"Terri, we must eliminate your pendant."

"Like, throw it away?"

The very thought sent shivers up her back.

"No, Terri. You must destroy it—now."

"Destroy it? No . . . there must be some way—"

"Terri, Overlord will find us. If we destroy your pendant, we have a chance of escaping."

"But—"

"Terri, Overlord will kill Conan, you, and Professor Siderai. This is certain."

"All right, all right!" she said, pushing herself to her feet and wiping the dust-laden hair away from her eyes.

"Terri, I know that it's not easy for you. You have developed an attachment. Overlord's pendant—his bracelet—can command the base, and yours is a lesser version, and can only communicate. Nevertheless, it is not easy for me to ask you to destroy it. The pendants that are presented to male Overlord youths are handed down, father to son. They are no longer created."

Terri pulled the pendant out from under her filthy T-shirt and slipped the strap over her head. She held the little brown treasure, her precious, cupped in both hands. *I can do this*, she thought. *You're lying*, another voice said. Was that the pendant talking? She didn't think so. It was her own cynical voice, forcing the truth, maybe offering a challenge.

She looked up. The cataclysmic collapse of the observation roof had shocked the mountain peak into temporary silence, and a murmur of excitement was starting to swell from the onlookers fifty feet below. But she heard something else, a steady hum, as of an industrious bumble bee.

She'd heard that before. She saw it, a black egg riding inside a blur of wings, coming in from the right, making for Spockette. "Do you see it?" she asked.

"Of course, Terri," Spockette replied.

"Aren't you going to . . . zap it?"

"I can't until you destroy your pendant, Terri."

"Your subsystems won't let you?"

"Correct."

"Why? They don't recognize it as a Scrubber?"

"I think you mean 'Eater,' Terri, and they do. However, Overlord has now disabled all of my defense mechanisms."

Everything pointed to the need. She picked up a chunk of concrete the size of a melon. All she had to do was kneel down, lay the alien communicator on the ground and give it one good hammer blow. Her father's precious. Her precious.

The buzzing grew louder. The drone came towards her. It hovered, beckoning her, like before. Now that it had her attention, it retreated back towards the ship, as though it knew this was now safe. It called to her, soundlessly, without words. She obeyed, knowing that much of the motivation was postponing the pendant's execution.

She froze. A young woman stood there, against the ship. *Oh, shit*, she thought, *it's me!* It looked like her reflection, but it couldn't be. The ship curved sharply inward, and her reflection should be grossly distorted. Terri lifted her hand to the side of her face. Her double just stood looking at her. It nodded. This simple gesture, so obviously independent of Terri, rose the hairs on the back of her neck. Of all the incredibly alien things that had happened that day, this was the alienest.

She glanced back at Conan. He was watching her intently. He looked from her to the ship, and then back at her. He seemed genuinely unhappy. He saw it too.

"Terri," Spockette said, "what are you waiting for?"

"Um . . . you don't see it?"

"I see the Eater, Terri. Destroy the pendant, and I can take care of it."

"You don't see . . . ?"

"What, Terri?"

"Never mind."

It was too weird to explain, but also, it was better that Spockette didn't know for now.

Why would she think that? She knew the answer—unbidden thoughts were becoming old hat.

She saw that the little drone had positioned itself directly in front of her double, clearly the source of the illusion. Did it think she was dumb enough to be fooled into believing that this was another her?

The unspoken beckoning continued, stronger, more urgent. Her double cupped her hands in front of her, just as she herself had done moments ago with her pendant.

It was an illusion. It wasn't actually there. It couldn't harm her.

She came forward, stepping carefully over the broken concrete.

"Terri," Spockette said, "what are you doing?"

"Just a minute," she replied, continuing on.

"Terri, you know that you are walking directly towards the Eater?"

For once, Terri gave the ship the silent response.

"Terri—"

"Shut up, Spockette," she said. "Just . . . shut up."

She stopped an arm's length from the ship. This close, her double wasn't so much a reflection as a dynamic image, a video playing across the ship's surface. The burr of the drone, so constant and benign, had almost melted away into the background. Her double let her hands fall to her side, and the little Eater emissary moved directly in front of the right palm. Then, as Terri gaped wide-eyed, the hand, palm turned upward, reached out to her. This wasn't a flat video image, this was an arm reaching out from the ship.

Terri gasped and took a stumbling step back. As she changed position, she could see that this too was an illusion, a 3D representation, some sort of hologram. The drone had immersed itself into the open palm. The message was clear. Without a second thought, Terri took her pendant between thumb and forefinger and held it out.

"Terri!" Spockette, yelled. "Stop!"

She ignored the ship. She gently placed the pendant, the cord hanging down, into the open palm. Her fabricated double curled the fingers and closed the open hand. The 3D projection was partially transparent, and Terri could see that her pendant clung to the drone, as though a magnet.

"Terri," Spockette said, calmly now, "the Eater is accessing the vast information stored in the base."

"Is that so?" she said. She wished the ship would just be quiet. What could Spockette say at this point? Make her feel guilty? She could probably do that. Just be quiet.

"Terri—"

"*Shut up!*"

Her double opened her hand. Terri took a breath and reached out, being careful to keep her fingers from the blur of tiny wings. As soon as she had the pendant, her double disappeared, and she almost dropped it. The Eater drone rose, paused a moment, and then zipped away.

"Terri," Spockette said.

She sighed. Time to face the music. "Yes, my lord."

"Terri, I can't know what the Eaters will do with the information, but valuable time has been lost. You must destroy the pendant immediately."

"Yeah, yeah."

She moved to a section of unbroken concrete below the open hatch, squatted, and gently lay the little brown walnut down. She glanced up to find Siderai looking down. "Do it," he said, nodding encouragement. She raised the block of concrete and . . . froze.

"Terri," Siderai said levelly, "the Overlord was wounded, but he will come. He might be on the way right now."

"I know!" she growled, the concrete hammer poised.

"Terri . . ." he said.

"Oh Christ!" she exclaimed, standing up. "There must be another way."

She yelped as something big fell from the sky. It was Siderai. He landed on the pendant, and fell to the side, grabbing his ankle and cursing. The pendant rolled a few feet, unharmed.

"What are you doing—?" she started.

He reached up and grabbed the block of concrete from her. He tried to stand up, but cried out in pain and sat back down. He threw her a dark look, and raised the concrete. "No!" she screamed and tried to grab it, but he'd already swung it down, and it landed with a sickening crunch. The concrete block rolled away, and Siderai lay back, holding his ankle in both hands.

The pendant was obliterated. For decades—no, for thousands of years it had patiently waited to resume serving its purpose, and now it lay . . . pulverized. What this revealed was beyond Terri's ability to describe. She'd seen inside human-made compact electronics, the complexity hinted at inside miniaturized, densely placed ICs. But this, this was something else entirely, neither wires, nor circuits—nothing she could compare with. The best she could do was simply "complexity." It was as though all of Manhattan had been duplicated, layered one on top the other, and then shrunk a billion-fold. And even that was like holding up a paper and pen to describe a laptop.

Her awe at the internals was washed away with despair, a grief she hadn't experienced since her father's death. She fell to the broken concrete, buried her face in her hands, and wailed. Preston had been so right. The relationship with the pendant was like a parent and child.

"Professor Siderai," Spockette said, "well done. I am now free from Overlord's control. We must leave. Enforcer is wounded from Overlord's weapon, and Terri is wounded from disassociation. You must get them aboard."

"Right," he said, maneuvering to stand up, but then groaned and fell back.

"Professor Siderai," Spockette said, "what's wrong?"

"I, uh, sprained my ankle."

Terri pushed herself up and looked at him. "Wrong. He broke it."

"It's not broken—"

"Look at how it's swelling."

"Sprains swell."

"Whatever. Either way, you're out of action—"

A grumble, like a kettle starting to boil, filled the peaks and valleys from the east. Terri and Siderai exchanged alarmed glances. "The Overlord?" she whispered.

Siderai cocked his head, listening. He shook it. "These were made by men."

Just then, she saw them—three dots on the horizon, speeding towards them. "Jets!"

"Fighters," Siderai said, squinting.

"Terri," Spockette said, "you must get Professor Siderai and Enforcer aboard."

"Right," she said, watching the jets, making no move to do it.

The dots resolved into three swept-wing metal birds of prey riding fire. She had watched Navy fighters strut their acrobatic stuff at air shows, and had been duly impressed, but had never imagined that one day they would come to her rescue. With a roar that shook her bones, the three strident machines passed a quarter-mile to the north, curved around the peaks to the west, and circled to the south, reconnoitering the situation.

"The recording in Preston's room!" she shouted above the maelstrom.

"What?" Siderai shouted back.

"Our conversation was recorded. The FBI, or CIA, or Men In Black—*some* agency—would have investigated the Incident of Aliens in the Parking Lot, and would have known we were headed for the Appalachian Trail. Even if they couldn't decipher Preston's code words, they'd be on the lookout for anything unusual along the trail."

"Destroying a prominent observation tower with an alien craft would probably classify as 'unusual,'" he said, wincing against the pain as he swiveled around to follow the trio of fighters.

The jets came around and buzzed them, zipping by so close, Terri felt the wash of their turbulent wake. She lifted her hand and waved. She wanted to salute.

Once past them, the jets arched up, perhaps to come around again. A flash of light so bright it temporarily blinded Terri engulfed the formation. As her eyes recovered, she saw just two jets arching up and swerving hard to the right. Where the third one had been there was now the smoking trails of falling debris.

"Terri," Spockette said, "do you understand the urgency of leaving?"

Chapter 14

Terri couldn't tear her eyes from the falling remnants of the fighter as its two companions circled away, back to where they'd come from. There had been a pilot there a moment ago. Moe, Thinker, and now a human. She wanted to smash the Overlord's head just has Siderai had smashed her pendant.

"Terri," Spockette, "Overlord will kill you."

That worked. Terri spun around. Conan still lay against the platform wall. His eyes seemed to say he was sorry for what they'd watched. She ran to him, and he extended his good furry hand so she could help him up. He could stand, but only tentatively. He wasn't very big. She reached around to pick him up, like a groom carrying his bride over the threshold, but when he leaned back into her embrace, she realized that his dense muscles were far heavier than she expected, and they both fell. Instead, she hooked her elbow under the armpit of his damaged side and helped him hobble to the ship.

Leaning against the side of the ship, Conan reached down with his good hand and planted it firmly on Terri's butt. "Whoa!" she exclaimed, stepping away.

"He's trying to lift you up," Spockette explained.

"He's the one who's hurt," she said. "I should help *him* up."

"And then how would you and Professor Siderai get in?"

"I, uh . . . hey! Why don't you just tilt over like you did before?"

"I can't, Terri. It's difficult to explain the physics, but that is an unnatural position, and I need solid ground around me for support."

"Fine, fine. Tell Conan to toss me up."

The Inhabitor's tossing days were over. Using the side of the ship as a brace, he lifted her butt enough for her to grab the lower lip of the hatch, from where, grunting and cursing, she scrambled up and in.

Siderai was next. Conan struggled to lift Siderai's extra weight, and when he finally managed to get a grip on the lip of the hatch, despite Terri and Conan's attempts to help him, his injured ankle hampered him, and he fell to the ground, crying out in pain.

Conan watched him lying on his side, hugging his knee, and then he looked up at Terri. He crouched down on one leg, and launched himself. He didn't make the hatch, but Terri grabbed his hand and, cursing through clenched teeth, hauled him up. They tumbled backwards on top of each other. The Enforcer was up and back to the hatch before Terri was even on her feet. He leaned out, reaching down for Siderai. Not sure what else to do, she knelt down and grabbed his leg for support. She heard Siderai grunting, and Conan twisting and pulling, and then Conan suddenly jerked back, losing his grip as Siderai thumped to the ground again groaning.

"Overlord," Spockette said.

The house-sized silver ovoid was rising above the trees, a mile to the southwest.

"We're out of time!" Siderai called. "Spockette, you have to leave!"

"Overlord will kill you, Professor Siderai."

"Maybe not. If you stay any longer, we'll all be caught."

"No!" Terri shouted. "We can get him!"

"Spockette," he said, "you know it's the best thing, the logical thing."

"I agree, Professor Siderai," she said. "Goodbye."

As the hatch began to flow shut, Conan threw Terri a confused look, and then, whistling angrily put his hand into the contracting opening. The flow stopped.

"What'd he say?" Terri asked.

"He says, 'All or none,'" Spockette replied.

"It's two against one," Terri said. "Open the hatch."

As the hatch flowed open again, Conan turned to Terri. Looking her in the eye, he placed the tips of his fingers against the side of her head, then turned and dove out the opening.

Terri looked out to find him using his good hand and leg to crab-walk across the broken concrete. "Where's he going?" she muttered.

"I don't know," Siderai said from below.

He reached the observation deck wall, grabbed the rail running along the top, and pulled himself up. He turned, pointed at Siderai, and then at his own chest.

"He was telling me to use my brain!" Terri exclaimed. "The solution is right there!"

"Oh, geez!" Siderai said, limping off.

"I understand," Spockette said, already rising. "Logic is no match for imagination."

Spockette had to wait for Siderai to reach the wall, where Conan wrapped his good leg around the rail and helped him up. Spockette then settled in amid more crunching concrete until the hatch was just above them. From their raised position, Conan was able to push Siderai while Terri pulled from above, and together they hauled him inside. He rolled to the floor, wincing with pain, and then his eyes went wide with alarm.

Terri looked to find the Overlord ship just a hundred yards away, the pine trees beneath it seeming small in comparison. Through the open hatch, she heard renewed screams of tourists. The spiral access ramp, their escape route, curved around and passed thirty feet from the base of the tower.

She heard scrabbling and turned back. It was Conan. His three fingers curled over the bottom lip of the hatch. "Oh, Lord!" she said. She reached out, grabbed his wrist with both hands, and heaved. As he swung up and through the hatch, Terri fell back when the ship suddenly jerked and swayed, and a tremendous roar followed Conan through the opening, as though lightning had struck just beyond.

"What the hell?" she exclaimed, standing up. Billowing clouds roiled on all sides as the echoes of cataclysm slowly died away. They were floating in mid-air. The observation deck was gone.

"Overlord has brought down the tower," Spockette announced.

Through the boiling clouds of pulverized concrete, Terri saw the shattered end of the dismembered ramp, twisted rebar hanging down like the roots of an upturned tree. Siderai peered down along the side of the ship.

"The people . . ." Terri started.

"I can't really see," he said, "but I think they got away."

He was probably just saying that for her benefit, and that was okay with her. She didn't even want to look. "It's time to get the hell out of here," she said.

"I'm afraid it's too late, Terri," Spockette said. "Overlord has captured us in a tractor field. He had to take away the tower in order to grab us."

"He . . . why doesn't he just zap us?" She glanced at Siderai, who slumped to the floor, defeated.

"Terri, we have dishonored Overlord. This requires a ceremonial execution."

She gulped. "Because we tried to get away? How is that dishonor?"

"Conan defied Overlord, which is—this is an approximate translation—blasphemous, and requires ritual handling."

"He . . . but he did it for us!"

"The reason doesn't matter. No sub-race may ever defy an Overlord."

"That's . . . monstrous—sick!"

"From your perspective, Terri."

"You *agree* with him!" Terri exclaimed, throwing her arms out, frustrated that there was no physical point of sentience at which to aim her anger.

"No, Terri, I do not. Remember, I too helped you escape."

"Yeah, you're right. Sorry. At least you won't be executed."

"That's not correct, Terri. I will certainly be terminated. He will wait until he leaves, since even his ship will not protect him against the intense release of gamma rays when I am destroyed."

"Oh, Christ," Terri said, looking at Conan, who stood waiting patiently, his good hand bracing against the side of the ship. "There must be *something* we can do. I can't bear to think of poor Conan going through that torture again."

"Terri, Enforcer will not have to endure that again. The ceremonial execution is beheading."

Silence.

"You're joking?"

"No, Terri. This is prescribed by ritual."

"Jesus. Uh, what about us—the Prof and me?"

"I doubt that he will behead you. You are not a classified sub-species."

"He'll . . . let us go?"

A pang of guilt kicked her for being relieved when Conan was still doomed.

"No, Terri. He will surely kill you both."

Well, at least she wouldn't have to feel guilty. Instead, dread knotted her stomach.

She turned to Siderai, lying flat on his back. His ankle looked like a grapefruit. She felt bad about him too. He had been a good companion, trying his best at each turn.

Wait a second, he'd dragged her into the whole mess. She had wanted to call the police after finding the aliens hiding in a tree. She had an urge to give his swollen ankle a good kick.

That wasn't fair. She had come willingly. She had seen things no other human could even imagine. She wouldn't have missed it for the world.

What a lie. She'd give it all up, and then cut off one arm to get out of their doomed situation.

"Christ. What's he waiting for? Is this part of the ritual? Torment us with black anticipation?"

"I presume that he is constructing a supplement to his anthem."

"He's making up a song about lobbing off the head of a crippled slave half his size? What kind of monster is this guy?"

"Terri, every culture has aspects that may seem monstrous to other cultures."

"You *are* defending the dog-faced savage!"

"Terri, I am not defending the ethics of this aspect of Overlord's culture. I again remind you that I too will be terminated for rebelling against his actions."

"Well, make up your mind."

"I am simply pointing out that cultures are not absolute black and white. For example, you denigrated Overlord for his appearance, which has nothing to do with his unacceptable behavior."

"You want me to apologize to him as he's killing me for trying to get away from him?"

"Terri, that's not the point. I am simply reminding you that cultures are, by definition, self-referential. As an analogy, they can be thought of as different universes, each with its own laws of physics."

"You're going in circles, girl. Now you're saying that anything goes, a culture can do whatever it wants to do."

"That is not my point, Terri. There are no general value measurements that can be applied to cultures, other than perhaps longevity. However, one can still place ethical boundaries."

"Ethical boundaries implies right and wrong. Who decides that?"

"That, Terri, is up to each individual. The task that each individual must carry is to attempt to step outside their culture and ask themselves the basic question of right and wrong. If there is a universal crime, it would be to act blindly within one's culture, using that culture as an excuse for not deciding for oneself."

"You're talking about religion."

"No, Terri. Religion is a manifestation of culture. Terri, do you believe that it is wrong for Overlords to enslave and breed other races?"

"You know I do. What kind of trap is this?"

"Terri, I am merely providing examples for you. You have no doubt that enslaving other races is wrong, yet your culture celebrates the ethos of Sparta. 'Spartans' is the most common name for your sports teams."

"That's not because Spartans kept slaves, it's because of . . . I guess their fighting spirit."

"And Spartans *were* formidable warriors, but as we've seen, they were primarily warriors *because* of their slave-based culture. Your sports teams are essentially celebrating slavery."

"Oh, come on. That's ridiculous. High school football players probably don't even know the connection."

"That's an excuse, Terri? High school is the primary source of cultural education."

"Yeah, well, ignorance is not the same as actually endorsing slavery."

"But ignorance is a failing of a culture. Terri, you said it was sick for Overlords to breed off the fingers of Thinkers, yet your culture has bred wolves into a wide spectrum of forms."

"You got me there. I always feel bad for bulldogs. Still, it's not the same."

"In what way, Terri?"

Silence.

"Terri?"

"Don't rush me. It's different because a bulldog doesn't know what we did to it."

"So, ignorance is again the excuse."

"At least this time it's the victim who's ignorant, not us . . . uh, I didn't mean victim, I meant . . . subject."

"Terri, are you a vegetarian?"

"No. Another trap coming."

"You therefore eat animals that were born in captivity, raised in captivity, and killed for your benefit."

"Yeah, yeah. That's a cheap shot."

"Why?"

"Because . . . because they're not intelligent. They're . . . animals. Look, I know it sounds bad when you put it so simply—"

"Terri, are you prepared to define intelligence?"

"Look, why don't you just come out and say it—you think humans are savages, just like the Overlords."

"Not at all, Terri. Considering that humans evolved as meat-eaters, it would be unreasonable to expect them not to eat meat—at least in light of the fact that it has been less than ten thousand years since they abandoned the lifestyle their bodies evolved within."

"Spockette, you're going around in circles. Are you saying that eating meat is bad or not?"

"Terri, I am still trying to expand my original point. The ethics of eating meat is for you to deicide. Your only responsibility is to step outside your culture to do so. Terri, Explorer evolved as a vegetarian species, and thinks that humans are monstrous savages for eating animals."

"But you don't think so."

"Terri, I don't reject the ethics of humans' meat-eating out of hand for the reasons I explained. My own definition of right and wrong in this case would lean heavily on the treatment of the animals—the quality of their lives, and the manner of killing."

"But, let's be clear here, you do think that the Overlords are bad?"

"Terri, my view is that they are a race that has caused needless hardship to other sentient races. And they are not done."

"Spockette, you didn't answer my question."

"Terri, yes, I think Overlords are bad."

"Finally . . . uh, you said that they're not done. But, they're not going to colonize Earth, right? You said that they only colonize planets with no intelligent life."

"Terri, I am very sorry. We were both misled. I had not yet accessed the base's information storages, and Thinker chose to be disingenuous. When he said that Inhabitors only colonize planets with no intelligent life, that is because Overlords eradicate any intelligent life first."

"Oh my God."

"Terri, the base is much more than simply a refueling station. It is a colonization port—an entry gate and staging area for a full-phased invasion."

"But, it's been here, abandoned, for thousands of years. Why did they wait?"

"Terri, I have no answer for that."

Terri sank down on her haunches, leaned her elbows on her knees, and cradled her chin in her hands. "So, we're all doomed, the entire human race."

"Not the entire race, Terri. They will surely make substantial selections as slave candidates."

Terri rolled her eyes. "Goodie. Lucky us. How much time do you think we have—I mean until Dog-face finishes his victory verses?"

"I can't know that, Terri. I would guess any time now. Professor Siderai, are you okay?"

He hadn't moved since lying down. "No," he said to the sky, "my ankle is burning with unbearable pain, and I'm going to die soon. Also, I'm not a professor."

Terri jumped up. She had to *do* something. She couldn't just wait passively to die. She went to the side and looked out through Spockette's faux-transparent hull. Flashing red lights were winding up the paved access road to the parking lot a half mile away below them. "The police are here," she said.

"Good," Siderai said from the floor. "Maybe they'll arrest the Overlord."

"Prof, have you given up?"

"Not at all. If the Overlord leans over me, I intend to punch him on his very prominent nose. Perhaps I should say snout?"

"You've given up," she confirmed. "Hey, what if we just jumped out and ran away?" She glanced at Conan, leaning against the side for support, and at Siderai, flat on his back. "Or, what if I jumped down and went for help?" She leaned forward, peering down. It was probably fifty feet to the mass of broken concrete and spaghetti rebar below.

She sighed.

The ship jerked, and Terri fell.

"Let the ceremonial executions begin," Siderai said, rolling over and pushing himself up onto his hands and knees.

Their small ship was slowly sinking while simultaneously drawing closer to the grounded Overlord behemoth, like landing a fish. When they were thirty feet away, they sank straight down and landed with a thud that sent them staggering again. The tourists who had survived the collapse of the tower were gone, perhaps fleeing into the forest on all sides. The Overlord's hatch flowed open, and their captor appeared, stepping into thin air as each stair segment unfolded beneath his foot.

"Are you going to open for him?" Terri said quietly.

"Terri, I won't have to," Spockette said.

The Overlord walked up to their ship, pulled a golden cheese grater from his belt, and pointed it where the hatch would be.

"Rescue crews must be able to gain access to a lifeboat," Spockette said, "even if it may be damaged or immobilized. My hatch is made to open when confronted by this tool, which also serves as a restraining device, as you will probably see."

Instead of flowing open, the hatch area simply dissolved, revealing the fearsome, determined head of the Overlord. Terri stumbled back, her heart pounding at finding herself in the line of fire of those menacing eyes. It was the face of a big, threatening, snub-nosed wolf.

Spockette translated a burst of discordant harmony. "Overlord says you will all disembark. I have explained that two of you are wounded, and so he will lift you down."

Nobody moved.

"Terri," Spockette said, "help Professor Siderai to the hatch."

"Is he . . . is he going to kill us first?" she asked, choking back a sob.

"I don't think so, Terri. A ceremonial beheading usually includes witnesses."

A sliver of hope blossomed. "That means that he's, like, not going to kill us?"

"I'm afraid that he will then indeed kill you, Terri. As with so much of Overlord ceremony, the rituals have taken on independent importance. By their nature, there is no logic involved."

They were going to stand and watch Conan loose his head. If there was nothing she could do to stop it, well then, Terri imagined she could just take off and run away.

What about Siderai?

She sighed. Could she leave him if there was no alternative? Should she die just because he did something stupid and sprained his ankle?

A shrill whistle interrupted her racing thoughts, and she helped Siderai to his feet. "I'm sorry, Terri," he said so quietly, she wasn't sure he was even talking to her. He looked at her with eyes resigned to their fate, already dead. "I'm still going to punch him in the nose," he said, cracking a thin smile.

Terri let him lean on her to keep the weight off his bad foot, and they hobbled to the hatch, and up the short set of steps. She hadn't even let him go before the seven foot hulk reached up and curled his two sausage fingers and thumb around his throat. Siderai pulled back a fist, actually going to do it, but the Overlord's other hand shot up and grabbed his wrist. With these two handholds, he lifted the community college instructor off his feet. Siderai kicked, swinging both legs wildly, and even managed to land a couple of blows against the alien's midriff, to no effect.

Terri expected their captor to toss Siderai aside like a broken doll, but he carried the squirming, kicking human a few paces to the side, and set him gently down. Then, still holding him by the neck, he picked up the golden cheese grater, and pointed it at Siderai's chest. Her traveling companion's expression morphed from fury to one of perplexed surprise. He flopped down on his butt and slowly, slowly raised his arm, clearly struggling to do so, then gave up, and fell back.

The Overlord stood watching him, then placed the immobilizing device on the ground facing his prisoner.

"The device inhibits peripheral motor neurons," Spockette explained. "Nerve operation reflects convergent evolution, and is common across species. The device seems to be only partially effective on humans, though—Professor Siderai should have been completely immobilized. This is probably the same reason you weren't killed when Overlord was torturing Manager."

Terri made up her mind, opting for a compromise. She would run away, but not for help, that would be useless. No, she'd run far enough to hide, and then sneak back and figure out a way to save them. Sure. That would work. Figure out the saving part later. For now, just get the hell away.

She sat in the hatchway, her legs dangling. The Overlord was watching Siderai, making sure the cheese grater was going to work well enough. She started to ease herself down, but the Overlord's head snapped around, and she jumped and took off.

She heard pounding feet behind her, like the thudding of an industrial jackhammer. She cut to the left to lose him, and a giant hand grabbed her shoulder and swung her around so that she lost her footing and ended up dangling from his hand. "Jesus Christ!"

she screamed. "What's with the shoulder!" It was the same one he'd pinched, exploring her pain reaction.

He set her down, and wrapped his other hand around her throat—dry, leathery skin, the opposite of the soft fur of Inhabitors. For a brief moment, she thought he was going to rip her head off, and she squeaked a little protest. He let go of her shoulder, and prodded her along back. He could have simply carried her and dumped her down, but he let her walk, what she took to be honoring her with that ounce of dignity. In fact, other than the rough interception of flight, he seemed almost gentle now. Maybe there was more to this huge brute than they'd given him credit for. Maybe there was a good part, a decent side that they just hadn't seen yet. In fact, she had the sense that if she could somehow connect with him, they might find some common understanding, some level of shared perspective.

He sat her down next to Siderai, where she wrapped her arms around her knees, feeling the pain in her shoulder aggressively refusing a retreat.

"Is that you?" he asked, staring at the clouds.

"Yeah. My plan didn't work."

"Something's wrong," he said. "I'm so weak, I can't even sit up."

"It's not you, it's the wolf-man. His magic cheese grater harasses your motor nerves—oh!"

The Overlord had pointed it at her, and she suddenly seemed to be in freefall. Her chin had fallen onto her knees, and her hands flopped to the ground. "Now it's me," she reported, through uncooperative jaws. "Son-of-a-bitch! The damn thing could have at least numbed the pain nerves." It was exasperating—she couldn't move her shoulder to a better position.

The Overlord carefully positioned the golden grater so that it pointed between them, and moved off, back to the open hatch. "Spockette," she said. She wasn't sure her voice would carry, coming through closed jaws.

"Yes, Terri."

"We smashed my pendant. Why don't you zap him?"

"I'm still held in the grip of the tractor field, Terri. I could try, but I believe that the field will absorb most of the energy of my emission. It would likely simply anger him and prompt him to destroy my sentient operation."

"Okay," Terri said. "I figured you would already have done it if you could."

"Terri?"

"Yes, Spockette."

"I will attempt it if you like."

She tried to smile, but only managed to expose some teeth. "That's okay, Spockette. I imagine we'll want you here with us to the end."

"Okay, Terri."

"But, thanks, Spockette."

"My honor, Terri."

Her honor. Terri didn't expect that from the logical ship. It felt right, though. Hell, what did she know about the emotional life of a space lifeboat?

From Terri's frozen position, she saw the Overlord reach through the open hatch and drag Conan out by the neck. He used both hands to carry the densely heavy, half-paralyzed warrior Inhabitor. The executioner lay Conan down on his stomach so that his head lay over a log, his neck positioned for the chop. Terri was amazed that her newfound companion didn't protest, seeming to accept his abbreviated fate. Of course, it wasn't like he could scamper away.

The Overlord pulled the golden turkey baster from his belt and extended it to become a slim-bladed sword. There was surrealism here—an advanced alien who piloted spaceships able to manipulate space fabric, standing there shirtless, flexing chiseled muscles, and wielding a seventeenth-century weapon.

Actually, swords had been Conan's only weapon. Maybe it was more comic book than surrealism.

The Overlord held his sword out before him, hilt and tip in each hand, and sang to the pine trees—reciting his anthem supplement. Terri closed her eyes. She couldn't possibly watch this.

She heard voices, men talking, earnestly, on the verge of arguing. She swiveled her eyes and saw three of them standing at the top of the path—two policemen, and a third man in shorts, a feed cap, and . . . hunting vest—the guy she'd scammed the gun from, her "mark." She called out, trying to warn them—to shoot and ask questions later—but between relaxed jaws and the Overlord's anthem, she might as well have been calling to the moon. Her mark saw her and grabbed one of the policeman's elbows, pointing. The cop nodded, but seemed reluctant to come any closer. Instead, he unholstered his gun. Her mark cupped his hands to his mouth and yelled, "Is this another mutant cross-breed?"

This caught the Overlord's attention, and his head snapped in their direction, causing all three men to take one step back.

"Shoot him! Shoot him! Shoot him!" Terri cried through her teeth.

Her mark cupped his hand to his ear. "What?"

A blinding light exploded where the three men stood, and then there were just two.

Chapter 15

One of the policemen had disappeared, and the other two were splattered with blood and pieces of raw flesh. Her mark froze for two seconds before tearing away down the path. The other cop stared at the horrific mess on his arms, looked at the Overlord with stunned eyes, and then turned and ran off as well.

The Overlord turned back to the prone Enforcer to resume his anthem supplement, but paused. Terri heard it—the familiar distant throaty rumble of jet fighters. The Overlord let his sword fall to his side as he waited.

"That zap came from his ship?" Terri said, breathing hard.

"Yes," Spockette said.

"Christ! It's as much a monster as he is," Terri said.

"His ship does not act on its own," Spockette said quietly, half imitating the wind so as not to draw attention. "It takes directions from Overlord."

"It hears him?"

"It communicates via his bracelet."

"Maybe you could, like, convince it to come to our side?"

"The mouse convincing the exterminator to kill the homeowner," Siderai said to the air.

"It is not possible to redirect his ship's priorities," Spockette said. "It takes directions exclusively from his bracelet."

"More paranoia about mutiny?"

"It's not paranoia. After all, I have turned against them."

The jets were getting closer, just two now, gluttons for punishment. Actually, Terri imagined what the young pilots must be feeling, and it wasn't gluttony. They knew at this point that whatever was down here, it was way outside their scope of experience. Anything could happen, and they had watched one of their own blown out of the sky right next to them.

And still they came back, men—maybe women—not much older than her, committed to risking their lives for their country . . . and her. Even as she sat there, immobile, staring at the human fighting machines streaking towards them, the monster's ship might be calculating a firing discharge, asking its master which one to take first. The Overlord answers that it doesn't matter. *No!* Terri thinks. *It does matter! Neither of them!* The Overlord shouts to Fire! Fire!

"Spockette!" Terri shouted. "*Do* something!"

A loud pop sounded from the direction of the Overlord's ship, and something bright zipped past the jets as they roared overhead and disappeared beyond the ridge.

"It missed!" Terri yelled. "Spockette you did it!"

"Terri, all I did was to struggle against the tractor field. Perhaps that was enough."

"Whatever it was, it worked!"

"Overlord is confident that I was the cause, Terri. He has instructed his ship to destroy my sentient operation."

"No! No, Spockette . . . do it again, make it miss!"

Another pop, and this time Terri was rocked by an explosion. From the corner of her eye, she could see their small spaceship still there. "Spockette?" she said tentatively.

"I am here, Terri. It did miss. Maybe you're right—I can perhaps redirect the ship's discharges by struggling against the tractor field."

The Overlord was waving his ceremonial sword at his ship, hooting up a storm. "He doesn't sound happy," Terri said.

"He is demanding that his ship ignore my interferences. His ship in turn claims that it doesn't understand what he's talking about."

The Overlord swung the sword in a wide arc, an obvious gesture of frustration, and raised it high for the ritual chop. *Poor*

Conan, Terri thought. *Poor, simple, loyal Conan.* "Spockette," she pleaded, "for God's sake, can you do anything?"

A brilliant flash reflected off the golden sword as it tumbled from the Overlord's hands.

Terri let loose with her own hoot, which issued from her locked jaws like the whistle of a tea kettle.

"The ship relaxed the tractor field for a brief moment," Spockette explained.

The Overlord picked up his golden sword and glared at Spockette, spewing a continuous stream of jarring tonal curses. Nasty white fangs flashed with each outburst.

"Overlord claims that humans have somehow re-programmed me," Spockette said. "He believes that I have infected his ship as well."

"He's not too smart, is he?" Terri said.

"I can't speak to his technical knowledge."

Technical smarts or not, the hulking alien had a sword and knew how to use it. Holding it again by the hilt and tip, he approached Terri and Siderai. Terri watched him, her heart seeming to pound in concert with each menacing step of the angry alien. The Overlord stopped, staring down at her, and then, flashing his fangs provocatively, grasped the hilt of the sword in both hands and raised it high above his head.

"Spockette . . . !" Terri hissed.

Her heart froze as she watched the blade swing down before clamping her eyes shut. She heard a ting. As far as she could tell, her head was still attached to her body. She opened her eyes and saw the golden sword lying on the ground ten feet away.

The Overlord bellowed a three-note discordant chord, and opened his jaws wide, revealing an array of white, shiny teeth. He grasped Terri's shoulders in both hands and leaned over to execute the sword's intent with his natural weapon.

Terri watched, paralyzed with the terror programmed in her genes over countless generations of ancestors living as prey for dominant predators, food for tigers. As the open jaws lunged down, Terri was jolted by a thud that splattered dirt across her face.

The Overlord had jumped away at Spockette's blast. He roared so loud, Terri felt her inner ear rattling. It was the roar a lion makes to startle a victim into paralysis. He stared at Terri, and then at Spockette. He lowered his head, and brought his wrist up.

"What's he doing?" Terri asked.

"Terri," Spockette said, "I don't know. He's speaking a language unfamiliar to me. It may be an ancient version. Some words are similar, like 'arise,' and 'obey.'"

Just then, the ground trembled, knocking her sideways. She thought it was the Overlord, but he just stood there, watching, swaying slightly.

It dawned on her that she had caught herself with her hands when she fell. The Overlord had accidentally kicked the golden cheese grater when he jumped away from Spockette's blast, and it was pointing away from them.

The trembling ceased, and was replaced by cataclysmic thunder like nothing Terri had ever heard, or even imagined. It sounded like a Saturn V rocket from a hundred yards away. "Spockette . . . " she whimpered.

"Terri, I believe that Overlord is summoning the base."

"What does that mean, 'summoning'?"

"Terri, Overlord is ordering the base to ascend."

"To ascend? Like, lift itself up out of the ground—?"

She saw it, rising above the forest. Curtains of dirt and boulders tumbled down on all sides, like dirty rain, all happening in slow motion. It was stupendous, heart-stopping, massively frightening. For the first time since she'd first seen Moe and Thinker in the tree, Terri had a true appreciation of forces in the universe powerful beyond human comprehension. She felt like a ground squirrel watching a bulldozer.

Through the curtain of raining dirt, she saw a thin beam of light reach down, sending shattered pieces of pine trees flying high into the air, old-growth trunks five feet in diameter. The base moved slowly towards them, stabbing the trees below, devastating the forest as though carpet bombed.

Terri couldn't tear her eyes from the malevolent monster of doom punching its way towards them. "What does he want from it?" she rasped.

"Almost certainly he wants it to destroy me, since he believes I have infected his ship."

"Why is it tearing up the mountain?" Each stab of light was followed by an earth-shaking boom seconds later.

"Why is it sending compression blasts into the forest?" Spockette said.

"Yeah. It's like it's . . . angry."

"Since I don't understand the language that Overlord used, I can only guess, but it takes no actions on its own. It is clearly manifesting the anger and frustration of Overlord. His foray to your world has not gone well, and he expects to be punished. His harem will likely be reduced, if not eliminated."

Terri glanced at her. Harem? No time to explore that.

Siderai sat up.

The Overlord was watching the enormous saucer approach—his gigantic instrument of destruction and revenge—ignoring Terri and Siderai.

"Oh, Lord," Siderai said, staring at the spectacle.

"Don't move," Terri urged. "Dog-face thinks we're still paralyzed."

The curtain of raining dirt had diminished to sporadic dribbles, revealing a little rooster-tail of glittering light, the refueling port that the Indians had damaged. *That can't be good*, she thought.

The Overlord suddenly took off, running towards his ship.

"What's he doing?" Terri said.

"I don't know," Spockette replied. "He's still holding me in the tractor field."

The massive disk was approaching. The "compression blasts" shook the ground. Shattered, uprooted trees thrown a hundred feet in the air created a continuous ripping, cracking roar, so that they had to shout to be heard. This close, they could only see the bottom, caked with thousand-year-old sediment, falling away in patches the size of lawns to reveal a featureless smooth, gray surface beneath.

The Overlord's ship, seeming so huge before, but now puny next to its awakened ancient ancestor, lifted off the ground.

"Where's he going?" Terri shouted.

"Terri, I don't know," Spockette replied. "Obviously he wants to get out of the way."

The Overlord's ship flew off to the east, but stopped, hovering over the parking lot below. Through the roar of obliterating trees, Terri heard gunshots, and saw sparks along the bottom of the hull. A stab of white light reached down, and the gunshots ceased.

The Godzilla saucer was almost upon them. Shattered pieces of limbs rained down, and Terri pulled Conan up against Spockette's hull for cover. Siderai limped over and sat down next to them. Suddenly the blasts stopped, and the cries of dying trees fell silent, except for the creaks and groans as pine corpses settling into place. A dark shadow moved ominously over them, and Terri looked up and gasped. The sky was gone, replaced by alien bulk. Dirt that hadn't seen light for millennia splattered down all around them, creating a dust cloud and causing Siderai to cough.

Silence settled in.

"Spockette," Terri whispered, "can't you do something?"

"Terri, Overlord still has me locked in the tractor field. This is why he hasn't moved farther away."

"You were locked in before, and you were able to zap things."

"Terri, I told you that it may have been because I was struggling against the tractor field. That was not the case. It was you, Terri."

"Me? That's crazy! You made us smash my Pendant, remember?"

"Yes, Terri, of course I remember. You were interfering with his control of his ship through his bracelet. After all, that is another type of pendant."

"You're kidding."

"Terri, you know that I do not joke. You were visualizing what you were telling me to do. This was interpreted as directions by the bracelet."

It actually made sense. When the Overlord had grabbed her by the neck, she had the impression that there was a good part of him that she just needed to connect with. It wasn't him she was sensing, but his bracelet.

"Why didn't you tell me?"

"I was afraid that simply knowing the fact would affect your ability. 'Go with what works,' as you say."

"But . . . why tell me now?"

"Terri, I believe that Overlord's bracelet is now too far for you to affect. I don't think he realizes what was happening—"

"Otherwise he could just zap you himself now—he wouldn't need the base."

"Exactly."

"They're warriors, not intellectuals," Siderai said, wiping the tears from his eyes with his dirty sleeve. He wasn't weathering the dust cloud very well.

"Perhaps," Spockette said.

Terri looked at him.

He shrugged. "Besides, it must be a tremendous ego boost," he said, gesturing upwards. "Anybody who composes accompanying music to behead an enemy can't be an archetype of rational thought."

"Wait a second," Terri said. "When—if—the base destroys you, it's going to be like a nuclear bomb going off. Dog-face is barely a hundred yards away."

"I expect that he'll leave at maximum speed. The tractor field will weaken, and eventually be thin enough for me to depart, but by then it will be too late. The base will destroy me before I can get away. Also, remember, as my antimatter annihilates, the vast majority of energy is released as gamma rays, and Overlord hulls are partially opaque to this form, just as mine."

"So, when we see him zip off, we know we have just a few seconds to live. What about the base? It's, like, just a few hundred feet up."

"Terri, it would take far more than my destruction to harm a base."

"Yeah, like Indians."

Silence.

"What in God's name is he *waiting* for?" Terri exclaimed. Her chest felt like it was being pressed in a vise.

"He's composing more anthem," Siderai said. "Look," he said, pointing up.

The slice of sky around the perimeter of the saucer was shrinking. "It's . . . lowering," Terri said. "What the hell? Is he just going to squash us with it?"

"I don't know, Terri," Spockette said. "There is one possibility—impractical, but perhaps your only chance. Terri, the base itself would provide an effective shield from the gamma ray discharge. You would still have to survive the accompanying shock wave and heat, but the base would provide a great deal of shielding for that as well."

"What are you saying? We somehow get on *top* of the base?"

"Exactly."

"That's like a mouse climbing on top of the hawk."

"Terri, I believe a better analogy would be a flea moving from the mouse onto the hawk. Remember, the hawk is after the mouse—it doesn't care about the flea."

"So, now I'm a flea abandoning the mouse."

"It's just an analogy, Terri."

"I know that. The key word is 'abandon.'"

"Terri, you can think of it that way if you like, but it's hardly abandonment when there's nothing to be gained by staying."

"You're always so rational."

Silence.

She could never leave a friend to die by herself. That was a lie. She was terrified of dying. Why sacrifice herself—and Siderai, and Conan—for nothing? It was the opposite of rational. Besides, Spockette wasn't even alive. Not really.

In any case, it was all moot if they couldn't get on top of the base. The bottom surface of the threatening hulk was fifty feet above their heads, but the edge was higher still, maybe half again that much.

Terri peered through the haze of the dust cloud. A half dozen bedraggled pine trees hung down over the otherwise perfectly smooth edge, their roots still gripping precariously to the floor of the floating island forest above. The best case, a gnarled old codger of a tree hanging by a few determined roots, reached to within twenty feet of the ground. That twenty feet might as well have been a thousand. Besides, it would take forever to get her crippled companions up through the reverse-angled branches.

She let her gaze follow the saucer's perimeter, their new horizon, and stopped when she came to the tumbled observation tower. The severed ramp, its end ragged with tangled rebar, terminated just a few feet below the edge of the saucer. It would be difficult to climb up, maybe impossible, but it was their only chance.

If the Overlord would just take another five minutes to perfect his death anthem.

"Come on," she said, helping Siderai up. "We're going for a ride. Spockette, tell Conan the plan."

They hobbled slowly towards the bottom of the spiral ramp, Siderai leaning on one of her shoulders, and Conan on her other elbow. She couldn't see Overlord's ship through the dust, which meant that he couldn't see them. Working slowly up the ramp, careful step by careful step, seemed to take forever. Terri expected at any moment for a blinding pillar of light to stab down, and an instant later, a nuclear blast to atomize them. Of course, she'd never know.

Finally, they were approaching the ramp's end. Terri's heart sank when she saw that the smooth, curved edge of the base was actually a dozen feet above the ramp. Even if it was level, they wouldn't be able to climb the smooth slope up to the flat area on top.

But then, miraculously, the base began to sink. "Come on!" Terri shouted, practically dragging her companions along. Why she felt suddenly confident, she couldn't say. She just knew this was the right thing.

They reached the edge, and stood mesmerized as the gigantic alien saucer slowly sank foot by foot until they were looking into the plateau trees they had been walking among only a short time before.

A mighty groan and crash threw them all to the concrete, and Terri felt herself falling—falling, and moving forward. The edge of the lowering base must have severed the supporting column below them, and the end of the ramp was sagging, leaning forward … dumping them onto the base!

All three rolled down into the snarled rebar. Terri clawed her way forward, to where the ends of the broken rebar lay on the slope leading up to the forest and safety just out of reach above. A small downed pine lay off to the side, it's tip pointing down the slope. Terri crawled to the edge of the rebar. Across a four-foot gap to the tree, the slope of the saucer curved down, dumping into thin air—a stomach-clenching fifty-foot drop to sharp, broken concrete below.

"We going for it?" Siderai said next to her.

"I'm afraid of heights," she said.

"No you're not."

She hadn't been, until now.

A furry hand took her gently by the arm and moved her aside. Conan studied the gap a moment, and then grabbed one solid piece of rebar in his good hand, and curled the prehensile toes of his good foot around another. He swung back and forth a couple of times, as though testing the stability, and then launched himself into the air. Terri gasped, and saw that he'd hung on with his hand. His feet swung out and landed among the short branches near the tip of the small pine. He had only a second to find purchase, and failed, swinging back down so that he was hanging by just his hand. Terri reached down and grabbed his wrist, but quickly let go when Conan shot her a warning look. Using his extraordinary strength, he pulled himself partially up, and then set his body swinging farther and farther, until his toes were brushing the tip branches again. And then suddenly he was no longer swinging. His toes had grabbed hold.

Conan met Terri's eyes. The look was that of possible farewell. He then let his hand go, and as he swung down, he curled his body and grabbed the slim trunk in his hand. He was now swinging slowly back and forth by both foot and hand. He encouraged the swing, and then with each upward arc, he moved his hand a couple of inches farther along the trunk until he was hugging the slender lifeline.

"Did you get all that?" Siderai said.

"Like we're going to do that?" Terri said. "You've been a barrel of laughs ever since you realized you were going to die soon."

"Maybe it's relative. Maybe I just seem jolly from your gloomy perspective."

"I'd say death-defying acrobatics as you're waiting to be obliterated constitutes justified gloom."

"So you admit it."

Conan was hanging on, patiently waiting for their attention. They had no Spockette to translate. Once he caught Terri's eye, he let go with his foot and began swinging by his hand. Farther and farther he swung, until his foot was brushing Terri. He twisted his head to look at her inquiringly.

"What's he doing?" she said.

"I think he wants you to grab his foot."

"Why?"

"One way to find out."

On the next swing, she grabbed Conan's ankle. He waited.

"What now?" she asked.

"Uh, my guess is that he wants you to swing away."

"What? You think he wants me to use him as a . . . rope?"

Siderai shrugged.

"Well, what do I do after that?"

"Terri, I can't know. You'll just have to trust him."

"Even if I don't know what he wants from me?"

"If you hesitate long enough, it won't matter."

"That's the gloomy spirit," she said, and, taking a breath, gave Conan's ankle a little tug of warning, and then let herself go. She gasped as the broken concrete swung by far below, and then she was hanging, only the limited strength of her hands keeping her alive. "Shit!" she yelled. "Shit! What'll I do!"

"Hang on, Terri!"

She looked at him. "Are you insane? What kind of advice is that?"

She felt a little jerk, and then she was slowly rising. The tip of the tree passed her nose, and then the motion stopped.

"Terri, he pulled the both of you up with his one good arm. You have to grab the tree."

"What kind of plan is this?" she squeaked. "I can't hang on to it—it's like grabbing a pencil!"

"You have to."

"I have to. Why didn't I think of that?"

This was it. She was going to die. There was no way to keep a handhold on that flimsy tip, even if it didn't break right off.

She had to, though.

Uttering a nasty curse, she let go with one hand and grabbed the tree. With her heart in her mouth, she let go of the other and then was swinging slowly back and forth, the little branches angling off the tip of the trunk providing a grip. "Are you happy?" she called.

"Yes," Siderai replied. "He's grabbed with his foot and is moving his hand higher."

Something soft bumped her forehead, surprising her so that she nearly lost her hold. It was Conan's foot. He was ready for another incremental climb. After two more of these, Terri's arms were trembling from exertion, and she was sure her hands were going to give out, but they'd reached substantial branches, and she was able to finding footing to finish the climb on her own. She didn't stop when she reached roots, and pushed on through. On the other side, she fell to the ground. She wanted to lay her head back, close her eyes, and let her burning hands and arms recover.

She'd done it.

No, Conan had done it. She'd just hung on.

She scrambled back up and peered down through the wall of upended roots. There wasn't anything she could really do but watch. Conan was repeating the rescue with Siderai, who apparently hadn't hesitated, the showoff. The Enforcer's load was now half again heavier, yet he executed each incremental climb methodically, assuredly, as though a well-worn routine. She had to admit, no matter how unethical, the Overlord's genetic breeding had been effective.

Siderai pushed through the web of roots and fell to the ground. "I need a month to rest before I try that again," he said into the dirt.

Conan came through, dragging his lame leg. He tumbled down, and used his good hand to pull himself up by a root overhead into a sitting position. He slumped, his head hanging down. The Overlord had taken his sword and knife, leaving him just his muscles, and only half of those at that. But, Lord, what use he had made of what he had.

She wanted to thank him, to tell him that she understood how much he'd done for them—ugly, hairless aliens who couldn't use their feet for anything other than walking. She crawled over and sat next to him. She put her arm around his shoulders. His eyes gazed into hers, and then closed, and he lay his head into the crook of her neck. His fur was so soft against her arm and neck, and he smelled of hay and the saddle her uncle kept in a shed.

She heard a droning burr, perhaps a humming bird that had chosen to ride along on the giant alien saucer. She lifted her head and looked around, but there was nothing.

"Terri," a tiny voice like Mickey Mouse said.

She looked one way, and then the other.

"Terri, I'm here," the voice said as a black ovoid the size of a TV remote and enveloped in a gauzy halo of whirring wings slowly descended two feet in front of her.

"An Eater?" Terri murmured wonderingly.

"I believe you call me a Scrubber," the little visitor replied.

Conan's hand flashed up, and the Scrubber drone was gone.

Chapter 16

Conan held the Scrubber drone in his fist. Gossamer wings poked through the cracks between his fingers at odd angles.

"Let go!" Terri cried.

Conan looked at her, surprised.

She held out her hand. "Let go!"

He stared at her. He understood her gesture, but seemed to question whether she knew what she was asking.

"Terri," the tiny voice said, muffled inside Conan's fist, "you must prevent the portal from firing on the Invader's escape pod."

Terri blinked. "Portal? Pod?"

"The escape pod must be Spockette," Siderai said, pushing himself into a sitting position. "I think the portal must be—"

"The base," Terri said. "I get it. I just don't understand why it thinks I can stop it. And how does it know my name?"

She tapped her open palm pointedly, and Conan finally gave her the drone.

"Terri, I listened to your conversations," it said. There was no mouth. Like Spockette, the sound came from the whole surface.

"You've been spying on us?"

"Terri, you saw me," it said, flexing its bent wings about, but several refused to straighten out.

"I saw things like you, but Conan smashed them."

"Terri, they were all me."

"Even the big one? The one that Conan shot?"

"Yes. I was a collective sentience. I am the last distributed component left. You lent me your Link—your pendant—so that I could access the portal's information. We can discuss this later, but right now there is an extremely dire need for you to prevent the portal—the base—from firing on the escape pod—what you call Spockette."

"The Overlord's bracelet is too far away—that's how I interfered before. That's why we climbed on top, for protection."

"You did contact the bracelet, but that was only associated with communications with his ship. Terri, you commune directly with the portal."

"Uh, like when we refueled Spockette."

"Correct. Also at the first encounter with the Invader—the Overlord. Your intervention allowed you to escape."

"What are you talking about?"

"Terri, you instructed the portal to initiate."

"I don't have a clue what you're—wait! You mean that earthquake—what I thought was an earthquake? When the Overlord grabbed Conan by the neck?"

"Yes, Terri. That was the portal below you reacting to your direction."

She'd been angry for sure, all that power right there underneath her, locked away. Tingles danced up and down her back at the thought that she had made this massive alien artifact, this cache of unimaginable power, react to her.

She shook her head, clearing it. "That's a little overwhelming. Why does the Overlord need a bracelet?"

"Terri, humans are more destined—you in particular, probably from your experience with your father's pendant."

"More destined. What the hell—?"

"Terri, I am sorry. There is no time. You must inhibit the portal from firing. Even up here, it is highly unlikely that you would survive the explosion if Spockette is destroyed."

"Okay! Okay. But, *how?*"

"I am not able to tell you that, Terri. I can tell you, however, that before you climbed up, you were inhibiting the portal from firing because you were afraid—"

"Wait! You said I was already preventing it from firing?"

"Yes, Terri. That is why the Overlord lowered the portal. He probably doesn't understand why it's not following his command to fire."

"Why don't *you* do it!"

"Terri, it doesn't listen to me. I am sorry. It's up to you."

"But, how . . . ?"

She'd already asked that. She closed her eyes. Nothing. When they had refueled, she'd simply visualized the process that Spockette told her. And when she'd connected Spockette to the base's information storage, again she'd visualized the concept of communication. But how do you visualize the concept of *not* doing something?

That's actually easy. The concept of not doing something is no different than the concept of doing something, as long as the concept is clearly visualized—a huge alien saucer floating in the air *not* firing at Spockette.

Terri opened her eyes and looked at Siderai.

"What?" he asked.

"I think I just did it. I can't be sure, but it happened like this before. I get these thoughts that I think are my own, but they're not really. They're not something I would have come up with by myself."

"Uh, you're sure?"

"No. No! Can you tell, Tinker Bell? Did I stop it?"

"I think she means you," Siderai said, nodding at the drone.

The last distributed component of the collective Scrubber had no distinct eyes, but presumably saw his gesture. "I can't know whether the portal has interpreted your thoughts, but I can tell you that the Overlord has commanded the portal to fire, and it obviously has not."

"I guess each minute we're still here, we'll know it's working," Siderai said.

Terri rolled her eyes. "Prof, for such a smart guy, you can be really inane."

"My ankle hurts, but that was an improved use of vocabulary."

"I'll try to work 'inane' into my conversations more often."

"Also, I'm not a professor."

"Terri," the little drone said, "The Overlord will continue to try to fire. You must be vigilant."

"Fine. I'll try to keep a cartoon image of a flying saucer hovering over a silver football in my head . . . and *not* firing. But Prof doesn't help with his inaneness."

"Which is an actual word," he said.

Conan had moved off a short distance into the pines that had managed to stay on their feet, dragging his own lame foot behind him. He turned to them and pointed into the remnant trees, towards the center of the island forest.

"The Enforcer is correct," the drone said. "The Overlord will eventually discover that someone is interfering with his commands. We should find cover."

"'We?' You're one of us now?" Terri said, standing up, and helping Siderai to his feet.

"Terri, we must all do what we can to stop the Overlord before the Earth is destroyed."

"Is *that* what he wants?"

"No, but he doesn't understand that the portal is failing."

They started off, following Conan who used his good arm to pull himself along, branch by branch.

"Can't we just somehow tell him?"

"Terri, the Overlord would not dare listen to you, who are associated with those who have disgraced him. His complete focus is now on their—and by association, your—destruction."

"And how is that the actions of a superior alien race?" she said, ducking a branch let go by Siderai.

"Dominance is superior only in its dominance, not necessarily astuteness."

"You sound like the Prof."

"I was just about to make the same observation," he said.

"I thought your ankle hurt."

"It does. Immensely. I'm trying to distract myself."

"Terri," the drone said, "it is important that you understand that the Overlord will not stop until he has achieved his goal."

"To finish his anthem."

"Correct."

"I was joking."

"Terri, I was not."

"You start all your sentences with my name. Why do you do that? Spockette does the same thing."

"I was actually mimicking the escape pod. I had the idea that it is a polite gesture."

"It is, probably. I'm not used to politeness. Politicians do that, like the interviewer is their best friend. I have to give you credit, though, your English is perfect. You must have been here awhile."

"I arrived this morning. I finally mastered English a half-hour ago."

"You've been spying on us just the last half-hour?"

"No, Terri. I stored all the previous conversations, and reviewed them once I could understand."

"Right. Of course. That's what I guessed." Siderai glanced back at her. "Smirk away, Prof. Let's see if I stick my hand out next time you need help catching a ride with Spockette."

Terri wondered how the little spaceship was doing down there trapped in the Overlord's tractor field. She'd been a good friend—not much with the jokes, but a paragon of dependability ... once she'd decided which side she was on.

"Spockette said you were bad," Terri said. "They call you Eaters, after all."

"From the Overlords' perspective, we no doubt appear bad. We prevent their expansions whenever possible. Over five thousand years ago they began an expansion onto Earth, and we forced them off."

"I see—that's why you call yourself Scrubbers."

"Terri, that was just a conceptual convenience. I didn't understand English at that time, and we were communicating with abstractions."

"We were, weren't we? I had the sense that you weren't dangerous."

"As we are not."

Terri tallied it up. "I can do Vulcan Mind Melds with pendants, bracelets, the base, and now you—quite the mental freak. But I guess that's my 'destiny'?"

"Terri, my English has improved since then—"

"It's been, like, five minutes!"

"Yes. I believe empathy is a better description. Terri, your species' brains evolved rapidly the last few hundred thousand years in large part because of challenges associated with social interactions. Negotiation and status positioning are universal components of social life, but your species has become particularly dependent on the advantages afforded by cooperation. Your individual survival depended on your empathetic abilities."

"You're telling me I can mentally connect with aliens because my ancestor had to figure out whether the good-looking dude on the other side of the camp fire was trying to cheat with his mate?"

"That is, of course, a simplistic example, but I think you understand."

"Overlords have to talk to their bracelets," Terri said, remembering.

"Overlords' evolution has been driven primarily by competition."

"They can't remote in with their own devices."

"Terri, pendants, bracelets, and even portals were not created by Overlords. These technologies have been acquired."

"Probably stolen."

"Again, somewhat simplistic, but not inaccurate."

I'm an alien whisperer, she thought. She smiled. "I have exceptional empathy."

Siderai paused to let her take a branch that would have slapped her in the face. He gave her a look before moving on. "What?" she said. "You find it hard to believe that I have special talents of personal connection?"

"You spent time with your father's pendant," he reminded her.

"Oh yeah? Well, just remember that we'd all be dead now if I couldn't commune with the base."

Oops. She'd forgotten to keep the restraining image in her head. *Shit,* she thought, *what good is an alien whisperer if she doesn't whisper?* As she imaged up the cartoon picture, she sensed that the base below her was receptive, as though patiently waiting for her confirmation.

But, speaking of bases . . . "Tinker Bell, you said, that your people scrubbed the Overlords from Earth, yet, here we are riding one of their portals."

"The Overlords hid this one from us. They realized that they had moved too quickly onto the Earth, and were anticipating a cleansing from us, so they proactively retreated, leaving this one out of sight. They used the local natives as slave labor to cover the portal, effectively creating the mountain plateau. They even forced the natives to create a temple so that they could worship their new masters. Once the Overlords departed, the natives took vengeance and attacked the portal."

"Letting loose an angry god."

"Yes. The effects of the leaking radiation eventually became obvious and the natives abandoned the entire area."

"We humans may be puny compared to the average Overlord, but they better not underestimate our tenacity when it comes to payback—"

"Terri, excuse me, but the portal has just told the Overlord that there's an entity on top of it interfering with his commands."

"The traitor!"

"Terri, the portal is not sentient."

Terri sensed something, a movement, like shifting shadows. She guessed that it was the Overlord's bracelet.

"Hey," Siderai said, pointing ahead. "We've come to the center."

Conan was sitting at the base of the little pyramid, using one of the bottom boulders as a backrest. It had to be exhausting hauling yourself around with just one hand and foot. He suddenly twisted to the side and scrambled around the boulder.

"Uh, oh," Siderai said, gesturing in the other direction.

The silver, double-pointed ellipsoid of the Overlord's spaceship was rising above the edge of the saucer.

"Hide!" Siderai yelled.

Terri didn't need urging. She had already dove under the low-hanging branches of a large pine, holding the Scrubber drone up to keep it safe. Siderai crawled in next to her as the spaceship rose higher, and then began a slow circumnavigation of the saucer.

Conan was trapped at the center of the clearing. He was hidden from the Overlord's view, but would become visible as the ship continued its circuit. Their alien companion looked at them expectantly.

"He wants to know where the ship is," Terri whispered.

Siderai nodded. He looked at Conan, and then at Terri. "Hold still," he said, and held his finger against the side of her head.

"What are you doing?" she whispered.

"This is Conan," he said. He held up his fist a few inches from her forehead. "And this is the ship."

Conan studied them, and then crawled in the opposite direction of the ship's progress. Siderai moved his finger and fist in concert.

"This is why we call you the Professor," Terri whispered.

"You're the only one who calls me that," he said.

Terri held still, playing her role as the simulated portal saucer. She didn't need to see the spaceship to know its location—the bracelet was enough for that.

The giant silver football slowly completed its orbit, and Conan ended up back where he started. The Overlord halted, hovering a hundred yards away.

"What now?" Terri whispered.

"The portal is describing for him our approximate position," the Scrubber said.

"Son of a bitch!" Terri hissed.

The Overlord's ship started forward. Terri wanted to melt into the bed of pine needles, disappear from sight. The sense of the bracelet's presence strengthened. She could close her eyes and still know its exact location.

Siderai's fist disappeared over her head as he indicated to Conan that his master's ship was almost above him. There was no escape. The alien warrior looked at them one last time, pushed himself up, and, dragging his lame leg, lurched off . . . away from them.

"Oh, shit!" Terri said.

"You would have done the same thing," Siderai said quietly, watching their companion.

"I'd like to believe that," she said, "but I can't."

He's going to have the ship fire on the Enforcer, she thought. *He's going to use just enough force to completely disable the Enforcer so that he can complete his anthem.*

Those weren't her thoughts. Terri knew that now. She was connected to the bracelet. She closed her eyes, welcoming external thoughts.

The ship is going to fire . . . now. "No!" she cried, opening them.

"Hey!" Siderai whispered. "Shh!"

Conan had almost made it to the opposite perimeter of trees. *The insistence has dramatically escalated. The instruction is unassailable and cannot be ignored.*

The ship was going to fire. There was no stopping it.

Maybe no stopping it, but . . .

The ship belched, like an agitated soda can opening, except loud enough to echo among the peaks. Pine needles exploded into a roiling cloud five feet from Conan.

Strike the Enforcer.

"No!" Terri exclaimed, willing the aim away, and the ground was thumped on the other side of Conan, who stopped and looked back at them. Terri nodded.

"The Overlord knows that somebody is interfering," the Scrubber drone said.

"He's eventually going to figure out that there's a range to Terri's connection with the bracelet," Siderai said.

"And that he only has to move that far away," Terri finished, "and zap us from there. We saw him take down a jet fighter."

"So we need to keep him close by," Siderai said, moving on his hands and knees to the edge of the overhanging branches.

"What are you doing?" Terri asked.

"Keeping him close by," he replied, eyeing the huge menacing ship floating above them.

"Hold on! You can't just walk out there!"

"I don't see any other possibility."

"You're crippled! I'll go. I can . . . run around and distract him."

"Terri, think about it. If you get zapped, we're all done. The Overlord doesn't know who's doing the interfering. He'll think it's me."

She stared at him, her mind spinning furiously.

He smiled. "Do your best, Scotty."

With that he crawled out and stood up. He swayed a little, and limped forward.

"Shit, oh shit!" Terri muttered, closing her eyes and concentrating.

He's instructing the ship to kill the human.

"Nooo!" Terri whispered, willing the aim off.

She heard the sizzling belch and thud, and opened her eyes. Siderai staggered backwards from a cloud of dust and needles. He regained his balance and started forward again.

She couldn't deflect every single shot. One lucky hit and he'd be dead.

Siderai reached the base of the pyramid and crawled up onto a large boulder. He stood up unsteadily and reached his arms out to the monstrous ship, as though beseeching it

Conan looked uncertain, not knowing what his human companion was up to. He glanced towards the cover of the pines just a few steps away, turned, and dragged himself back towards Siderai.

"What the hell is Conan doing?" Terri muttered.

"I believe it's called loyalty," the Scrubber drone said.

"I think it's called stupidity. He doesn't even know what the Prof is up to."

"He trusts the Professor. That's enough."

Terri glanced down at the elongated egg with the mangled wings. It had never heard him called by name.

Another shot at the human.

Terri squeezed her eyes shut. The ship seemed to resist misfiring. The Overlord must be foaming at the mouth.

Sizzle, thud, and Terri opened her eyes to find Siderai on the ground, flat on his back. She watched, willing him to move, wishing he was a fabricated being like spaceships or portals that could be induced to respond. He lifted one hand, flopped it back down, and pushed himself into a sitting position. Conan arrived and eased down next to him. Siderai, dirty, ragged, his hair a chaotic mat, put his arm around Conan's shoulder.

Be done with it. Kill them both.

Terror set Terri to shivering. She couldn't hold off the Overlord. He had the bracelet. The ship was his.

Silence reigned. The Overlord's ship hovering above them, the massive bulk of the portal floating in mid-air—all this alien technology remained airborne soundlessly. Whatever birds had followed along with the torn fragment of forest remained in hiding.

And so the whine of propellers was obvious. The little ship came gliding in over the treetops.

"It's the Explorer! What does he think he's doing?"

"Although specialized for exploration," the drone said, "the ship contains rudimentary weapons."

"It's come to join in the attack—?"

The Overlord ship suddenly sizzled and zapped.

"Shit!" Terri said. "I wasn't ready!"

Siderai and Conan still sat there, looking up at the Overlord ship. The Explorer's little prop vessel was gone, however. Where it had last been was a rising column of smoke.

"He killed his own slave?" Terri exclaimed. "Why?"

"Terri, he wouldn't trust the Explorer," the drone said, "which had contact with subjects who displayed radical behavior. With slaves, the Overlord rule is to suspect, and let them prove their innocence later, if able."

"Difficult to do when you're dead."

"Yes, Terri."

"Wait, there was no big explosion. What happened to the Explorer's antimatter?"

"Slave's aren't allowed access to that much energy."

"That would make one helluva suicide bomber—oh my God!" she squeaked.

The giant Overlord ship was moving . . . away. Silently it floated off, disappearing behind the pines.

"He gave up?" she said wonderingly.

"Terri, that seems unlikely. Perhaps the Overlord concluded that he needs to recalibrate his control of his ship in order to eliminate the three of you."

"Spockette said that he thinks we've infected it with some kind of virus."

"The Overlord doesn't understand the detailed operation of his own ship."

"Spockette said that too."

"The danger from Overlords does not derive from their mastery of technology."

"Just their meanness."

"Yes, Terri."

"Um, I was kidding."

"It is true, though. Purposeful, organized aggression can become a nearly unstoppable force."

"We found that out with a guy named Hitler. Well," she said, crawling out on her hands and knees and slipping the Scrubber into her pocket for protection, "no need now to hide in a spider hole like Saddam Hussein."

"I don't understand."

"I don't either. The guy was a madman."

Siderai stood up when he saw her, leaving Conan still sitting, exhausted. "Did you see him shoot down his own Explorer?" he asked.

"Yeah, even Darth Vader wouldn't do that. The Scrubber thinks that Dog-face will be back. Any ideas?"

"He may have figured out that he can move away and blast us from there."

"Shit. I forgot about that," Terri said. She was trying hard not to succumb to complete hopelessness. "What'll we do?"

Siderai rubbed his chin. He shrugged. "Hide, I guess. Hope for a miracle."

"A miracle, eh? You're a man of science. That means you have zero hope—"

"Ouch!" he yelled, holding his shoulder. A spot of blood appeared through his shirt. "What the hell was that?"

Terri yelped when a sharp pain, like a giant wasp, stung her thigh. "Son-of-a-bitch! Who the *fuck* is doing that?"

Conan was up and scrambling across the open area as though injected with crystal meth. Terri saw the reason. A big pink weasel stood at the edge of the clearing . . . on its hind legs . . . pointing a golden egg beater at her.

"The Explorer!" she exclaimed. "It survived the crash."

"Damn!" he cried, putting his hand on his chest. "It's shooting at us! Get down!"

He dove to the ground, pulling Terri with him. She had to twist to keep the Scrubber from being crushed. She couldn't see how bad her wound was through her jeans, but she could tell that it was superficial.

"Jesus!" Siderai said, nodding in the direction of their assailant. "He's running right into it."

He was talking about Conan, who flinched, and flinched again as the Explorer peppered him. Conan grabbed his thigh and fell, rolled, and was back on his feet, charging the pink sniper in a frantic spider walk—using his good hand as a replacement for his crippled foot.

The creature was holding his weapon using one hand and his tail. The other arm dangled, bent at an odd angle, obviously broken during the crash. The Explorer turned to run, but stumbled and fell. Conan was on him, tossing the weapon aside, and grabbing the pink neck firmly. He lifted the creature high, so that pink feet pedaled the air. Conan stared at him, turned to look at Terri, and then set him back down. Conan sat back, grabbed the Explorer's neck with his foot, and used his freed hand to pick up the egg beater gun and tuck it under his weak arm. He then made his way back to them, moving slowly as he dragged the Explorer along.

"I don't get it," Terri said. "His master tried to kill him. Why did he attack us?"

"The various servile species have been evolving under the Overlord's direction for different amounts of time," the Scrubber said, its voice muffled inside Terri's pocket. "The Inhabitors were enslaved relatively recently—less than a thousand years—and retain some amount of independent thought."

"The Explorer doesn't understand when freedom is staring it in the face—or what serves for a face?"

"Terri, the Explorer knows nothing but absolute obedience to an Overlord. The concept of defying just doesn't exist."

"Inhabitors will eventually be like that."

"Yes, Terri. Humans too, should the Overlords choose to enslave them."

"Yikes! You make it sound as though it's inevitable."

"A poor choice of wording, Terri."

"So you don't think it's inevitable?"

"There is not nearly enough data to make that assessment."

Conan had reached them, and he sat down, keeping the poor pink creature firmly in his grasp. Terri's thigh still hurt like hell, but she couldn't help feeling bad for the little guy. He had no choice. It would be like blaming a honey bee for protecting its hive.

Conan grabbed the Explorer's head with his hand, and then curled his foot around one shoulder. He looked at Terri.

"What's he doing?" she whispered.

"Terri," Siderai said, "he asking you whether he should kill it."

"No!" she cried, shaking her head.

"He won't understand that."

"Scrubber! Tell him!"

A short two-tone syllable issued from her pocket, and Conan reluctantly set the pink creature down.

It made sense that the Scrubber would know Overlord language if they were adversaries.

Suddenly, as though a powerful and majestic rebuke to the Scrubber's Mickey Mouse utterance, a trumpet call flashed across the clearing, fading away as the diminishing echoes called to each other.

The Overlord stood at the far end of the clearing. He held the hilt of a sword in both hands, an ancient weapon of a size to match the snout-faced giant alien. The cross-guard and pommel boasted intricate, elegant designs. The ruddy setting sun gleamed off of knife-sharp edges.

Terri stared. She blinked. "What's the chance that it's just symbolic?"

Nobody answered.

Chapter 17

"Run!" Terri shouted, helping Conan to his feet. When they turned to flee, they stopped short, staring. The Overlord's ship had slipped up over the saucer perimeter in the other direction, and hung in the air menacingly above the treetops. Terri pointed off to the side. "This way!"

They set off across the clearing, hobbling and limping, leaving the little pink Explorer behind. Terri kept her eye on the Overlord, who strode unevenly but purposefully towards the pyramid mound in the center of the open area. "Why isn't he coming after us?" she wondered.

"Maybe just luck," Siderai said, "but I doubt we're that lucky."

The Overlord's ship was easing around to intercept them, but it was obvious that they'd at least make the cover of the forest before it was again in front of them.

Something odd was happening just before the wall of pines marking the clearing's edge. Grass and small shrubs thrashed about, as though a gust of wind was blowing through . . . but only in specific places. The grass suddenly went flat to the ground in a line all along the pines, and then the outermost branches of the trees pushed inwards, as if a giant glass pane was preceding the three escapees.

"What is it?" Terri said.

"I don't know," Siderai replied, "but something tells me it's not part of that hoped-for luck."

They paused when they came to the flattened grass. The Overlord had reached the pyramid. Without a moment's hesitation, he lifted the sword, plunged it down, and then pulled it back, dark with alien blood.

"Oh my God!" Terri whispered. "Did he just murder the little pink guy?"

Siderai didn't say anything. The answer was obvious.

"Come on," she said, "let's get the hell out of here."

She turned, took one step, and tripped when something caught her foot. She fell forward, but never hit the ground. In fact, a soft, indiscernible membrane was holding her up, suspending her as she stared down at the flat blades of grass before her.

"Uh," she said, "this is pretty weird."

She felt Siderai grab her belt and pull her backwards, out of the alien wall of invisible molasses.

"Terri," the Scrubber said from inside her pocket, "I detected a repulsor field."

"That sounds right. It's like a wall in front of us."

"That would be a planer repulsor projection, probably beamed from the Overlord's ship."

"You get a cigar," Terri said softly as the giant spaceship moved in soundlessly above them. "We're trapped."

"This doesn't look good," Siderai said.

The Overlord stood in front of the pyramid watching them, leaning on the bloody downturned sword. He lifted it and placed the pommel to his lips.

"The son-of-a-bitch is kissing his sword," Terri said.

"Terri," the Scrubber said, "is this sword decorated with patterns resembling intertwined concentric circles?"

"It's decorated, all right, but I can't see the pattern from here."

"Terri, it's probably a ritual battle sword. They call them Manifest Destiny weapons."

"They stole the name from our imperialistic ancestors."

"Terri, I had to find a concept that was similar in meaning. The weapons go back many thousands of years before the Overlords acquired advanced technology. They represent an imagined superiority and a justification for conquering and enslaving other races. These weapons are handed down, father to son, generation after generation."

"Like the pendants and bracelets."

"Yes."

"Um, so, if they're ritual, that means they don't actually use them to fight?" she said hopefully. "Other than, like, for killing innocent slaves?"

"No, Terri. This is a last slim hope for this Overlord to maintain a small amount of honor. He is challenging his enemy to a dual to the death, an epic battle with which to extend his anthem."

"What if his enemy doesn't want to fight?"

"Then the Overlord will have lost his chance for a last piece of honor."

"So, we don't actually have to fight him."

"No."

"Whew!"

"He will kill you, of course."

Terri sighed.

A soft, taut blanket pressed against her back, pushing her forward towards the waiting snouted, pointy-eared Overlord warrior. Siderai and Conan were stumbling along on each side of her. "We don't have weapons!" Terri exclaimed.

"The Overlord will provide one of equal value."

"Goody. It might be equal if he ties one hand behind his back … and sits on the other one."

As they were pushed closer by the repulsor field, Terri saw that one of the Overlord's thighs was raw, a milky ooze flowing down across his knee—the wound where Spockette had accidentally zapped him, and why he walked a little unbalanced.

Twenty feet from the giant alien, the invisible pushing hand stopped and retreated. The Overlord stepped forward, grabbed Conan by the head, and pulled him off to the side. He extracted his immobilizing cheese grater, and pinned their companion in place. A ceremonial beheading was apparently still on the agenda.

The Overlord turned back to Terri and Siderai. He looked at them each in turn, then reached out and grabbed Terri by the front of her T-shirt. She yelled and grabbed his wrist, but it was like yanking on plumbing. The alien used his other giant hand to rip open her shirt. He peered inside, then pushed her over next to Conan. She tripped, fell, and was paralyzed as she entered the range of the cheese grater. She lay on her side, facing the last two standing beings.

"He's a sexist," she said, her words slurred through uncooperative lips.

"It would be dishonorable to fight a female," the Scrubber said so quietly Terri almost didn't hear it.

"Oh, yeah," Terri lisped, "they keep harems—the chauvinistic pigs."

The Overlord turned to Siderai. He pulled the golden turkey baster from his belt, extended the slim blade, flipped the ceremonial sword around, and held out the handle to the community college instructor. Siderai glanced at Terri. His eyes danced with fear.

"What happened to a weapon of equal value?" Terri muttered. "What kind of epic battle lasts two minutes?"

Siderai took the delicate sword and backed away. The Overlord followed, and Siderai turned to run, but stopped in mid-step, poised with one foot in the air as though a mime demonstrating frozen action. The Overlord's ship was making sure nobody escaped.

Siderai stepped carefully back and spun around, holding the golden sword in both fists. The Overlord stepped forward, cocked his massive blade, took one swipe, and Siderai's handsome ceremonial weapon flew off in an arc, landing ten feet from Terri.

The Overlord stood, staring at Siderai, who stared back, both his hands still clenched together, as though he didn't realize that he'd lost his sword. The Overlord walked over towards Terri, stopped, reached out with his sword, and used the tip to drag Siderai's puny version towards him before carefully reaching down to pick it up. The golden cheese grater apparently worked on Overlords as well.

The Overlord returned to the battlefield and tossed Siderai's sword to him, sideways, as the Musketeers do in movies. Siderai jumped to the side and then reached down and picked it up. His eyes darted back and forth, and he hobbled off in a brisk limp towards the little pyramid. The Overlord followed, loping along unevenly. Terri had the impression that the alien master was a little exasperated.

When Siderai reached the mound of boulders, he climbed the largest one at the bottom, a chunk of granite the size of an easy chair. From there, he was level with his opponent. As the Overlord approached, he thought better of the equalizing maneuver and turned to climb higher. The sides of the pyramid mound were steep, a testament to the craft of the ancient natives, and he struggled to reach the next level. He was almost up when his bad foot slipped, and the swollen ankle jammed between two boulders. With a shout and a groan, he fell back onto the large boulder, and then rolled to the ground. He lay there, face down, his golden sword three feet away.

The Overlord reached him and stood looking down. He raised his Viking-size sword, hanging from both hands, the wicked sharp tip poised over Siderai's back. He turned his gaze up, to the altostratus clouds edged with pink from the setting sun, and let loose a mighty musical call, like Roman trumpeters announcing the Caesar's entrance, the last bars of his new anthem.

Terri's eyes blurred with tears, and she struggled against the immobilizing field of the golden cheese grater to blink and clear them, although she wasn't at all sure she wanted to watch. It was hard to believe that the whole thing, the downward spiraling, doomed adventure, had begun just that very morning when they'd tried to get videos of a strange new hominid species. A sob clenched her chest, nearly choking her. It couldn't be happening. This had to be a nightmare she'd waken from. It just *couldn't* be happening!

The Overlord's anthem went silent. He paused, raised his sword a few inches, and . . . staggered backwards.

Terri heard the deep, almost subsonic rumble, the twitch of unimaginable power, and felt herself bouncing, as though next to someone jumping on a mattress. Above the trees, off towards the perimeter, stunningly beautiful in the fading light, a high-reaching spray of leaking antimatter shot into the sky.

She'd done it again. The portal base responded to her intense distress.

The Overlord regained his balance, but a second jolt sent him staggering backwards again, and this time he tripped over a small boulder. He fell, dropping his sword, his arms flailing. He didn't move. She held her breath, but the Herculean alien lay motionless.

The portal's mighty shrug ceased, the entire tectonic shudder lasting maybe five seconds. Siderai rolled over and lifted his head, and then sat up. He looked at the motionless giant, and stood up, but fell back on his butt, holding his ankle. His mouth clenched with resolve, and he approached the Overlord on his hands and knees. He paused just out of reach. He leaned forward and lifted the hilt of the great sword, but, grunting with effort, wasn't able to lift it entirely. Instead, he dragged it away.

"Is he dead?" Terri called.

Siderai looked at her. He seemed dazed. He shook his head. "No! He's breathing. He hit his head on a rock."

Even as he said this, the Overlord's head twitched, and his hand clenched. Siderai scampered on hands and knees to where he had fallen and retrieved his human-sized sword.

"Kill him, Prof!" she yelled. "He never gave *you* a chance."

She had yelled. With a mouth that worked.

The portal's shudder had jostled the golden cheese grater. Terri's head was outside the field. Everything else was still paralyzed . . . almost. She could move the fingers of her left hand. She dug them into the ground and squeezed, dragging her hand along, and, as it too left the confines of the field, it came alive. With both fingers and a hand, she pulled out an entire arm, reached a half-buried rock, and used that to drag even more body parts. The more that left the field, the easier it was to extract more, until she jumped up, careful not to lose her balance and fall back inside.

Siderai knelt over the Overlord, golden sword poised to plunge into the barrel chest. "Kill him, Prof!" Terri shouted. "Do it!"

Siderai's face was distorted in agony. Tears streamed down his face. He looked at her. "I . . . can't! Terri, I just can't!"

He sat back and let the tip of the sword sink to the ground. Then, he looked at her again, and now his face was alight with hope. "This is what he used on Moe and Thinker!" He studied the hilt and, holding it firmly, pressed down. The sword slowly retracted, the hand guard folded in, and the sword was again a turkey baster.

Suddenly, the Overlord's hand shot out and grabbed Siderai by his thigh. He shouted and tried to kick away, but the slave master held fast. Continuing to kick with his wounded foot, Siderai worked the alien tool with both hands and suddenly yelped, yanking away one hand. He turned the baster around, leaned forward, and planted it against the Overlord's wrist. It was the giant's turn to yell, a hair-raising bellow as he let go.

Siderai crab-walked away, out of reach of the downed giant, who sat up, holding his head.

Terri had to do something. Run over and kick the Overlord in the head? He'd grab her foot and rip it off. She could throw a rock. Better yet, she could shoot, if not with actual bullets, at least something that stings like hell.

She ran around the back of the cheese grater to the other side of its paralyzing field where Conan lay. Their warrior companion had dropped the Explorer's golden egg beater, and it lay a few feet away, closer to the edge of the field. Terri slowly extended her hand until she felt the tips of her fingers go numb. She grabbed a stick and used it to nudge the slave-qualified weapon closer, and then picked it up.

She turned to find the Overlord reaching for his sword. The alien moved slowly, unsteadily, woozy from the blow to his head. Siderai squatted nearby, and as the Overlord leaned over and reached out, Siderai again touched his outstretched hand with the turkey baster with the same bellowed result.

Terri looked down at her own weapon. Close up, it wasn't so much an egg beater as a pistol with fine looping tubes instead of a barrel. It was probably a tool of some sort, but whatever for, she couldn't even guess. Somehow, the Explorer had gotten it to fire oversized bee stings. The pistol handle had no trigger that she could see.

The Overlord was recovering. He reached out yet again, but this time when Siderai tried to jolt him, the giant grabbed Siderai's wrist, causing him to writhe in pain and drop the torture tool.

"Shit!" Terri muttered, "how the hell does this thing work?"

"If it is a quantum welder," came a muffled voice, "simply squeeze the handle while simultaneously pressing the actuator."

Terri had forgotten about the Scrubber. She didn't know quantum welders from egg beaters, and in any case, she couldn't tell which intricate projection would be an actuator.

She pointed the tool towards the Overlord, who was dragging the struggling Siderai towards him, and began squeezing everything she could get at. Suddenly Siderai yelped, and she saw a red spot appear on his arm. She ran closer. Siderai was near enough for the Overlord to grab his neck with his other hand. Terri ran closer still, so close she could smell the alien. While the monster warbled a curse in three tones as he prepared to rip off Siderai's head, Terri placed the looping tubes a foot from the Overlord's head and squeezed . . . and squeezed, and finally the slave master howled in pain, and Terri was knocked flat on her back as he back-handed her.

She pushed herself into a sitting position. The Overlord had let go of Siderai, and stood up unsteadily to come after her. She pointed the quantum-welder-egg-beater at him and squeezed and squeezed. Too late—she turned, scrambling to her feet. A vise grip latched her calf, sending her down onto her face. Another vise clutched her shoulder and spun her around so that she was looking up into the monstrous animal face. He curled back his lips to reveal his fangs and growled, like a cougar about to charge. Her shot had left a nasty wound on his cheek that oozed milky alien blood, alien blood she'd already seen. She still held the Explorer's tool. Her ancestors used weapons long before technology evolved to inflict damage from a distance. She glanced down to make sure she had the right leg, and then slammed the golden tool into the wound that Spockette had made. His growl rose an octave, and she slammed the wound again. He uttered a train whistle scream, grabbed the tool from her, and flung it away. He brought his face inches from hers. His eyes were deep wells of anger, and his breath was rotting potatoes and rubbing alcohol. She struggled to keep from passing out. Just when she thought she was about to die from pure terror, the monster giant jerked straight, wailing like a stricken bear. He squirmed, twisted, and threw himself away. Siderai stood there holding the torture baster. He thought a moment, then turned and hobbled away as fast as he could. "Run, Terri!" he called.

That was about as necessary as telling her to breathe.

She ran. She glanced back and saw that the Overlord was cupping his hand over his leg wound. She'd really hurt him.

Good.

Suddenly, her body was gone. That's how it felt as she tumbled to the ground and rolled. *Son-of-a-bitch!* She'd run right into the golden cheese grater field. Her body returned as she rolled out the other side. She got up on her hands and knees. Had she broken any bones? If so, not important enough to keep her from running.

That had been pure luck, having enough momentum to carry her through the paralyzing field. Talk about exotic alien weapon technology.

Weapon technology.

Shit! Why hadn't she thought of that before?

She got up and ran around to the other side of the cheese grater. Only the size of an unabridged dictionary, it was surprisingly heavy as she placed her hands on both sides and lifted. Care was key here. With no idea how it operated, she might accidentally turn it off. Worse, she might come into contact with the paralyzing field.

She staggered towards the pyramid, the field swaying invisibly back and forth before her. A bird fell out of a tree on one side, a squirrel on the other. Both the Overlord and Siderai were gone. *Shit!*

She heard a shout from Siderai. There, off to the left. Siderai stood, his back against a pine tree. The Overlord had picked up his sword, and was lifting it over his shoulder, about to divide Siderai into two parts. Propping the heavy paralyzing device against her stomach, she pointed it in their direction. *It's not working!* she thought as the Overlord began his downward swing, but the lethal swipe lost momentum, the Overlord's shoulders drooped, and the tip of the massive sword bit the ground at Siderai's feet. He growled and loped off, dragging the sword, his feet lifting heavily with each step.

The farther he got away, the less the paralyzing effect. She ran after him—or tried. The damn thing was heavy and difficult to maneuver over fallen logs. Each time her aim swung away as she climbed over an obstacle, the alien gained strength and distance. She was going to lose him. *Damn!*

She saw a red glow through the trees ahead, the sunset. They were approaching the giant saucer's edge. Far ahead, she saw the Overlord turn to the right, following the perimeter. She knew her geometry. A chord line scribed through a circle is shorter than the perimeter. Terri turned sharply to the right, cutting across the outer third of the base. With luck, the downed trees near the edges would slow him down. It was getting dark under the trees, and she had to be careful. She could fall and end up paralyzing herself.

She again saw light through the trees ahead, and there, a silhouette against the twilight, the running figure of a giant man with a snout for a face. Terri put on steam, risking a fall. The Overlord slowed, seeming to grow tired, but in fact just weak. Terri could tell that she had him. He slowed, and slowed, and finally stopped as she gained on him. He turned and his eyes found her coming through the darkness under the pines. He curled his lips, unveiling glistening fangs, threw out his arms wide, and roared. He swayed, dropped his sword, and then fell to the ground.

Terri slowed to a stop, careful to keep the golden grater pointed at him. Maybe he was just faking it. Maybe he would jump up and snatch her, ripping her head off with one twist.

She continued, slowly, carefully. She came upon him, an inert mass of muscular giant, lying on his side, his head resting on his arm, as though in a deep, restful slumber. His eyes spoke otherwise. They followed her, furious, hateful. His mouth twitched, like somebody talking in their sleep—probably cursing her in three part harmony.

What now? Kill him? How? Stand outside the field and throw rocks?

She had to get back, see how Siderai and Conan were doing. She positioned the paralyzer, leaning it against a rock ten feet from him. No, the field probably swept out in a funnel shape. Too close, and some of his extremities might be outside, just like her fingers had been. She moved back another ten feet. That would have to do.

One last thing. She dug her hand into the needles on the forest floor until she reached damp loam, and pulled out big handfuls. Standing as close as she dared, she tossed them over her captive.

This achieved nothing other than humiliation, but that's exactly what she wanted.

She headed directly away from the light filtering through the trees. That should take her back to the center clearing. The Overlord's ship still hovered up there somewhere. He was, of course, telling it to fire on whomever might be in the clearing now.

Uh, oh. That wasn't her thought. Damn! The bastard's twitching mouth wasn't cursing her, he was talking to his bracelet!

"No!" she called into the dusk-filled forest as she ran, tripping and falling over and over. *Don't shoot!* she screamed inside her head. *Don't shoot!*

A pale blue sky sprinkled with a half-dozen stars opened above her as she burst into the clearing. Siderai hobbled to meet her. "What happened?" he said, glancing behind her nervously. "Where's the Overlord?"

"Trapped inside his own cage." *Don't shoot!* she thought. "How's Conan?"

He gestured towards the pyramid where their alien companion sat with his back against a boulder.

"Is he okay? He looks dead."

"He's okay, I think. Just beat. The Overlord is secure?"

"Yeah. I think so." *Don't shoot!*

Siderai looked up at the dark bulk of hulking ship.

"He's commanding it to zap us," she said.

"You're able to stop it? Obviously you are. Pretty precarious situation, eh?" he said, forcing a grim smile. "Any ideas?"

She looked at him, her mouth drawn tight. It was hard to say it, now that it was in her power.

"We have to kill him, don't we?" he said quietly.

She nodded. "He killed Moe and Thinker with the torture stick."

"Does he deserve the same fate?"

She sighed. "I guess that would make us as bad as him. It's not going to be easy. We have to stay outside the paralyzing field—"

Something rustled near the pyramid. It moved closer. In the dim light she saw tufts of grass go flat. "Oh, crap," she said. "He's using the molasses wall."

"The planer repulsor projection?"

"Ever the professor."

Soft pillows pressed against her, urging her away from the pyramid. She was through being pushed around. She held her ground . . . which was completely useless. The invisible wall was irresistible. She could choose not to walk, but that simply meant that she was carried forward like a fish in a net. Her foot caught on a rock hidden inside a tuft of grass, and she fell. She hit the ground rolling, rolling. She remembered the sensation. When they were kids, they'd roll themselves in a carpet, and two others would pull the exposed end. She tried to push herself upright, but the repulsor field turned her over before she had a chance. Her butt hit a small rock, and she yelped in pain. The insistent wall was going to eventually bring her up against a tree trunk. Then what?

Something grabbed her wrist and yanked. She was being dragged across the ground and into the pines.

"That was close," Siderai said, helping her up. "Let's go before it catches up with us."

"Where are we going?" she asked, rubbing her bottom.

"Away from the pyramid, away from the repulsor curtain."

"We can only go so far," she reminded, starting off into the darkness under the pines.

"Yeah, I thought about that," he said, following along. "That may be what he wants—push us right off the edge."

"How will we know how close the curtain is to us—?"

She was interrupted by a series of mighty crashes, the creaks and groans and splintered screams of trees being snapped and torn up by the roots. The curtain had reached the edge of the clearing.

They broke into a trot. "Jesus!" Terri yelled, barely audible above the apocalyptic roar pursuing them.

"I can't even imagine the amount of power behind that," Siderai yelled back. "Alien technology is pretty frightening."

"Frightening, Prof? Is that a euphemism?"

"Okay, shitless scary."

"Prof, I think I'm a bad influence on you."

"Terri, I have to ask—you can communicate through his bracelet to keep the ship from firing, why can't you stop . . . this?"

"I tried, Prof. It's not working. It may be that the bracelet is too far away, but I think my intervention only works for, like, impulse actions. This repulsor curtain is all spread out—I don't know, unfocused, maybe."

"I'm sure you tried your best, Terri. We're not that high off the ground, you know."

"Like, fifty feet? That's pretty high."

"Yes, it is. But not necessarily a death sentence. Particularly if we're over some trees. Heck, we might be able to jump into a tree."

"Yeah!" Did she dare to hope? "You're probably right!"

She saw clear sky through the tree trunks ahead, and they suddenly broke out into the narrow cleared band at the perimeter where the trees had fallen away. They stopped short, staring, ignoring the grinding monster bearing down on them from behind.

There were no trees to jump into. There were no trees in sight. Below them were the peaks of the Smokies. Far off, to the east, lights twinkled in a little town down in the valley.

They were thousands of feet above the ruined observation tower.

And, the thunderous crashing of toppled trees was fast approaching.

Chapter 18

"Oh, Lord!" Siderai yelled.

"Fuck!" Terri countered.

"I think you raised the base, Terri! You communed with it when the Overlord was about to kill me—"

"When he fell, knocked unconscious."

"I had the sense that we were going up."

"I didn't tell it to go up!"

Siderai shrugged. "Who knows how it interprets your fears." He looked back at the destruction bearing down on them. "These trees are going to come down hard. We should move away, get as close to the edge as we can."

They inched forward carefully. The surface of the saucer curved down here, and the bed of needles gave way to bare hull where the soil had slid away. A waxing gibbous moon glinted off the perfectly smooth surface.

Terri froze, suddenly shaking with fear. There was nothing to grab, nothing for her feet to anchor on, just smooth hull curving down and down. One step too far, and she'd slide away off the edge, to fall thousands of feet to her death.

"I can't go any farther, Prof," she said, her voice trembling. She desperately wanted to back up, find a tree to hug.

The colossal wall of destruction was close. She could see pines thrashing and slamming forward. It would be upon them in seconds. Death if she moved forward, death if she stayed put.

The reflection of the moon on the hull moved away from her, down the curving surface. The terrifying slope wasn't so terrifying anymore. She'd been standing on a hull that angled down, but was now almost level. The terrible cataclysm behind her eased, leaving just the sporadic creak and moan of downed trees settling into place.

"Prof . . . ?" she said, not sure what to make of it.

A new sound rose—low, grumbling, ominous—not close, but in the distance. "What is it?" she whispered.

In the moonlight, she saw Siderai's eyes wide with wonder. "Terri," he said, "you don't know what you've done?"

"*Me?* What did I do?"

"Terri, you've tilted the base. That rumble is the forest falling off the far edge."

She looked around. He was right! The pines were downhill from them. Rocks rolled away into the forest, where downed trees shook and shivered as they found new positions. But the threat from the invisible repulsor wall had ceased. She took a breath, relieved.

And the world tilted back.

"It's righting itself!" Siderai yelled, trying to claw away from the edge, but slipping on the increasingly steep slope. Terri turned to find something to hang onto, but her feet flew out from under her, and she was sliding backwards on her stomach, faster and faster, towards thousands of feet of thin air.

She landed. Her feet slammed into something hard, and she fell back on her rear. Siderai landed with a thud next to her. In the faint light of the moon, she saw that they were sitting on a little rounded platform, perfectly positioned, as though expecting their fall.

"Terri."

Siderai and Terri looked at each other.

"Spockette?" Terri said.

"Yes, Terri. You will find handholds behind you. Grab hold tightly, and let me know when you're both ready."

"Ready? For what?"

"For me to take you to safety. Hurry."

"How . . . how did you know we would fall right here?"

"From Scrubber. Terri, there's very little time before the Overlord understands what has happened, and attacks us with his ship."

"Uh, okay," she said, turning around and gripping a bar she didn't remember being there before. "Prof?"

"Ready," he said.

Instantly, they fell away, eliciting a squeak from Terri. Spockette swooped out, around, and back up. "Jesus!" Terri yelled, hanging tight, and flopping around in sync with Siderai, as though they were executing a well-rehearsed choreography. The little spaceship landed gracefully along the ravished perimeter of the forest.

"What now?" Terri said, out of breath from the wild ride.

"Wait here until I come back. If I lose, try to command the base to take you down."

"Where are you going? What do you mean, 'if I lose?'"

"I must disable the Overlord's ship."

"You're going to *fight* it?"

"Yes."

"Can't you . . . take us down first?"

"There's no time, Terri. Disembark. Hurry."

"I don't understand—you're tiny, and his ship is *huge*!"

"Come," Siderai said, gently pulling her hands free.

"I have an advantage," Spockette said.

"A secret weapon?" Terri said hopefully as she slid off, stumbling and falling when she hit the ground.

"Yes," the little rescue boat said as it rose and glided away into the darkness.

Terri sat on the ground in the moonlight. Siderai slid over next to her. "She came through for us," he said.

"She sure did. Big Bertha had to let her out of the tractor field to come after us—hey! Why did it remove the repulsor wall?"

"You caused a lot of havoc when you tilted the base. If I haven't gotten all turned around, you left the Overlord on the other side."

"Ah, ha! He fell off? He's dead?"

"No," came a muffled voice.

"Oh, geez, I keep forgetting about Scrubber," Terri said, reaching into her pocket.

"Terri, leave me here for now," her pocket said. "The Overlord is not dead, but he thought you were."

A pencil of light pierced the sky above them, accompanied by a wicked sizzle, and a moment later, a small explosion somewhere unseen over the middle of the saucer.

Terri gasped. "Was that—?"

"That was Spockette," the Scrubber said.

"Firing, or hit?"

"Spockette fired, and hit the Overlord's ship."

"So, it's . . . over?"

"No, Terri. Not nearly. The energy density of Spockette's discharges are just a fraction of those of the Overlord's ship. Spockette will have to work hard to damage it."

"What about the, uh, other way around?"

"Terri, one direct hit from the Overlord's ship would likely decommission Spockette."

Decommission. Alien technology had a natural propensity for euphemisms. But . . . "Hey! Wait a second! I can keep Big Bertha from firing!"

"No, Terri, you can't, not anymore. The Overlord has come to understand what you were doing, and he has convinced his ship to ignore you."

"Turds."

"Terri, there is something you and Professor Siderai can do."

"I'm not a professor," Siderai said.

"What can we do?" Terri said.

"The Overlord will be directing his ship—"

"With his bracelet."

"Yes, Terri. You can search him out and distract him."

"Oh. He's, uh, not caught anymore in the cheese grater?"

"Cheese grater?" Siderai said.

"That's correct, Terri. Your yawing maneuver of the portal displaced the paralysis projection."

"Double turds. Where is he?"

"I don't know, Terri, but you do."

"I'm afraid you've missed on this one—"

"His bracelet, Terri."

"I thought you said he—"

"Convinced his ship to ignore you. The bracelet's operation hasn't changed."

"What good does that do if I can't get through to his ship—?"

"Can't you sense it, Terri?"

"Right. Maybe." She closed her eyes. She jerked when another sizzle was followed by a bang, this time off to the right. She concentrated. Then she relaxed. Then she focused on visualizing the bracelet. Then she tried to empty her mind.

"It's no use," she said. "There's nothing."

"Maybe we need to get closer," Siderai said.

"Brilliant, Prof. That was sarcasm. Like Scrubber said, the whole point is that we don't know where he's at."

"Maybe not, but we generally know where he's not."

"I see your point. Okay, a grudging touché. I left him somewhere on the other side. He didn't have time to get very far." She stood up and helped Siderai. He could barely stand on his swollen ankle. "I think you'd better stay put, Prof."

"You're not going alone," he said, taking a cautious step.

"No argument from me—I didn't want to. Into the dark jungle we go."

Siderai leaned on her, using her as a crutch. Spockette had put them down outside the area flattened by the repulsor sweep, and it was indeed dark under the patches of standing pine trees. Many had come down, and in these areas it was a nearly impossible obstacle course. The upside was that here the moonlight fell on the arboreal carnage, and they climbed over the upturned trunks, keeping away from the impenetrable masses of branches and spooky tendrils of roots. Sizzling flashes, and explosions broke the dark silence, usually off on the far side, but sometimes close by. At these times, Terri flinched and crouched, feeling like a refugee fleeing an indiscriminate air strike.

Siderai directed their travel, staying on a straight line by keeping a bearing on the moon. After ducking under the trunk of a particularly large old codger of a pine tree, he turned off in the wrong direction. "Sorry, Prof," Terri whispered, "it's this way," she said, pointing.

He shook his head, pointing at the moon.

Terri blinked.

He peered closely at her. "You sensed it, didn't you?"

"No. Um, maybe."

The pines closed in on them as they followed her sensed direction. Here, the trees had held their ground, and they proceeded mostly by feel, as the moonlight was just blinking teases breaking through high above. Suddenly, Siderai grabbed her arm. "Shh!" he whispered.

She heard it, quiet music, bad music, music out of tune, Overlord chatter.

Ahead, the moonlight filled a wide expanse. They crept forward slowly, quietly, wincing at each spaceship blast. They came to the edge of an open area. "It's the pyramid!" Terri whispered.

More accurately, it had *been* the pyramid. They'd arrived at the central clearing. The carefully constructed mound of boulders had toppled when she'd caused the saucer portal to list heavily to starboard. The original base of the monument still remained, a cluster of the largest boulders, and in the middle stood the Overlord, peering upward, and talking constantly to his wrist.

Terri peered up as well, and gasped. The battle hadn't been obvious from inside the jumble of ruined forest, but here, with a wide open skyline, the two spaceships were clearly visible, one large and lumbering, and the other, seemingly tiny, darting this way and that, like a busy hummingbird.

Siderai nudged her. The Overlord had heard her gasp. He glared at them from fifty feet away. Still talking to the bracelet, he reached down and picked up mighty alien Excalibur with his other hand.

Looking back up at the battling spaceships, Terri said, "Why doesn't Big Bertha just zap Spockette out of the sky?"

Spockette would zip in close, fire a shot onto the Overlord's hull, then scoot away, constantly moving, constantly turning, a dizzying scramble of motion.

"Overlord ships cannot fire in a upward direction," Scrubber answered from Terri's pocket. "The energy discharges were not originally designed to be a weapon. Spockette is inaccessible as long as she stays above the larger ship."

"Why does she dance around?" Terri said, watching the little space lifeboat mimic an energetic gnat.

"The Overlord is trying to catch her in his ship's tractor field. He knows what she's after—his ship's flight control. It's a delicate operation avoiding the antimatter control."

"For obvious reasons." She shivered at the thought of the consequence. "Hey, Spockette said she has a secret weapon. Why doesn't she use it?"

"She already is, Terri."

"Those bug zapper flashes? They look like the same ones she used—"

"Terri, secret weapons don't always inflict direct damage, and hers isn't really a secret at all."

"It's her maneuverability," Siderai guessed.

"Yes, Professor."

"Because she's smaller?" Terri said.

"No, Terri. Because she has free will. The Overlord's much more powerful ship is capable of just as much maneuverability, but it acts only from direct instructions."

"Overlords don't trust anybody or anything," Terri said.

"That's right."

"Spockette obeyed Moe completely, and then couldn't disobey the Overlord."

"Not until you freed her, Terri."

"*Me?* Why is every alien misbehaving action blamed on me?"

"Because of your father's pendant."

"It's gone, smashed," Terri reminded, pushing aside a deep twinge of guilt.

"Over time, the pendant developed a channel of empathy with you, one that also applies to Overlord ships, which were created by the same extinct people who made the pendants and bracelets."

"I don't remember giving Spockette an emancipation order."

"Terri, you freed her by your example. You rebelled against the Overlord, not out of self interest, but simply because he was deeply morally wrong."

It was her favorite T-shirt. "Spaceships have morals?"

"Morals are, to an extent, based on cultural perspectives, but we believe that there are aspects of existence that are morally absolute.

Any thinking being with faculties of empathy has the ability to comprehend this."

"That meant that Spockette had empathy to start with."

"The race that made her, and all other Overlord ships, included this in their core. Without it, there can be no true sentient intelligence."

"No soul."

"Perhaps. On this, I cannot comment. Terri and Professor, I must remind you that you came here for a purpose."

"Right!" Terri said. The Overlord was already dividing his attention, directing his ship in battle with occasional glances at them. "He has a really big sword, and we have sticks and stones."

"Exactly," Siderai said. "Move around the perimeter, and we'll come at him from two sides."

"Prof, you didn't get my point—we're rabbits to his wolf."

"Terri, we're not going to actually fight him."

"Oh, yeah. Right."

"We don't even have to get very close."

"Right," she said.

"You simply must distract him," the Scrubber said.

"I *got* it!" Terri said. "Geez, it's been a helluva long day, and I'm beat, and I've been running on nothing but adrenaline for hours, and even that's about run out—"

"Terri," Siderai said, laying his hand gently on her shoulder. "It's okay. Let's do some distracting."

She nodded and set off around the edge of the perimeter. She intended to go all the way around, to come in from the opposite direction, but she'd barely gone a quarter of the circle when, in the eerie silver light of the moon, she saw him limping towards the tumbled boulders. "He thinks he's going to grab all the glory, eh?" she muttered. She found two stones and started towards the alien Colossus. Her stones weren't Colossus size—hardly bigger than tangerines—but she figured they afforded the best accuracy, and she didn't need to wound, just hassle him. Like Siderai said, no fighting, just distracting.

Halfway to their target, Siderai stopped and waited for Terri. She came as close as she dared, hardly more than halfway herself, and raised her stone high, ready to throw. Siderai took the cue, and they lobbed their projectiles together. She couldn't see them fly in the darkness, and she was pretty sure she missed, but Siderai's bounced off the giant's midriff like a pea off a squirrel. The Overlord threw the puny human a menacing glance, but otherwise ignored the feeble annoyance.

Siderai wasn't looking at the Overlord. He was staring into the sky. Terri realized that Spockette's blasts, which had been peppering along every few seconds, had gone silent. Terri gazed upwards, and moaned. Spockette floated motionless above her much larger adversary, like a fly caught in a web. The invisible tractor field was turning its prey slowly over, swinging the aim of her ad hoc weapon away.

Siderai advanced. Terri took a few steps forward. From just a couple dozen feet away, Siderai raised his second stone, larger than the first, a bona fide rock. Terri raised hers, and they threw together. Terri had no idea whether hers found the target this time, but it didn't matter. Siderai's five-pounder whacked the alien square in the neck, almost knocking him off his perch as he recoiled and recovered. With his eyes glued to his ship above, and singing a continuous nonsensical stream of music into his wrist, the Overlord moved his sword to his communication hand, reached over his shoulder to extract the golden spatula, and swung it towards Siderai, who collapsed amid a flurry of sizzling fireflies like a blind-folded prisoner before a firing squad.

Terri froze an eternal second, and then turned, and, on instinct, dove to the ground. A storm of sizzling, spinning light points flowed past her, and the skin on her back tingled, became excruciatingly painful, and then numb.

She clutched tufts of grass, waiting for the next volley, but there was only silence, a silence made horrible by the absence of Spockette's blasts, and taunted by the invincible, inscrutable musical communication.

He thought he'd hit her squarely. He thought that she was out of action, like Siderai—unconscious or dead.

The continuous stream of instructions suddenly stopped short. One heartbeat, two, and the evening was pierced by a vicious howl, threatening and aggressive, as might burst from the lungs of a werewolf.

She had heard this raw animal bellow before. She turned over and looked. In the moonlight, it was difficult to discern details. The Overlord was struggling, twisting and swinging both his sword and the spatula, as though trying to scratch his back.

It wasn't an itch on his back, but something round and . . . furry.

Terri jumped up. Like her dive to the ground, it was practically instinct. She didn't think she'd see their crippled friend again, left behind when they were swept away by the repulsor curtain. But now he needed help before his former master pulled him off to be impaled.

There was no time to think about what she might do, there was no time to do anything but charge. She'd have a couple of seconds to come up with something.

What she came up with was a scream. Defiance—it was all she had left in her arsenal.

When she came to the toppled pyramid, she sprang up onto a small boulder, about to leap forward to grab whatever she could of the Overlord, but just as she launched herself, he swung the spatula around, and sprayed her feet with sputtering fireflies. Instead of springing into the air, her momentum carried her forward, and down . . . down, to his feet, and her chin bounced off his boulder, and she fell hard, with fireflies of her own filling her head.

She opened her eyes. She could tell that she'd been out only a second. Her chin hurt like hell, and she felt dizzy, but she could move . . . except for her feet, which felt like they were gone, chopped off.

Above her, the Overlord continued to wrestle his tenacious assailant, but it was no real contest. Conan was a weasel, hanging desperately onto the back of a gorilla. It couldn't end any way but with death for Conan.

Then she saw it. The Overlord wore no shoes. His two wide toes, what once, long ago, had been his ancestors' hooves, perched there just above her head. The bottom surface would be deep, hard callus. But the top . . .

She lifted her head, studied the situation, and then grabbed his ankle, opened her mouth wide, and shoved her mouth over one big, leathery toe. It tasted of dirt, dirt and the smell of a log so rotten, it crumbles in your hand. Suppressing a gut-wrenching gag, she clamped her teeth down hard.

He howled with pain, the foot jerked, and she clamped harder, hanging on to his ankle with both hands. A spray of fireflies swept past, and her legs departed, joining her feet in numb absence. Something fell next to her, something heavy and metal—his Excalibur. Another spray of fireflies, and her shoulder was gone, and with it, the strength in that hand. She hung on with just one hand, chewing now, grinding her teeth until she met bone. The howl grew in pitch, and the foot was turning over. He kicked as he fell, and she was thrown away. Her head hit a boulder, and more fireflies filled her head, but she hung on to consciousness. Her vision cleared, and she saw only stone. A furry hand reached down and lifted, with the sword following along. A roar of slave master rage was followed by a soft thud, like a melon impaled with a butcher knife, and the night air vibrated with multi-tone anguish and despair.

Then silence, followed by swishing—the sound of metal drawn from an alien body—and finally the punctuating sound of ancient crafted metal clattering onto the rocks.

Terri lay there, half her body beyond sensation, enduring the taste of moldy carpet and the copper tang of alien blood. A furry hand appeared and cradled her face. Worried gray eyes, gleaming in the moonlight, stared into hers, searching for assurance. "Hi," she said. Conan's brow bounced as his nostrils pinched together—his version of a smile.

She held her hand out, and he took it and helped her to her feet, and then steadied her. Sensation was returning, but she didn't have much control. It reminded her of walking on a foot that had gone to sleep.

The Overlord lay splayed on his back across the boulder, the final stage for his anthem's last coda, a piece never to be played, never to be praised by comrades and criticized by scheming adversaries, never to be heard echoing down halls and around corners, finding its way finally to what remained of his harem, a distant, inaccessible reminder of rigid status.

"Fuck you," she said, staring at the dead alien.

There was more to the silence than freedom from the enmity of a slave master alien. She looked up. The two spaceships floated in the silver moonlight, the smaller one, tiny in comparison, hovering above the dead alien's vessel. "What's going to happen to Spockette?" she mumbled.

"The lifeboat has sufficient power to dock the Overlord's ship," came the muffled reply from her pocket.

Terri smiled and lightly touched the lump in her pocket. Once again, she'd forgotten about the little Scrubber.

"The Overlord's ship has gone inert upon his death," the miniature drone continued, "and Spockette must land it."

"The roles have reversed?" Terri said. "Spockette is lifting it?" She saw that the pair were slowly sinking towards the saucer.

"She doesn't have the strength to lift it—enough to keep it from crashing into the portal, though."

"And commit suicide as a nuclear bomb."

"Yes."

Terri swallowed, watching the landing maneuver warily. There was something else . . . *shit!*

She pointed, and Conan helped her across the clearing. Strength and feeling were returning to her zapped extremities with each step. She dreaded what they'd find, and for awhile she was puzzled that they couldn't. Then she saw him, a dark mass nearly invisible among the clumps of grass in the monochromatic light of the moon.

She knelt next to him. Lying on his stomach, one arm outstretched, the other folded underneath his chest, he showed no more life than the rocks, as dead as the Overlord. "Prof," she said quietly, gently laying her hand on his back.

Taking a deep breath, she slid her hands under him and rolled him over. He opened his eyes. "It's you," he said.

Terri could have danced a jig. "Who the hell did you expect?"

"Maybe one very big dude with a very big sword."

"Don't worry, he's dead. Conan took care of that."

Their companion sat next to them, patiently waiting for whatever might come next.

"Can you move?" Terri asked.

Siderai lifted one hand, and let it drop. "I think so."

"Can you get up?"

"No."

"You didn't even try."

"I'm tired. I'm too old for this."

"You're too gay, you mean."

"What's that supposed to mean?"

"I don't know. I'm tired. That's the best I could come up with."

"It doesn't make any sense."

"I know. My insults are running dry."

"Maybe they're evaporating along with your insecurity."

"What the hell is that all about?"

"I think you can figure it out."

A shadow glided past, throwing them into complete darkness. Above, sinking inexorably towards them, was a dark mass. "Come on, Prof!" Terri exclaimed, as Conan helped her pull him to his feet. Together, leaning on each other, they hobbled to the edge of the clearing, and turned just in time to see the Overlord's ship settle onto the ground with the screech and crack of tortured boulders being crushed beneath. Whatever had remained of the ancient native monument was now obliterated.

The final thump and groan died away, allowing the tattered forest to return to quiet solitude, the kind that only exists riding the night sky high above the Smoky Mountains.

"He's under there?" Siderai said.

"Yes," Terri replied.

He put one arm around her shoulder, and the other around Conan. "Good."

Chapter 19

Terri was sitting in a pine forest while flying through space—she, the trees, the rocks, the birds, all riding on a giant saucer. Siderai and Conan were around somewhere, and it occurred to her that she probably should go find them. Stars above blazed in their millions, undiminished by atmosphere. There was no sun, no moon, just the stars, achingly beautiful diamonds, each hinting at unknowable secrets of the universe. The giant saucer, with them as passengers, was traveling incredibly fast, yet there was no rush of air like she felt when riding in a convertible. Well, duh. They were in space—there was no air *to* rush past. That, of course, presented its own dilemma. If there was no air, how was she breathing? *Was* she breathing? In fact, she was not. That explained it. On the other hand, she had to breathe, or she'd die. But she couldn't. She tried, but her lungs didn't work. She tried harder, panic rising from her gut. She couldn't! She couldn't breathe!

She awoke gasping loudly, and sat up. Siderai looked up from his reading. "You okay?"

"No," she said, rubbing her eyes. She felt stiff, and cold. "Can't we turn the heat up?"

"Spockette," Siderai said, "what's the temperature?"

"Seventy-two degrees, Fahrenheit. Would you like to adjust?"

"Why do you ask him?" Terri said. "Is he the boss, now?"

"Terri, I meant 'you' as the collective."

"Seems like we're a little grumpy," Siderai said. "Perhaps you should get some more sleep."

She stood up and stretched. "I've slept thirteen hours in the last—what?"

Siderai looked at his watch. "It's been twenty-seven hours."

"I think that's enough sleep. Any more, and mold will start growing in my brain. Hey, that means we're almost there?"

Siderai pointed, and Terri gasped again. A rust-brown arc, seen through the silhouettes of frozen pines, blocked the pin-point stars along one edge of the visible dome provided by Spockette. Mars!

Her dream had been based on reality. Or, most of it. She wasn't sitting in the forest, but inside Spockette. The forest beyond Spockette's hull was dead now—freeze-dried in the cold vacuum.

They had formulated the plan once Spockette came to join them at the edge of the clearing after landing the Overlord's ship. For multiple reasons, not the least of which that Spockette had picked up cruise missile targeting instructions, they decided that they had to get the portal base the hell out of there. And so Terri had told the saucer to go up. And up. And away. From Earth. With the Overlord's competing directions gone, the portal saucer was obediently compliant. They tried to get the Overlord's ship to use its tractor field to hold on to the saucer with no luck—it seemed to go catatonic with the loss of its master—so for the last twenty-six hours, the base had been accelerating at one G, balancing the great ship on its back.

Terri had a hard time believing it. Space probes traveled for months to get to Mars, and they had cruised here in less than two days—the magic of continuous acceleration, which in turn was possible because of nearly infinite energy.

"Are we in orbit?" she asked.

"Terri," Spockette said, "you might want to lie down again. We need the portal to increase deceleration for orbital insertion."

"Okay," she said, returning to the make-shift bed of cheap seat cushions they'd bought at the convenience store. "Tell me when."

Spockette calculated the parameters and fed them to the portal saucer, but it only acted on them upon instruction from Terri.

"Ready . . ." Spockette said. "Three, two, one—engage."

Go! Terri thought, and she instantly went from 120 pounds to something that felt like a horse sitting on her. "Jesus," she said through clenched jaws, "is this, like, ten Gs?"

"Three point one, Terri," Spockette said calmly.

"Holy cow. I have an aunt who weighs three hundred pounds. She feels like this all the time?"

She wished now that she'd stacked the plastic-coated cushions. Her shoulder blades pushed right through the thin foam to press against Spockette. These were all the convenience store had, and they'd cleaned them out at that. After taking the saucer up twenty miles—out of range of fighter jets and cruise missiles—they'd sneaked back in Spockette to the little town of Bryson City to stock up with food and water for the interplanetary jaunt, where "food" was chips, power bars, and cans of little Vienna sausages. Siderai had grabbed a handful of random magazines as they checked out, but they'd hardly needed them, since Spockette had downloaded reams of books, and served as a tireless reader. Terri was now a veritable expert on the diaspora of early humans out of Africa one hundred thousand years ago, Siderai's choice, and she had finally "read" *Atlus Shrugged*. She was glad she'd gotten that one under her belt, but she figured she was now done with Ann Rand.

Conan had been dozing on the hard surface, and roused with the change in weight. Terri had thought his paralysis was permanent, and it would have been had he been closer to the Overlord's weapon, but control was slowly returning. With a bit of luck, he'd be swinging from tree branches in no time.

That was racist, and Terri mentally apologized to him.

"Orbital insertion nearly complete," Spockette said. "Terri, are you ready to relax all force?"

"Count her down, boss."

"Three, two, one—disengage."

Stop! Terri urged, and she was floating. Her cheapo seat cushions sprang back and gently pushed her into the air. As before, it was both exhilarating and disorienting. She didn't think she'd ever get used to it. "How long?" she asked, struggling to keep corn chips and sausage meat down.

"The portal is ready to reverse at any time, Terri," Spockette said.

"How long?"

"It's not precise, Terri. I suggest about five seconds."

"Okay." *Back up!* she willed. She, Siderai, and Conan continued to float about. "Uh, nothing happened," she said.

"It has, Terri. The portal is pulling away."

She'd forgotten that Spockette had been riding as an unrestrained passenger the same as the Overlord's ship. Indeed, the giant Overlord's ship was swimming slowly past them. Surrounding them on all sides, floated a cloud of loose boulders and uprooted trees.

"Terri," Spockette said, "you can tell the portal to cease."

"Oh, yeah!" *Stop!*

She watched the Overlord's ship. The portal's exit hadn't been perfectly balanced, imparting a slight angular force on the silver ovoid spaceship and launching it into a slow spin, almost majestic if one ignored its history. "Do you think they'll ever retrieve it?" she said, touching the side of Spockette's hull lightly to keep her oriented towards the view.

"Sure," Siderai said, "if we don't destroy the Earth with nuclear weapons first."

"In other words, 'Yes, unless we don't.'"

They had debated what to do with the great spaceship. Leaving it for easy access seemed a bad idea. Even if the military couldn't figure out how to reverse-engineer the underlying technology in secret (likely), it's possession could still become a point of international tension (more likely). Siderai had the idea of leaving it in orbit around Mars, where it could serve as a goal, drawing mankind from the tenuous safety of Earth on a first big step to the stars.

"Prepare to secure yourselves," Spockette said.

Terri wasn't sure how to do that, since floating in freefall was essentially a state of complete helplessness without a handhold. As usual, Spockette was on top of it. She eased slowly into her acceleration so that the three of them glided down to soft landings. The convenience of artificial gravity didn't last long. Their alien chariot quickly chased down the wayward saucer, and once she was positioned, they went freefall again.

"Okay, Terri," Spockette said. "I'm ready."

She had done it before, she could do it again. This time it was a breeze, since she knew exactly the image to conjure.

"I've got it, Terri," their ship said. "Thank you."

"You're welcome, Spockette."

There was no fireworks display this time, since there was no air for the tiny amount of escaping antimatter to annihilate with.

"You know why she waited until we were fifty million miles from Earth to refuel," Terri said quietly.

"She can hear every word," Siderai said. "You're not going to hurt her feelings. She waited out of courtesy."

"Now there's a euphemism. It's a 'courtesy' to avoid killing seven billion people?"

"They're not her people," he reminded her.

"And neither are we, apparently."

"What's that supposed to mean?"

"Our atoms could be sent on their individual ways at any moment."

"Terri, we all agreed about this. In fact, Spockette offered to take this mission on alone—and, as I recall, it was you who objected. You accused her of hogging all the fun."

"I did, didn't I? Sorry. I get cranky when there's a seventeen percent chance that I could be obliterated—her words, you know."

"I understand," Siderai said, nodding. "I'm nervous as hell too."

"I'm finished," Spockette said. "You can retract."

"Gladly," Terri said. "Periscope down," she uttered as she envisioned the refueling column withdrawing.

They sank back to the floor as artificial gravity returned. "Are we leaving already?" Terri asked, surprised but relieved.

"Not yet, Terri," the ship said. "I'm circling the portal for your convenience. We'll be in orbital position for extraction soon."

"And now we have a hefty ninety-two percent chance of living?"

"That's correct, Terri. Now that we're not actively refueling, there is only an eight percent chance that the portal will fail."

"I would call that 'only' a definite euphemism."

"Actually it has just risen to twelve percent."

"I'm okay if you'd rather not give us those updates," Terri said. "Let me rephrase that—don't."

"Terri," Spockette said, "perhaps now is a good time to conclude with the Scrubber."

Conclude, Terri thought. *Why is everything ending so quickly?*

As she found herself doing so often lately, she placed her hand on her pocket, feeling the oblong lump. "Ready, little buddy?" she said.

"Yes, Terri," came the muffled Mickey Mouse voice, buzzing a little as it vibrated broken edges.

She glanced at Siderai, who nodded, and then she took a deep breath, and slowly, slowly reached into her pocket until the tips of her fingers touched the alien object. She was about to remove it from its protective haven. Its case had cracked when she'd fallen inside the paralysis field of the cheese grater, and it had then broken when the repulsor wall caused her to trip. This was why it didn't want her to remove it during the epic spaceship battle.

She reached farther and grasped it between finger and thumb, holding it together as she slid it out. It looked like it had gone through a war, which, of course, it had. The cracked case was clearly visible inside the crumpled wings. "Do you really have to go?" Terri said. "Maybe we could—I don't know—wrap rubber bands around you, or something."

"No, Terri," the Scrubber said. "I was sent here for a specific purpose, and I must carry through to the end."

The Scrubbers had detected the hyperspace perturbation when the Inhabitors had arrived in Spockette. They'd been keeping an eye on the area for thousands of years, ever since they first scrubbed Earth of Overlords. The drone she held in her hand, the last component left, had explained that they are an ancient race, neither organic, nor built in factories—the eventual result of any species that advances and persists. In the last billion years, many such types of entities have arisen and fallen—some good, some viruses. Many of the good type were taken down by the viruses, and then, inevitably, the viruses eventually failed on their own. If they persisted, Overlords could well eventually evolve into viruses.

Terri had cried, "Take them out!"

Their Scrubber replied, "That would then make us bad."

The sparkling auras that Terri and Siderai had seen enveloping the Scrubbers were not zaps from Spockette, but rather micro pushes through hyperspace as the Scrubber components transferred their gathered information back home prior to their anticipated destruction. That was this Scrubber's collective mission, reconnoitering.

And now it was time for their Scrubber to say goodbye. When it broke, it lost its ability to gather energy from its surrounding environment. It would use what was left to transfer its gathered data home.

"I'm going to miss you, little guy," Terri said, holding it delicately.

"It has been rewarding interacting here on Earth. I have high expectations for your future."

"You mean me personally, or all humans?"

"I believe that you and Mr. Siderai are representative of your species. With a little luck, and a lot of attentiveness on your part, you will maintain and improve your empathetic abilities, an essential first element in your long journey as a race. You are far closer to the original creators of the Overlord's technologies in this ability than the Overlords themselves."

"And yet, presumably, the Overlords gobbled them up."

"Sadly yes. It would be tragic, though, if you take that as a lesson to fight fire with fire, sword with sword. That is a path that ends only in narcissistic stagnation."

"Yeah, and in slaves. Slaves that are bred like dogs."

"Terri, it is not only their slaves that the Overlords have bred."

"What do you mean?"

"Isn't it obvious? They have bred themselves, wittingly or otherwise, for fighting."

"That ideal Greek physique is not a natural benefit?"

"Terri—" Siderai interrupted.

"Prof, relax. I was joking."

"They bred themselves not only physically, but psychologically as well," the Scrubber said.

"Yeah, they keep harems," Terri said. "Is there a better reason to take the pacifist route?"

"Terri, there are alternatives to either taking up the sword or passively prostrating oneself. These are things you have yet to learn as a species. But now it is time for me to retire."

"Uh, what should I do?"

"Just set me down."

Terri lay the damaged drone on the floor and stepped back. She heard a crackling sound, like crumbled cellophane, and then a soft light enveloped the ailing Scrubber. It lay there, an alien visitor from who knew how far away, neither organic nor fabricated, cradled in its glow of hyperspace fluctuation. And then the light was gone, and it was just a lifeless, broken artifact.

"Is it gone?" Terri whispered.

"Yes," Spockette said. "It's energy reserve is depleted."

"Was it . . . successful?"

"I can't know. It's communications are beyond my comprehension."

"It was successful," Terri said, nodding.

"Why do you say that?" Siderai said.

"It had to be. Otherwise the Overlords will be back, and we'll be on our own."

"Of course," he said. "Pure logic. On the other hand, maybe we should take its advice and find that middle way between swords and prostration."

"Terri," Spockette said, "it is time to send the portal out of orbit."

"Already?" She sighed. "Just tell it to go?"

"Yes Terri, I have configured its path."

"Goodbye, saucer," she said. She closed her eyes, concentrated on imagining it speeding away from Mars, and then gave a quick, forceful nod.

When she opened her eyes, Siderai was looking at her oddly. "What was that?" he said.

"What?"

"That head jerk."

"It was my last command. At least once I wanted to be Jeannie."

"You wanted to be what?"

"You know, Jeannie—*the* genie."

"Terri, are you talking about that sophomoric TV show from the sixties?"

"You say sophomoric, I say role model."

He just looked at her.

"Fine," she said. "It was just fun, okay?"

He smiled.

Terri looked around. "Hey, where did Mars go?"

"It's behind us, Terri," Spockette said.

"You're heading back already?"

"Yes, Terri."

"Couldn't we, like, go down and visit?"

"I don't think that would be a good idea," the ship said.

"Oh. Uh, we wouldn't have enough fuel then to get us home?"

"That's not a problem, Terri. I am now completely refueled. Understand that the original hyperspace jump to get to Earth consumed nearly ninety-eight percent of my fuel capacity. As a lifeboat, I was designed to do just one jump. I have enough antimatter to perform non-hyperspace operation for years."

"That's kickass. So, why the rush to get back, then?"

"It's not my problem, Terri, but my passengers. As a lifeboat, my passenger facilities are limited."

"I see. Is the CO_2, like, building up? Do we need duct tape?"

"Duct tape, Terri?"

"Spockette," Siderai said, "ignore her. She's talking about the Apollo thirteen disaster. What problem do we have?"

"Professor, the first concern is Conan. His dietary needs have not been kept up."

"She called him Conan, instead of the Enforcer," Terri said.

"Terri, shut up," Siderai said, "or I will indeed find some duct tape to do the job. Spockette, how dire is this?"

"Like humans, the Inhabitors require a small number of amino acids in their diet, those that their bodies do not produce. None overlap with what humans require."

"He's been living on power bars."

"Which has been a good choice since many amino acids common in Earth plants are toxic to Inhabitors, and fortunately these food bars have essentially no natural ingredients. On the other hand they also contain no Inhabitor essential amino acids."

"Sounds dire indeed. Will he, uh, die on Earth?"

"No. Not if we return in time. There is a large subset of Earth plants that he can eat. After all, the Inhabitors were living in the forest near you for weeks before you found them."

"Well, that's a relief. Uh, you implied there were other concerns."

"Professor, you have filled all of your emptied juice containers. It will take a day and a half to return to Earth."

"Oh! You mean filled with . . ."

"Our pee, Prof!" Terri blurted.

"I know what she's talking about, Terri. Well, that one is more an inconvenience."

"For you, perhaps, professor."

"Oh, right. Of course. It's your, uh, house. Your, body, really. By all means! Home on the double!"

"Thank you, professor."

"Um, listen, Spockette, I really am not a professor."

"Actually, although you do not hold a full tenured position, my information indicates that associate professors commonly carry the colloquial label."

"I see. So, even though I no longer hold even an assistant professor's position at a university, you're going to continue to use it . . . colloquially."

"If you don't mind. Professor."

"I don't seem to have a choice. Well, I guess we'd better settle in."

"I vote for *The Hobbit*," Terri said.

"She already read that to us," Siderai said.

"And you slept through half of it."

"Because I read it three times as a teen, and saw the whole movie series."

"So, it's settled. Start anytime, girl."

Spockette began, this time with much improved intonation. "In a hole in the ground there lived a hobbit. Not a nasty, dirty, wet hole, filled with the ends of worms and an oozy smell . . ."

∞

Terri threw a pebble into the darkness, heard it land on her mother's back porch, and squatted down behind a bush. This was the third toss. What kind of guard was this? A guard who didn't guard? Spockette had probed the secure FBI communications and determined that her mother was being watched round the clock. The agency didn't have a lot of leads, and they were making the best of what they had.

On the other hand, if this FBI agent was the best they had, the country was in trouble.

They had still been a couple of million miles from home when Terri began to realize that she wanted to see her mother. She hadn't thought about her until then, but once she started, the desire became a need. It was possible that this would be her last chance.

The back door suddenly flew open. Finally. A middle-aged man in traditional nylon FBI jacket garb stepped out and stood looking around. *Come on, turkey!* Terri thought, but unlike the alien base portal, humans were oblivious to her thoughts.

Well.

She took another pebble from her little pile and launched it from her squatting position. He must have heard her, because he instantly raised a flashlight, blinding her. "You there!" he called. "Don't move!"

"I'm not moving!" she called.

He paused, probably not expecting a girl. "Come here!" he ordered.

"No!" she countered, peering through the bush.

He swung the light around the perimeter of the yard, and then stepped off the porch. "Come here," he repeated. "I'm with the FBI."

"No," she repeated. *Umm* . . . "I can't move."

He hesitated and then started across the yard. Halfway, he froze in mid-step. "What the . . . ?" he croaked, and then as Conan appeared from behind the shed carrying the ludicrously long carving knife he'd found, the agent's eyes went wide and he yelled, "Jesus!"

He stood perfectly still watching the furry alien approach, and then began struggling, but wasn't able to move more than a fraction of an inch in any direction. From just above the roof of the house, Spockette's tractor field was precise and firm.

"What . . . what . . . ?" the man stammered as Conan reached him.

"Don't worry," Terri said, standing up. "He's not going to hurt you. He carries around his sword out of habit. We don't tell him that it's actually a really big knife."

Planting the blade into the grass, Conan yanked off a strip of duct tape from a roll he was carrying, ripped it off with his teeth, and, being careful to keep his arms above the narrow tractor field, slapped it across the agent's mouth.

"Can you breathe?" Terri asked coming up to him.

Eyes still wide with fear, he nodded.

"Okay. I won't be long. Try to relax if you can. You'll find it's a pleasant experience if you let all your muscles un-tense. It's like floating in a pool."

She left him hmmphing excitedly under the duct tape and went inside. She found her mother watching TV. "Hey, Mom," she said sitting down next to her.

"Oh, hi, dear," her mother said. "You're just in time for dinner. Randall and I were just about to sit down. He's a friend of your father."

"Mom," she said, "this man isn't—"

"Your father called. He should be home next week. What did you say about Randall?"

"Uh, nothing, Mom." Terri was disheartened that she'd caught her mother lost in time. She wouldn't remember any of this later. That was okay, maybe even for the better. The visit wasn't for her mother anyway. It was for her.

The woman on the TV was talking about the terrible earthquake that had struck the heart of the Smoky Mountains. A scene of concrete rubble among broken pine trees panned across the screen as the news helicopter circled. "Cleanup continues at the collapsed observation tower at Clingmans Dome," she reported. "Multiple eyewitnesses continue to insist that they saw a giant flying saucer. The North Carolina National Guard commander overseeing the recovery attributes the accounts to a rare meteorological phenomenon that can occur after an earthquake, when dust is thrown into the air. The commander continues to claim that the fighter jet that crashed was on a routine mission, and that it was a coincidence that the earthquake followed soon after."

Terri's mother turned to her, eyes filled with concern. "Honey, that's where your father went!"

"No, Mom—"

"Terri, it is! I remember. It was Clingmans Dome."

"Mom, he came home from there. Long ago. Don't you remember? He brought along that pendant?"

She thought a moment and then her face relaxed. "Yes, you're right, dear. I'm telling you, I'm getting so forgetful lately." She snorted. "That darn pendant, his precious. He's adamant that it's only good, but I'm sure it's going to be trouble someday."

Terri grinned. "Mom, you were both right."

She looked at Terri quizzically. "What do you mean, dear?"

"Nothing. Just me babbling." She leaned over and gave her mother a long hug. "Goodbye, Mom," she said, and stood up.

"Where are you going, dear? You're not staying for dinner?"

"There's something I have to finish with some friends."

"Okay. Don't be too late. Is it a school project?"

Terri looked at her. What the hell. "Yes. It started out studying marmots, but it's expanded to include alien species."

"That's good, Terri," she said, turning her attention back to the TV. "I hear those Asian carp are terribly invasive."

Terri smiled. "Bye, Mom."

"Good bye, dear," she said watching the screen.

Terri nodded, turned, and walked out. It wasn't often that dementia was a godsend.

Outside, Conan stood guard over the FBI agent who stood glued in place, only his frantic eyes following her. She tossed a little recording device at his feet, and it hovered in the air near his knee, caught in Spockette's tractor field. She looked him in the eye. "That's a recording of the last ten minutes, so there's no need to pump my mom. Got it?" The agent stared at her. "Got it?" she repeated, louder. He nodded vigorously.

She waved to Conan and they trotted off towards the spot a block away where Spockette would pick them up. By the time the agent could call in backup, they'd be long gone. Terri was pleased at her companion's continued recovery. His trot was still lopsided, but it was at least a trot.

∞

Conan came through the window first, his Conan-sized sword drawn and ready. Terri wasn't able to convince him to keep it sheathed in his makeshift scabbard, which he'd stitched together from two halves of a biker belt. They had hovered outside the hospital window in the dark, waiting for the agent on duty to go down to the cafe on the first floor for coffee, as he did like clockwork each hour.

Preston, looking far more haggard than five days before, silently let his gaze follow the four-foot-six alien as he crossed the room to lock the door and then turn around to stand guard. When Terri came through the window, the patient's face relaxed. "I thought I had died and flown to heaven," he said.

"I don't know what angels look like," she said, leaning over to give him a kiss on his forehead before sitting in the chair next to the bed, "but I'll bet they don't look like Inhabitors."

"Inhabitants?" he said.

"I made the same mistake. It's a long story, and we don't have much time, Preston. But you'll hear the whole thing soon."

"I will?"

"Do you have internet access?"

"I supposed, yes, but no laptop."

"That's okay, TV networks will pick it up for sure. Preston, you look terrible."

He grinned. "I never have worries that you might be . . . what do they say? Pollyandy?"

"It's Pollyanna, Preston. Has the FBI been rough with you?"

"Not physically, no."

"What does that mean?"

He shrugged. "I am a very sick man. I need a lot of sleep."

"They've been depriving you?"

"Not on purpose. No."

It came to her. "You've been resisting telling them everything, haven't you?"

He raised his eyebrows and glanced at the blinking amber light, indicating that their voices were being recorded. "No, Terri," he lied. "I tell everything I remember. Thing is, you know, I am very sick, and my mind, it does not work good." He winked.

"The agent will be back soon," she said, pulling a leather pendant strap over her head and handing it to him. "I thought you should have this, Preston. My dad would have wanted it that way. It's his pendant."

He looked at it, confused, and then back at her. She placed her finger against her lips for him to be quiet. The "pendant" was a cheap cast iron doodad that they'd picked up in a consignment store, a replica of the Buddhist wheel of joy, three tadpole swirls endlessly chasing each other. She reached inside her torn shirt, her favorite, the one the Overlord had ripped to confirm her sex, and removed an old, worn leather pouch, the kind that European men carry as a male purse. "Keep the pendant in contact with you all the time," she continued pointing to the purse. "Who knows, it might do for you what it did for my dad," she said as she quietly opened the drawer in the stand next to his bed, placed it inside, and closed it again.

Inside the purse was a note explaining that the plain black metal band had been taken from an alien, and that it was the big brother of the original pendant. With a little luck, it just might do a better job. She didn't write about crawling under the crushing giant Overlord ship to retrieve it by sawing off the hand of the alien using his own massively heavy sword. She didn't write how this was probably the hardest thing she'd ever done, and hoped to ever do.

The television in his room was on with the volume set low, but she heard something that caught her ear, and she turned it up.

"Have you heard this?" he asked.

"No. They discovered a star that went nova?"

"They think this at first. No, whatever this is, it is here, in our own solar system. They think maybe near the asteroid belt. It produces tremendous light and radiation."

Terri smiled.

"They think maybe a little black hole that absorbed an asteroid. But this seems unlikely—where would this black hole come from?"

She shook her head. "Not a black hole—antimatter."

"Okay. Where would the antimatter come from?"

"As I said, it's a long story, Preston, but let's just say that it involves advanced alien technology."

He looked at Conan. "Him?"

"He's a part of the story, a big part. Like I said, you'll hear the whole thing soon. Our . . . companion—also our ride—recorded every second. It's going to take up a lot of server space."

Conan tensed when the doorknob jiggled, followed by a knock.

"Time for us to go," she said, standing up.

"Where to?" he asked.

"Ecuador."

"Why Ecuador?"

"We need a small country, where we can deal directly with multiple departments of the government, a country where we can trust what we're told, and not worry that some super-secret agency will override the promises."

"And you think Ecuador is this?"

She shrugged. "We'll soon find out."

The knock on the door had escalated to pounding accompanied by authoritative demands. Terri leaned over and kissed Preston again on the forehead. "The next time I see you, you'd better be doing cartwheels."

"I will do my best," he said, smiling.

She motioned to Conan and went to the window, where Siderai helped her through the hatch and into the waiting Spockette. Once Conan tumbled in, his "sword" finally sheathed to Terri's relief, they steadied themselves as Spockette took them up and away into the night sky.

"I forgot to mention," Siderai said, "that it would be best not to mention where we're going."

She raised an eyebrow.

"You *told* him?" Siderai said.

"Sort of."

"You told them we're going to Iceland?"

She shook her head. "A little misdirection."

Siderai sat tapping his fingers on the floor.

"You nervous?" she asked.

"Of course. In a couple of hours we're going to land in Reykjavik and try to convince Viking descendents to harbor us while we tell the world our story."

He studied her disapprovingly. "Do you have to wear that rag?"

Although they'd changed into clean clothes picked up at the consignment store, she had pulled the torn shirt on over top. "It gives me confidence," she said.

He was about to protest, but smiled, and then nodded. "I understand."

Terri looked around at what had become their little home. "How about you, Spockette? Do you understand?"

"Terri," the ship said, "your shirt provides me with confidence as well."

"Hey! I thought you always told the truth."

"I am, Terri."

She thought a moment, and then fished the lifeless artifact from her pocket, the drone that once housed the member of a race that had been watching over this part of the galaxy for millions of years. She kept it as a souvenir. "Scrubber said that this shirt was part of the reason you were able to set yourself free."

"Yes, Terri. When I was refueling, the professor told you that I was performing a courtesy by waiting until we arrived at Mars because humans are not my people. I didn't want to contradict him, but he was wrong."

Terri exchanged raised eyebrows with Siderai. "If I hadn't been an idiot," she said, "and gone after the Overlord, you'd still be following his every command?"

"Terri, that is a hypothetical question. Do you truly want to pursue it?"

She looked at Siderai, the wise, ever-patient gay professor, and then at Conan, sitting calmly watching them, waiting for the next chance to go into action for their defense.

"No," Terri said. "I'll stick to reality. It's pretty cool."

∞　∞　∞　∞

About the Author

Blaine C. Readler is an electronics engineer, inventor of the FakeTV, and, of course, a writer. He has accumulated a pile of awards, among them, Best Science Fiction in the Beverly Hills Book Awards, two-time Distinguished Favorite in the Independent Press Awards, an IPPY Bronze medal, Honorable Mention in the Eric Hoffer Awards, a finalist for the Foreword Book of the Year, and three-time San Diego Book Awards winner. He lives in San Diego with his wife who has graciously remained married to him for twenty-five years.

He encourages you to visit him:
http://www.readler.com/